The McKinnon Legacy

By

Anthony Ashpitel

ISBN 978-0-9569003-1-9

Published by Anthony Ashpitel
Email: tonyashpitel@btinternet.com

Revised in 2011, from an original novel by Anthony Ashpitel.

This book is dedicated to my wife, Anne, who is a boundless source of help and encouragement.

AA

Prologue

He was going to die.

He had known this certain truth for some days. At first he'd felt panic but this had soon abated. After struggling through one night of deep anxiety he had become too tired and in too much pain to care much beyond a numb acceptance of his fate. In part to distract himself from his pain he tried to sum-up his life and found himself dwelling primarily, predictably, on his mistakes.

There had been many mistakes, the most important being the one that had brought him to this place. He ran over this most recent memory from its beginning some eighteen months before and for the most part his wasted facial features remained closed. But when he reached that point in his memory, which unknown to him through his occasional delirium had occurred only two weeks before, the haggard pastiness of his face creased into the trace of a smile that knew both chagrin and resignation.

From the camp-bed where he lay he eyed his surroundings once more. The late afternoon sun, providing his only light, shone in dusty rays through the reed doorway to brighten an area of the earth floor near his bed. The room was a hut, functional and nothing else: a temporary lodging. He believed he had been in the hut for four days, but again the lapses into delirium denied him exact recollection of time. He did, however, remember his arrival at the guerrilla camp and something of his subsequent collapse. There too, in the hazy memory, was the picture of his attendant, a native girl, and he seemed to remember her frequent visits to his bedside. An earlier memory, which recalled the help given him by his friend, was very clear. Particularly, he remembered that his friend had promised to meet him here but, not yet receiving news of the man's arrival, felt he would probably be too late.

Although he would never feel panic again he experienced something strangely similar, deep and urgent regret. Regret that here, thousands of miles from anyone who knew him, he would die a very lonely death. What was more, he knew he would die without his only surviving relation, his child, knowing of it and, perhaps more important, why.

It was with this very much in mind that he spent the remaining daylight and all of his failing strength in what was to be very nearly his last act. On the floor by his litter lay the few oddments of luggage he had been able to bring on the long and hurried journey. Among this rubble was his compact tape-recorder, an item which had rarely left his side for some years. He lurched, sore and dizzy, striving to reach it. Then, when the sickness had subsided a little, his trembling hands were able to operate the familiar controls.

In a voice weak and shaking, but backed with determination, he dictated until both sides of the cassette were used. When he was finished he re-trieved the tape and marked it in a spidery scrawl.

Then he lay back exhausted, his only activity now thought, as he mentally ran through his story to check he had got it right. In particular, he dwelt upon his account of the symptoms of the sickness to which he had succumbed: first came the severe headache and muscular pain, to be followed by the fever, the alarming measles-like rash, and the nausea which meant he had been unable to keep anything down for long.

The sequence from then on had been difficult for him to fix with any accuracy as the symptoms experienced to that point had debilitated him physically and mentally to the point of prostration and hallucination.

It seemed only possible to list what he could remember: the wracking cough and bleeding; bleeding to the point where he had seemed to be leaking from everywhere. Now, satisfied he had got his story on tape, he could rest. He was well aware that this period of lucidity wouldn't last. He had seen the final rally of a dying person too many times. For brief moments, drained as he was of all reserves of strength and emotion, he heard the myriad night-sounds a jungle makes. Then his eyelids drooped slowly to a close and he was asleep.

In the morning he was dead.

Chapter One
(Thursday: 1000-1230)

Summer was barely half spent when it was already being reported as the most extreme the United Kingdom had endured in living memory for its ferocious heat and consequent drought. Here, in late July, the heat was fast becoming unbearable for a British public historically unprepared for such blistering weather.

Even before London's great commuter army had settled to the day's work the temperature in the street was moving towards the uncomfortable. Already pedestrians were shedding precautionary raincoats and motorists were lowering the windows or otherwise wresting what air-cooling they could from their vehicles. In general only purveyors of ice-cold confections and drinks, and the inhabitants of the newer office blocks, would remain cool and comfortable through this day: the first with their swollen profits; the others with their air-conditioned environments.

The Department of Health was located in one such office block, one with installed air conditioning. Unfortunately, those who worked here were suffering unaccustomed solidarity with those populating less opulent premises and had been for the last twenty-four hours, ever since the air conditioning plant had packed-up.

As the Chief Medical Officer of Health looked out gloomily onto the swirling traffic below, the prospect of another hot day of unbroken sweat vied with the other contestant for his depression, a man called Marshall. Not that he was easily depressed: throughout the course of his career he had applied himself to all manner of medical and administrative problems with a level of cheerfulness only possible in one who is devoted to his work.

His response to the present problem was an exception. The difficulties thrown up by the outbreak of a viral infection, as yet unclassified, he could tolerate; but that he should have to withstand the intrusion of a security man in medical matters, albeit at the personal direction of the Minister, would have accomplished a rise in temperature in his somewhat substantial frame even on a cold day, especially as he was keeping him waiting. A last glance at the cloudless sky, before he turned from the window, reminded him that he would be melting shortly come what may.

Plainly overweight, Sir Roland Fletcher stood in complete contrast to the aims of the National Health Service's latest publicity campaign, Preventative Medicine. Even though his two-hundred-and-forty pounds had a frame a shade over six feet upon which to distribute itself the resultant shape was such that it would always be beyond the sartorial art. Dressed in a three-piece suit despite the heat, his appearance of one who has tried in vain to climb out of his clothes by way of the collar was not pretty.

Frequently he pawed the dampness of his face and neck with a handkerchief as he surveyed the scene before him. Occasionally he looked fixedly at a perfectly innocuous area of the far wall. At such times he saw nothing. It was his habit, when in deep thought, to stare straight ahead in an un-flickering, unseeing gaze. To wander by chance into the full glare of this was, at least, disconcerting: the stern countenance he affected, his face framed in the full thatch of unruly white hair and punctuated by the satanic eyebrows, drew startled reactions from all but his most constant acquaintances.

Perhaps there was something in this daunting visage which, when consciously used, had been instrumental in part for his rise to such a prestigious position. Perhaps. The fact was that he had spent over thirty years of his fifty-six in getting to the top. Six years later he was still number one in the Health Service.

The room in which he stood now was the boardroom in a suite that was effectively his private wing. It was a long room with windows on three sides and a single door in the centre of the fourth. The decor and furnishings were that mixture of new and vaguely archaic which seems to be the way with government establishments. Serving the principle that circulating air is better than non-circulating baking, even if the former carries with it the pollution and noise of traffic, almost all of the windows were open; the exception being the very highest panes, which had been crudely taped shut. Driving a principle further, the door was also open, exposing the narrow corridor off which branched several other rooms. At the end of this corridor was the outer door connecting this section with the rest of the building. Now shut, the door functioned as a barricade against intrusion by the masses which frequented the other administration departments. More recently the door was found to be of some use insulating against the repeated hammering noises from workmen in the outer corridor.

Reluctantly terminating his gaze into the middle distance, Sir Roland looked around the room. The nine people with him in the boardroom formed a group made up of doctors and administrators of varying seniority. They all had three things in common: they all claimed allegiance to the mighty NHS; they had all been summoned in connection with the reported outbreak and; they were all waiting. Conversation among them was minimal, as reading and cogitation were optimal. In part this was due to the noisy portable circulation fans, dug-up from some pre-war habitat, which made a din sufficient to discourage chatter. The main reason for silence, however, was that they were mostly strangers to each other.

Against this background the CMO stood out as the obvious leader if only because his imposing figure was in the vertical plane. His survey of the scene before him quickly located his aides, professional associates and subordinates. Almost all of those who sat or lounged around had paperwork with them and were engaged in various degrees of industry. Those who had nothing to do read or looked on disinterestedly.

Among the onlookers was the man who automatically drew the CMO's attention. Browning, his right-hand man, was almost totally inactive to the point of being asleep. A most orderly administrator, if he was in that room for a meeting then all other work would be allotted another slice of his time. Now, with the meeting delayed, he was inert, an efficient machine switched off.

Both he and his boss were of a height but there the comparison of their physical appearance ended. Browning was slight of frame, having some experience of athletics in his none-too-distant past. His clothes also were different, a faithful reflection of the man; smart but not flash and, if regularity of features were the foundation of good looks, the tanned complexion, deep brown eyes and jet-black hair gave him a Latin handsomeness. All of which helped to conceal at least some of his forty-six years but, even though vanity played no part in this deception, all in the NHS hierarchy knew his age anyway: they knew almost everything about him. Browning was a whizz-kid and, as such, had been watched since he had first made good impressions after struggling with his balancing act, the one between his career as a surgeon and that of an administrator. Arthritis had tipped the scales. Now, some years on, he held the post of Principal Medical Officer at the Department of Health, was number two to Sir Roland and it was widely tipped that he would be the next Chief Medical Officer.

Sat to the left of the PMO was the Chief Scientific Officer, Professor Prendle-James, who was at present reading his 'comic', The New Scientist. Gangling is a term normally applied to a youth; it was also the first word that leapt to mind when confronted with this thin, angular body, six-toot-two-inches tall, whose hands would wave about at remarkable distances from his body in the course of a discussion. Together with the thinning grey hair atop an emaciated head, he cut a comical figure on first sight. But it only required one further look, at his eyes, to see the shining intelligence of the man and dispel first impressions. At sixty, 'Hector', as he was known, was the oldest person in the room.

The two youngest members present were sat at the furthest distance from the CMO, along the far wall. One of them, the only woman present, was a microbiologist in whose head was a report direct from the site of the outbreak. The nervousness which she felt may have been due to unease in the presence of such senior company but was probably specifically because of the darted glances from the CMO who seemed to be trying to wrench information from her by telepathy.

The other junior member was Gibson who, in his mid-twenties, was the assistant Public Relations man for the section. It was a post he had held for a mere six weeks and his attendance at the meeting was due entirely to the absence of his immediate superior who languished, at that time, in his sick-bed. Callow youth Gibson may have appeared but it certainly wasn't the look of inexperience that Sir Roland intercepted being directed at the unsuspecting woman.

The CMO may have pondered further on the PR man's behaviour but his train of thought was interrupted by an increase in the level of hammering noise outside and instead he winced. Among the faces of those who responded to the noise he recognised that of Robins as he looked up from the shuffle of papers on his lap. Henry Robins was the Regional Health Authority representative, whose fellow committee members were responsible for feeding whatever funds and experience were available into a sizeable portion of East Anglia. In addition, the RHA strove to maintain a comprehensive organisation to meet the demands of all health matters in their area. More local control was obtained by the use of Area Health Authorities, of which there were several to each region, whose function, again by committee was to determine the more specific needs of a locality, feed these requirements back to the RHA, and distribute their response as directed. Ferguson, who sat in conclave with Robins, and who, incidentally, was an ex-secondary school teacher bereft of any medical experience, was the AHA's representative for the meeting.

Three of the remaining four people were very nearly strangers, having been introduced to the CMO only that morning. Even now their names were lost to his memory. He did, however, know the names of their departments, having summoned representatives from Public Health, International Health, and Overseas Development departments himself, with a view to their providing input wherever possible.

'Mr Marshall, Sir Roland,' the voice of his secretary, a middle-aged woman who had been with him for some years, brought him back to the moment.

'Thank you, Claire,' he replied quickly. Then, following her glance to the open door, he saw a stocky man of medium height.

At first glance, the newcomer gave the impression of authority by the way he carried himself. Presentably dressed in sports-jacket, cavalry-twill trousers, open-necked shirt and shoes that made no sound as he approached, Marshall directed himself towards the CMO.

'Sorry if I've kept everyone waiting,' he said. 'Bit of a rush... and London traffic being what it is... '

It had taken no more than five seconds to say those words, which had trailed off into deliberate vagueness, but it was sufficient for Sir Roland to form an opinion of the man before him; disturbing as it was. His second glance had almost gone the way of the first in confirming to the CMO that the newcomer seemed an agreeable type. That is, until he scrutinised the face and saw two things which surprised him: unusually the eyes didn't yield to his inquiring stare and, beneath the grey eyes, smudges of blue, forming half-circles, showed through the pale tan. Not in the best of health, decided the CMO.

These impressions so surprised the CMO that it prompted him to cancel the torrent of abuse he had promised himself, however diplomatically gift-wrapped, and allowed himself instead a tinge of sympathy and at least a fair hearing. 'Quite! Can't be helped, I'm sure,' he said.

He turned quickly to his PR man then, who was now hovering close by. 'Gibson, the windows. One or two, I think. And switch off those dreadful fans. Can hardly hear meself think!'

'Harry,' he said quietly, this time to Browning. Then he made a circular motion with his hand and the PMO called everyone to the long central table.

The large blades of the caged fans had barely clanked to a stop before Sir Roland, the last to sit down, had squared the slim folder before him unnecessarily and begun to address the meeting. 'Gentlemen...and Lady,' he said, belatedly remembering that his microbiologist was female, 'you all have some idea why you are here. The object of this meeting is to pool all the information and expertise at our disposal for the containment and eradication of a viral disease which has mysteriously appeared in Dent. In short, it is up to us to sort it out.' He paused, adding: 'Dent is a small community of some fifty-odd inhabitants situated in an isolated position in the Fen district of Norfolk.'

'It is just forty-eight hours since Doctor Lewis, the local GP, called on a patient during his rounds there. At first he diagnosed 'flu. All the signs were there: headache, sore throat, high temperature, et cetera. The fact that they seemed more severe than usual at first had him believe the patient, a youth, was just hypersensitive. At the same morning rounds, however, he was called upon to visit three more patients displaying the same symptoms. When a further plea was received that afternoon he, quite rightly, called in the Public Health people.'

The CMO looked down the long table to the Public Health representative. 'Anything you can add at this stage, er...'

'Selby, Sir Roland,' supplied a sprightly chap. Then he frowned. ''I'm afraid not. I'm in the embarrassing position of being completely in the dark on this and, if any of my colleagues had heard, I'm sure....'

'No need for you to feel embarrassed, Mr Selby,' interrupted Marshall. He turned to the CMO. 'You see, Sir Roland, before the local Public Health Laboratory could report to London we intervened - in the interests of security, of course.' The smile he attempted didn't quite come off. 'In fact, excepting your department here, all possible outlets of information are being watched for leaks.'

The glance thrown at Marshall by the CMO appeared to break the policy of compassion he had decided upon earlier. If Marshall was in any doubt as to Sir Roland's disgust he had to be in a far worse state than he appeared. But, reminding himself of the Minister's directive, he went no further than wiping his brow before picking up the threads of his narrative. 'Anyway, the lab sent off the usual whole-blood samples to the Special Pathogens Unit at Porton Down, obviously taking no chances. At the same time isolation and barrier nursing techniques were instituted. The area has been sealed off for the last,' he checked the wall-clock, 'thirty hours and no-one has been in or out. Except for, of course, Doctor MacKenzie.'

'Doctor MacKenzie?' prompted Marshall.

'Doctor Anne MacKenzie, gentlemen,' said the CMO, nodding toward the young woman. 'She is a member of the team of microbiologists and epidemiologists I dispatched as soon as we heard the news. For reasons that may or may not become apparent I instructed her to return with a report, meant for this meeting, on the progress made. She arrived two hours ago. If you please, young lady...'

'Yes, Sir Roland.' Now that the assembled men had a *bone fide* reason, indeed duty, to look and listen to her as she launched into her report, they made a meal of it. To be honest she was not beautiful. She was much more than beautiful, she was attractive. In that sweltering room her gentle voice joined forces with her good looks to seriously contest the concentration meant for the information she strove to impart. Put quite simply, her audience was sympathetic to her presence here, or rather, that was the mood of most of those present.

'Our team,' she said, somewhat meekly, 'arrived to find that the isolation organisation was well established and field nursing was well on the way to being so. After setting up the portable lab we obtained our own acute-phase whole-blood samples and began fluorescent antibody tests.'

'What is the purpose of these tests, doctor?' interrupted Marshall.

Slightly off-balance, the microbiologist hesitated for a moment.

'Please, Mr Marshall,' intervened the CMO, 'you must let Doctor MacKenzie finish her report.' He turned to her. 'Perhaps it would be better if you couched your report in layman's terms for the moment. We can go into the technicalities later.'

'Of course,' she agreed. Then, trying to answer the requests of both, she continued: 'Fluorescent antibody techniques are simply tests for the rapid detection of viral activity in blood. A further refinement is their application in discovering the precise disease but only limited success has ever been achieved. Such is the case with our tests on site: we know there is virus activity and that is all.'

Marshall nodded.

'Clinical diagnosis,' she said, now back on track but carefully choosing her words for the benefit of the non-medical members, 'that is, the symptoms noted by the doctors at Dent, indicates an acute febrile illness, certainly not any of the influenza strains, but whose identity cannot yet be ascertained. A number of possible viral diseases are indicated at this stage but it will be another thirty-six, or maybe forty-eight hours before we begin eliminating non-runners. What we do know is that the indications are pretty gloomy.

'On the other side of the shop, in the lab, the time-scale for virological isolation of the virus - when we will know its identity and can begin any treatment - may be anything from five to seven days.'

'Can't they work around the clock to find out sooner?' queried the security man.

Anne MacKenzie shot a glance at her boss expecting his intervention. Although the CMO tensed, he said nothing. It was up to the microbiologist to answer. 'They are working around the clock. There is no quicker way of doing it,' she replied, irritation in her voice.

'Then it seems we may as well forget the lab and leave it to a clinical diagnosis at the site and an answer in thirty-six hours,' responded Marshall.

'Maybe,' retorted the girl. 'Maybe in thirty-six hours. Maybe a lot longer. And you can't forget the lab, Mr Marshall. Once we discover the identity of the disease, assuming it isn't a previously un-encountered or very rare type, we shall still need antibody, convalescent plasma and interferon, all substances which have effect against a specific virus, to fight or protect against it. The lab is the only place where you can obtain these in sufficient quantities. Also, their work over the next few days will not only confirm the diagnosis in broad terms, it will establish the exact strain.'

'And if it is an unknown or very rare type?' asked the security man, unashamedly picking up the weak points.

'Then the need for the facilities at Porton Down is greater than ever. In fact, the lab there would be our only hope,' she corrected, and something in the way she said it drew a quizzical look from Sir Roland.

'So,' she continued, looking back to the CMO, 'until we see the signs all we can do is keep the patients comfortable and watch. That, with the news that the latest count is eleven, concludes the basic details of my report.'

'I see. Thank you,' said Sir Roland, following a brief period when the loudest sounds were the muffled hammering outside the suite and the traffic noise below. 'And what are these diseases we're looking at?'

'Seven altogether. All tropical diseases: Yellow Fever, Dengue, Marburg and Ibola, Lassa, though this last is almost discounted as the clinical symptoms aren't as well indicated as in the other diseases, and the two South American diseases, Junin and Machupo.'

'Good God. Are you serious?' said Prendle-James, alarmed. 'No, I'm sorry, of course you are.'

Seeing the same expression, a mixture of alarm and surprise, among all the medical men present, Marshall turned to the Scientific Officer. 'Do you mind explaining what you mean?' he asked.

'Not at all. The young lady has just named some of the most infectious diseases to affect the human race. And if that isn't enough they're among the most deadly too - or used to be. Yellow Fever and Dengue seems to be stretching it a little too far,' supplied the professor, his hands even now punctuating his speech. ''Course I know that chap Reed established a domesticated mosquito could transmit the disease from one infected man to another. But East Anglia? No, I'm not too worried about those two.'

'East Anglian fens, perhaps, at the height of summer?' prompted Browning, making his debut in the conversation.

'Hmm. Still stretching a point, though,' replied Hector.

Marshall moved impatiently in his seat. 'The others. What about the others?' he demanded.

'Oh yes,' said the professor whose brain had still been scanning for information on Yellow Fever and Dengue. 'The others. I don't know much about the South American ones, Junin and Machupo. Haemorrhagic diseases discovered in Argentina, I seem to remember. Marburg and Ebola? The less thought about, the better. Reported fatality rate of around ninety per cent. The 'papers were full of it a few years ago. Almost front page stuff. I hope they're wrong.' This was the product of his brain operating in automatic: no effort, general information dressed in a conversational manner. It allowed him to think of other things at the same time. Now he was looking at the security man and the major part of his concentration was focused on him. 'Are you alright'?' he asked.

'Perfectly, thank you,' responded Marshall. Then, as if to prove his well-being, he ignored the professor and turned again to the microbiologist.

'Would you,' he demanded, 'care to leave the safety of hindsight, or rather that of seven-or-so days' time, and go daringly into speculation now as to what you think this virus is?' His tone was harsh; it was meant to be, it was meant to crush speculation on the state of his health.

'Certainly,' retorted the young woman, two spots of colour, which were not as innocent as a blush, blooming in her cheeks. 'But I could be as near or as far away from the truth as it is possible to be. Perhaps if I gave you a few factors concerning viruses you would care to come to your own conclusions.'

'Please do,' invited the security man.

Her questioning glance brought a nod from the CMO.

'Firstly, you must realise just what a viral particle is,' she began. 'Viruses are organisms which exist only in living cells, although they can, and are, kept in suspended animation by being freeze dried to a temperature of minus four degrees centigrade. That they can only multiply in living cells is one of the major differences between them and the other organisms the layman tends to confuse them with, bacteria. Another major difference between them is size: bacterial agents of all types may be seen by using the standard high-powered microscope. Viral particles are very much smaller, requiring the use of an electron microscope to study them, a device so powerful as to be capable of revealing the structure of the heavy atoms such as Uranium. As the electron microscope is a comparatively new instrument, and the major source of information on the structure of viruses, so it follows our information is fairly recent and far from comprehensive.'

Unknown to those around the table Marshall cast surreptitious glances at each face as Anne presented her discourse. His reward from this activity was to see a look of respect in their eyes at her knowledge and delivery. For himself his interest in what she said was minimal. He knew what she would say already but he was very interested in her delivery and the impact on those around the table.

'But we do have other means of detecting the activity of viruses,' Anne was saying. 'Indeed, because we may have seen the specific damage done before by a particular virus we can tell if it is encountered again from the specific trail of destruction it leaves behind it. Cells can easily be seen through a normal microscope and therefore the particular damage done to it, together with other information such as the parts of the body affected, blood count, age of the patient, environment and the standard clinical information of temperature and blood pressure will very often provide conclusive evidence of the presence of a particular virus.

'However,' she continued, and the emphasis she placed on the word left nobody in doubt that things were not as simple as they seemed, 'there are numerous viruses that are normally encountered in the blood at any time. Some have been attenuated, weakened, by constant reproduction, whereas others do not last long against the body's innate or acquired defences. Therefore cell damage may very often be due to several different viral agents whose presence tends to camouflage the identity of that which is causing the symptoms of illness in the patient. As if that isn't sufficient, it sometimes happens that two, different viruses attack a cell simultaneously. The outcome can be a completely new strain that has a mixture of the properties of both. This is called recombining, a process that, incidentally, is one reason why influenza cannot be pinned down and eradicated; every time the body gets used to one strain, another, well-travelled but perfectly harmless to man, meets up with the first in the same cell which starts off a new strain against which the body hasn't had time to develop natural defences.'

'Something of a jigsaw puzzle,' said Marshall.

'A gross understatement,' responded the microbiologist. 'The nearest I get it to a jigsaw puzzle is one where you've no picture to go by, you don't know if all the pieces are there, or if you will see a picture at the end of it.' She may have scored off Marshall; she may not have. There was no telling from his inscrutable expression but she felt better for the retort.

In a calmer voice she went on. 'The task facing Porton Down is a problem of elimination. Firstly they must apply small amounts of the patient's blood to a variety of substances which will react according to the type of virus present. This will eliminate some of the strains. Secondly, they will conduct more specialised tests, some requiring many hours of repetitive filtering, and through these will discover, then eliminate the majority of viruses. At the end of a period stretching some days hence they will have accounted for all the previous encountered viruses present but will still be in the process of searching for new ones.

'Having narrowed down the field they will then take another blood sample from the patient. This they will apply to cultures, most likely tissue cultures, in which they have kept particular viruses alive. Certain substances which fight a specific virus and are produced during the course of the patient's illness will react when in contact with the isolated virus. If there are amounts of these substances in superior numbers or potency to the virus then the virus will be destroyed, if not then the reverse will occur. Whatever happens, the reaction will be plainly visible under the microscope. The particular virus which is shown to attract higher concentrations of the substances, known as antibodies, as the illness worsens, can be considered the cause of that illness.' She paused for breath after the hurriedly spoken lesson, for that was what it was. At the same time she looked directly at the security man, a challenge in her eyes.

Marshall, however, did not respond as expected. 'I would like to say: I see what you mean,' he said. 'I can't. Because, although you have obviously simplified a complicated process, I couldn't possibly know all the technical problems Porton Down face in not only tracking down the virus but destroying it.' He tried again his misshapen smile. 'But let's say I believe you.'

It wasn't a flowing apology, for having demanded the impossible, it was too awkward to be flowing, but it allowed the dust to settle between the two people temporarily. Ferguson was one of the few who didn't see it for what it was. In fact he missed it completely. He was still frowning in the way he had been doing for some time.

'One thing I don't understand,' said the ex-teacher-turned-AHA representative, 'is this: if you know it's a virus and you've got an electron microscope capable of revealing a virus's presence, why haven't you used it?'

'Because, Mr Ferguson,' replied the girl, 'at this stage it would be a pointless exercise.' When the baffled expression remained on his face, she continued. 'You see, when the specimen blood samples are taken for analysis, as soon after the symptoms appear as possible, there is relatively little viral activity to be seen. In the sample taken there will only be minute traces of the virus and, with the necessarily limited view of this device, the task of locating a viral particle, likened to searching an area the size of London for a particular object a centimetre square, is extremely difficult if not practically impossible.'

'So you grow them in culture until they have multiplied to fill the Petrie dish. At that point you have a complete layer of the virus and can therefore locate a virus to study far more easily,' added Prendle-James.

Both Anne and Ferguson nodded their understanding.

Perhaps it was the atmosphere of gloom prompted by the realisation, at least for the laymen, that this was to be a drawn-out affair, which nudged her into adding: 'There is one other use for the electron-microscope at this stage. It is the examination of acute serum which has first undergone ultra-centrifuge. Unfortunately it's only enjoyed a limited success in the rapid detection of some of the viruses on our list, but you can be sure it doesn't stop us from trying.'

The silence that followed was some seconds old before the tinkle of ice on glass captured the attention of those sat around the table. Animation, barring that of Prendle-James, had been lustreless until that moment; the occasional movement as someone adjusted his tie or wiped his brow, the odd shifting of weight as someone strove to avoid the dazzle of the sun. It was incongruous that, in the hot atmosphere, they should be so formally dressed, for only Anne was free from the glistening patina of sweat. Half-an-hour had elapsed since they had sat down at the table: it was enough for the CMO. The arrival of chilled fruit-juices might well have been the signal he had been waiting for. 'Shirt-sleeves if you wish, gentlemen,' invited Sir Roland, who rose quickly to take the lead in his own suggestion.

It took less than five minutes to demolish the contents of two large pitchers which Claire had brought in. In that short space of time the scene almost reverted to that before the meeting: again the fans breathed fresh air noisily into the stuffy room and, after the initial stretching of legs, people sat around, silently sipping their drinks.

But now Marshall was in their midst. As they relaxed, he watched. Unashamedly he scrutinised each person from the isolated vantage he had selected away from the rest. Only the CMO, Browning and Prendle-James did not notice the surveillance; they belonged there and had no cause to feel the slightest unease at their surroundings. For the rest, including Gibson, whose tenure in his job was still too short, they were naturally sensitive to the situation and felt uncomfortable at the security man's pointed looks. They were all the more uncomfortable at the change in Marshall from the one, brief though the period had been, who had loudly dominated the meeting until the break, to the one who they sensed rather than saw quietly staring. It was with relief that they answered Browning's call to return to the table.

With one quick traversing look the CMO satisfied himself that all were ready. 'The next item we must discuss,' he began, again checking the neatness of the folder before him, 'concerns the steps necessary to ensure the containment of this disease. But first we must know just how such viruses may be transmitted from one human to another.' He turned to the young woman.

'Perhaps I might say something on the subject,' offered the professor, quickly. 'I don't want to step on the toes of our specialist,' he added, indicating the girl, 'but I think I'm entitled to play in this discussion as well. No doubt the young lady will correct me where I go wrong.'

That the young lady would find no fault with his knowledge the audience were certain, as certain as they were of the real reason for his intervention: to ease the pressure on one unused to such high-power company as was in evidence around the table.

'The viral agents mentioned,' he began, without waiting for comment, 'have several vehicles for the transmission of infection. I've already made clear my view on Yellow Fever and Dengue so, apart from mentioning that their primary means of infection is through inoculation by the mosquito, I'll say no more about them.' A dismissive wave of the long-fingered hand verified the unproductiveness of further discussion on the subject.

'Transmission, because of the virulence of these diseases, may be by simple contact only: that is, by simply touching someone. There need be no broken skin to allow this as the normal antisepsis of the epidermis isn't sufficiently, er, powerful as to afford protection against such pathogens.' He paused then but only to look at the girl. When he spoke again it was to her. 'In fact, I cannot see how any of the suspected diseases could be present, here in England, without the presence of a carrier; someone either suffering from the disease or recovering from a bout of such. He or she must have brought it into the country.'

'You're saying someone walked into Dent and merely by shaking hands or accepting change in the village shop infected a person there?' queried Marshall.

'Possibly,' responded the professor. 'But even articles of cutlery and crockery, and all sorts of personal items which have been used very recently could undoubtedly support viral agents for onward transmission.'

Marshall seemed satisfied with this for he said nothing.

'Droplet infection is another vector,' said Hector. 'What this means is this: as I speak now minute vapour particles, droplets, are being thrown into the atmosphere. In this way infection can very easily be transmitted to another person within intimate speaking range.' Again gestures combined with inflexion of speech to enrich the Scientific Officer's expression.

'Incidentally, a sneeze involves a tremendous amount of droplet transmission, to distances of up to thirty feet, hence the government health warning slogan of some years ago: coughs and sneezes spread diseases.'

Prendle-James looked around at the rows of faces which returned blank expressions at his revelation. He shrugged his shoulders. 'Ah, well, I remember the slogan.'

'Lastly, there is direct inoculation either by hypodermic syringe or, as I've said before, through insect bite.' He looked around at the decidedly pessimistic expressions and, as if in agreement but unable to see a way out of the situation, shrugged his shoulders again.

'I think you would have been better asking by what means it couldn't be transmitted,' said Marshall.

The CMO nodded. 'I think we've established there is little we can do at the moment. We will need to control our impatience and wait until the position clears. All that can be done is being done. In the meantime we will continue taking reports from Dent every four hours and prepare contingency plans for an escalation of the problem.' He looked at the security man then, leaning forward onto his arms in anticipation at the same time. 'Perhaps you would like to tell us what progress has been made in your line of business?' he asked.

In truth, that had not been the question on his lips a second before he had spoken. What he had really wished to inquire was: 'What the hell is a security man doing here?' Again, it was only the telephoned agreement with the Minister which had persuaded him to frame the question more diplomatically; it was a procedure relatively alien to his normal manner and only as permanent as he, himself, wished.

Marshall, looking marginally better than he had on arrival, ironically spoke in a softer tone which was almost inaudible to those sat at the end of the table. In order that they might hear better they stretched further over the table and nearer the speaker. ' ...so, naturally,' Marshall was saying, 'when we heard the infection could be serious, we clamped down on all possible lines of communication, with the exception, of course, of connections with this section and Porton Down. Since that time, twenty-four hours ago, we've had men in the village investigating possible outlets for the disease. These measures include tracing visitors to Dent, consignments of anything transportable, and even the layout of the local sewerage system.'

'Isn't this normally a job for police and medical teams?' queried Walsh. It was the first time he had spoken at the meeting but he had been following what was said keenly. Now the unobtrusive administrator from the Department of Overseas Development was the focal point for all eyes. The little man, standing no more than five-feet four-inches when upright, shrank inwardly from the interest his quiet voice had drawn. Only constant application of willpower kept the impassive expression on his face. The ruddy cheeks, frizzled sandy- coloured hair and eyes of indeterminate hue, were set in a stone mask which rarely changed from an expression wholly inoffensive.

'Yes, indeed,' said Sir Roland, before Marshall could answer. 'I, too, would like to know why this isn't the case at present.'

Marshall replied without hesitation. 'Security,' he said, simply. From the silent, cynical looks he received it was obvious to the security man that this alone would not suffice for explanation. 'You've had a spate of small outbreaks over the last two years,' he continued. 'No more than is normal, perhaps, but one or two concerned very dangerous infective agents. We saw the reaction from the media as well as the public: concern bordering on panic. So when we heard that the present outbreak could be potentially lethal we took action. The security clampdown will give us the time to trace all contacts within hours. The alternative, gentlemen, is the descent on Dent of a horde of media-men who will not only frustrate containment precautions by their presence in the vicinity of the outbreak, but will send back inflammatory stories to their editors. The latter may cause widespread panic and would certainly frighten the people living near Dent into flight, and into possibly taking the infection with them. The problems would escalate to terrifying proportions.'

'Aren't the antics of your men going to alert suspicions?' asked Gibson, the PR man. 'Surely it doesn't matter under which guise your men make their inquiries, police, Public Health Department or security men, people will wonder why you need to know their movements and so forth.'

'No problem,' returned Marshall. 'It just so happened that at the very moment we heard the news of the outbreak another, one of foot-and-mouth, was reported in the very same area.'

Even Walsh cracked the studied seriousness of his expression to register quiet understanding that the foot-and-mouth outbreak was purely an expedient to cover the problem in Dent.

Marshall continued. 'A few posters here and there, plenty of disinfectant swilling around, manned road-blocks, and a tame vet to keep the local farmers occupied, was enough to camouflage the real situation. Naturally, our inquiries were slanted towards those asked during such a cattle crisis. The information required is, after all, very similar.'

'I'm afraid I didn't think it out,' replied a nervous PR man, who, at the warning glance shot in his direction by the CMO, quickly returned to silence.

'But we digress,' continued Marshall. 'Our position at present is much the same as yours, waiting for something to turn up. I am, however, optimistic and believe that the containment and destruction of this menace will depend upon the close liaison between investigation and medical teams. Or, put another way: we track them down, and you kill them off.'

It was two or three seconds after the security man had finished that Sir Roland spoke. It was in his mind to wind up the meeting by injecting a note of optimism into his final words. He searched in those brief seconds for the words to accomplish his aim: none came. In the end he resorted to a paraphrased version of all that had been said, reiterating his remark that they would need to wait and see what developed. He knew it was pointless to say anything else: every one of them understood that the problem was, at its simplest, one of a battle between organisms measured in nanometres and human cells. Through Porton Down they could see the battlefield but might not locate the attackers until too late, when the defenders were destroyed, the human body dead and when the attackers had, perhaps, moved on.

'The situation here,' prompted Browning, when the CMO had finished.

'Ah, yes. With the obvious exception of Robins and Ferguson, all medical staff will attend a further meeting in,' he consulted his watch, 'two hours' time, that's two o' clock, to sort out a few things. Any further business?'

'Just a couple of points,' responded Marshall. 'As I'm going to need a medical specialist as an assistant during my investigations and, as Doctor MacKenzie has already answered my many stupid questions with such superb clarity, I should like your permission to borrow her. Would that be possible?'

Momentarily the CMO was taken aback, but two conflicting interests were uppermost in his mind: if this liaison between his people and the security men was going to work he needed to establish a working relationship. But he knew, from the microbiologist's expression, that she wasn't exactly happy at such a prospect. In the mental battle that ensued for Sir Roland, diplomacy and practicality won.

'Naturally, I see your need for expert information and the fact that you may be moving around. I'll need to check with the School,' he said, meaning the London School of Hygiene and Tropical Medicine, 'but if they and Doctor Mac-Kenzie raise no formidable objection, I see no reason to refuse.' His use of the word formidable obviously made the right impression on the microbiologist, for she replied, in the tone of one who may have wearied of life: 'I have no objection.'

'Thank you,' responded Marshall. 'My second point really concerns those returning to East Anglia. I have a helicopter standing-by to leave for Dent. I have a few phone calls to make first but I shall be leaving this building in, say, twenty-five minutes. Anyone who wants a lift is welcome.' Marshall rose. 'If you'll excuse me, Sir Roland?'

The CMO nodded. 'You will find a telephone, and privacy, in my office. First on the right,' he said.

When Marshall had left the room Browning joined the CMO, Prendle-James, and Gibson the PR man in a little group some way from the rest. 'What's the betting,' said Browning, 'that if Marshall's lot had got to hear of the outbreak before the GP called Public Health, we wouldn't be in the loop.'

'How do you mean?' asked Gibson.

'Security,' offered Prendle-James, never one to hold back an opinion. 'Marshall is only including us because the cat got out of the bag. He tolerates our involvement but would rather we weren't involved.'

'I agree,' said the CMO. 'However, we are in so we will do our job. We're medical men. We'll leave the security aspects to Marshall. Just one thing though....' With that the CMO turned round to address the others in the room. 'Can I have your attention, please,' he called. He waited while they settled to silence from their subdued conversations. 'I don't want any of you talking to anybody outside this room about the content of this morning's session. Is that clear?' A chorus of agreement greeted this question. 'Good.'

By now the CMO and PMO, Browning, were alone.

'Just one thing,' said Browning. 'Why didn't Marshall say what you just said? Unless we're already in a sort of quarantine.'

The CMO checked around him before returning to look at Browning. He tapped the side of his nose with his finger and spoke quietly. 'Mum's the word, Harry. Eh?'

Within fifteen minutes Marshall was back in the boardroom.

Gathered at one end, furthest from the noisy fans, a group of people, dominated by Sir Roland, were in discussion. Among them the security man noticed the three 'advisers' who had yet to find an opportunity to inject their expertise into the situation. A figure broke away as he watched. It was Browning, who came over to join Marshall. Behind him he left a voluble Prendle-James.

'Do you have room for four on this trip?' asked the PMO once he was sure he would be heard above the fans.

'No problem. Who are they?' returned Marshall.

Browning ushered the security man into the passageway. When he had shut the door it was much quieter. 'The RHA and AHA reps, Robins and Ferguson, will be going. As, I assume, will your new assistant.'

'Good,' said a relieved Marshall.

'Not all that good,' smiled the PMO, 'Sir Roland wants his own report on Dent. He's chosen Gibson to get it for him.'

'Sadist. Don't you think I've got enough problems without having to put up with that schoolboy?'

Browning grinned but said nothing.

'Are they ready to leave now?'

'Almost, I should think,' said the PMO. 'Your assistant hasn't had time to unpack so her overnight bag is with her. Robins and Ferguson don't need anything as they're going home and Gibson won't be staying long enough to endure any lasting damage.'

'Right,' said Marshall moving slowly down the passage, 'if you could give them the tip, please, we'll leave now.'

The four passengers filed out of the PMO's office and through the main door. As they crossed the threshold of the suite *en route* for the exit, they may have noticed the presence of the workmen, busily active but unproductive, at work around the entrance to the section. What they were unlikely to have noticed, however, with the exception of the security man, were the workmen's hands: hands with a smooth appearance, not at all the hands of those normally engaged in manual labour.

Chapter Two
(Thursday: 1400-2000)

The flight to Dent, or more correctly to Barton's Farm some half a mile outside the village, proved to be uneventful. The noise of the aircraft's engines prevented all but the briefest conversation and most of the passengers fell into silent reflection or took in the excellent view below. Marshall was the exception: he neither looked through the window nor thought grim thoughts. In fact, he was asleep.

'Wake up, Mr Marshall,' shouted his newly-appointed assistant, above the roar. As one or two disinterested glances came their way she nudged him gently on the shoulder, repeating her plea. An answering grunt told her she was getting some reaction so she continued: 'We're on our way down. We must be landing shortly.'

Marshall blinked awake then, fixing his glare on her, and said: 'This is much too formal. Why don't you call me Paul?'

'Alright, Paul it is,' replied the woman smiling. 'Call me Anne,' she added, and the now interested spectators took in just what they wanted to see and hear from the exchange before returning to their gloomy reflection.

Marshall shifted his position slightly and almost immediately winced. The pallor of sleep was still on his face but even this and the expression of

41

pain could not detract from the fact that he looked much better than before. As he finished tidying himself up the helicopter tilted up by the nose before bumping down onto the uneven ground.

Outside, a Range Rover was already drawing to a stop some yards from the aircraft. The vehicle had ample space for the five passengers but the run down to the road was by no means comfortable. As they approached a manned road-block they were waved to a halt beside a barrier. To either side of this was a litter of posters proclaiming the presence of foot-and-mouth disease and warning against entry. A halt of thirty seconds was enough to check their names before they could continue along the narrow metalled road.

Dent, like a number of Norfolk villages, appeared at first glance to have little in common with the twenty-first century. The acutely pointed roofs of the cottages were something from two or three hundred years ago. In all, some dozen buildings, all very old, were packed into the area that was almost surrounded by the close but extensive drainage system so necessary in the flat county. This, together with Dent's location, well off the beaten track, was the reason for the lack of new building and expansion.

'Quaint,' decided Ferguson aloud, as he waited for the others to climb down from the vehicle. However, quaint was somewhat wide of the mark as a word to describe the scene before them. It was a term that applied to the scene before the public health circus had come to town. There was now a bustle about the village that wouldn't normally be there. Clustered around the church, like chicks to a mother hen was a rather drab looking group of large, muddy-brown, tents and trailers. But it wasn't difficult to see what Ferguson meant; the buildings which rose above and surrounded the temporary structures, the church, the public house, the rows of cottages, still managed to project a character from another age.

'Quaint, perhaps,' said Robins, 'and no doubt this outbreak is a tragedy for such a community but, looking through the eyes of someone who must do something about it, I am almost happy that, of all possible places, it happened here.'

Nobody rebuked him for this. Nobody remarked on his seeming callousness. They all knew, possibly with the exception of Gibson, just what a similar outbreak could mean in a city.

Instead they began to move, approaching the village through the sign-posted pathway which led to The Swan. Anne sighted and waved to someone as they drew nearer and Marshall saw the response from a middle-aged man dressed in white PVC overalls and gumboots. This tired but friendly wave, however, was replaced by something more menacing as he moved towards the group.

'What the hell is this, Anne?' he demanded. 'We're not running this as a tourist attraction, you know!'

'Hold it, Don,' pleaded Anne, hand raised in defence.

'Does Browning know about this?' he persisted, obviously not good at holding.

'Even higher,' replied the young woman, 'The CMO himself.' She forgot to mention Marshall's hand in things. Quickly she moved on to introduce the visitors to the epidemiologist, somehow forgetting to give Marshall's occupation with his name. By the time she had finished the stranger, Don, had quietened noticeably.

'Look, you'd better come inside and tell me what we can do for you,' he advised.

'What a good idea,' said Marshall, whose complexion seemed to be improving all the time, in pace with his humour. 'Listen. Have you seen a chap called Henderson?'

'What's he look like?'

'Greying hair. Medium-build. No sense of humour. Security man.'

'Oh, him,' groaned Don. 'Yes. Never did get his real name. We call him Himmler. You'll find him in the back room of the pub, grilling some poor mass-killer.'

Marshall left them in the saloon bar. 'Don't go anywhere,' he said, to nobody in particular. 'I promise to be back in ten minutes.'

The way Marshall said it he might have been submitting a request rather than issuing an order. Don didn't misunderstand the command, however: 'Who the hell is he?'

'Security,' responded Ferguson, with the trace of a smile.

'Oops. Should've guessed.'

'Yes,' agreed Robins. Then, reflectively, 'But the state he's in he doesn't exactly instil confidence, does he.'

Contrary to the gospel according to Don, Henderson was not grilling, mass-killers or otherwise, at the moment Marshall entered the room. The small room, which had until so recently been the public bar, bore little resemblance to its former employment. Being that type of pub for which one counter is considered sufficient, a hatch serviced custom in this bar. With the hatch shut and all but two tables stacked in a corner it only required a large-scale map of the area to be draped over the darts-board for the transformation to be complete.

It was in deep study of the map, an area of which was spotlighted by the dartboard lamp, that Marshall found his colleague.

'What news, old buddy?' asked Marshall, after the brief greetings of two who have only been parted for twenty-four hours.

'Not a lot,' replied Henderson. Then, as Marshall sat heavily and showed no sign of response, he continued in a brisk fashion: 'Primary and secondary contacts have been interviewed and the results collated by the two of us.'

'The whole two weeks?' injected Marshall, surprise in his voice.

'Well of course, the boss has had everyone on the beat, as you know. As for the collation, I certainly didn't get these eyes from too much sleep.

Young Bob looks even worse. To look at him you'd wonder why he's still walking.'

'Anything come out of it?'

'Zero,' answered Henderson, resignation in his voice. 'Okay,' he continued, seeing the questioning look in Marshall's eyes, 'we've accounted for every person in and out. The medical side of all contacts is being chased at the moment. We reckon we've got everyone except the carrier.'

'Who is?'

Henderson took a deep breath and shot a glance to his colleague that was shy and somewhat out of place for a man of his vocation. 'Black African. Six-feet-two. Scar. War wound, from nose to left ear. Looked the none-too-friendly type.'

'Good God, Ian!' Marshall stood up, quick to display a temper uncharacteristic of him.

'I know, shouldn't have even needed to look. With a description like that someone was bound to trip over him. But it hasn't happened. The man has simply vanished.'

'Sure your information isn't from someone in delirium?' Marshall wasn't in the mood to be diplomatic.

'Four sources of information,' said Henderson, quietly, the angry glint of his eyes and tense frame giving way to patient professionalism, 'confirm the description. This man arrived at the pub around eighteen-thirty Saturday before last. Surly character, apparently. Although he stayed 'til chucking-out time he didn't have more than a couple of drinks. He had a cold and was forever sneezing.

That, and the fact that he is the only one not accounted for, is enough to make him the prime suspect.'

He gestured to the map. 'He almost certainly hasn't left the area but, if you take a look at the map,' he paused to shake his head, 'there isn't much cover around here.'

'I won't take a look, but I see what you mean.' Marshall rubbed his eyes then blinked at the discomfort caused. 'Look, I don't mean to take it out on you, Ian, but Christ, he's about as inconspicuous as a man painted in coloured spots.'

He sighed. ''Well, just keep up the good work, eh?'

'Naturally. What will you tell them,' he nodded to the door that connected them with the saloon.

'I think I'll play this one straight. It can do nothing but good. All set with Bob?' It was Marshall's turn to nod toward the room in which the visitors sat.

'Sure thing….'

Marshall nodded and made to leave.

'….and, Paul. I think I know what strain you're under. At least tell the bloodsuckers to lay off a while.' But he was talking to himself. Marshall had left.

The saloon of The Swan had suffered less from its change of circumstances than the public bar. The decor, mainly exposed beams and copper-brass ornaments, was completely intact. The bar stock, however, was safely stowed under lock and key. Now the only liquid refreshment came in the shape of a tea-urn sat, ironically, upon the copper counter. To one side a brand of utility cups were stacked upon a tray.

Marshall joined the group of visitors who were now sat at a table by a small window. In response to questions on the situation he informed them of the progress made so far, his tone quite firm in discouraging conjecture on the carrier's movements. 'So when do we begin our tour?' he asked, finally.

It was Anne who spoke first: 'Don has agreed to take us round but I want to turn my work over to him first.   Then I will be free to help you.'

'Good idea,' said Marshall and then, as she made leave, added: 'Will you be long?'

'About ten minutes I should think,' answered Don. 'Safety precaution, really. With the type of organisms we may be dealing with here it doesn't pay to take chances. We'll just double check what is being analysed and come back here.'

The silence that followed their departure was almost total, only the bustle outside invaded the room in muted tones. With the addition of a coolness, in both the temperature and relationship of the room's occupants, Marshall found nothing in his waiting that might keep him awake. But, though nobody had anything to say, his quite unashamed lapse into sleep was to be of very short duration.

Even when he heard the bang of a door, thrown back with such force that it rebounded at the end of its swing, he kept his eyes shut. The clatter of crockery and a gruff 'hello' followed, to which a voice responded courteously.

'You must be the group who came in with Anne,' said the voice of decidedly Australian ancestry and, one whose tone didn't quite tie in with a social call.

'That's right,' replied Gibson, self-nominated spokesman for the four.

'My name's Dawson and I'm the other half of the team you've just wrecked,' said the newcomer, having some difficulty in containing his emotion.

'Sorry, I don't understand,' replied Gibson, nervously.

'Anne, the other half of our team,' reminded a now irate Dawson. 'She's just told me she's now somebody's assistant. A man called Marshall, I think she said.'

Marshall, realising that peace would continue to elude him until he sorted out the problem, opened his eyes. The man standing by his table was immediately noticeable by the gleaming white overall he wore. The young face, beneath short curly hair, had a number of laughter lines around the eyes. But they were not indicating good humour now, as the blotchiness of his suntan could not be confused with anything but anger.

'That's me, Dawson. You seem to be saying that you've some prior claim, is that it?' said Marshall, calmly.

'Too true,' responded Dawson, hastily, before fully realising that he was no longer talking to someone as malleable as the inexperienced PR man. When he'd had chance to take in Marshall's stocky frame and the no-nonsense glint in his eyes, he continued in a voice more pleading than the previous dominant tone: 'I'm sure you would feel the same if, after eighteen months of hard work, and the successful conclusion of your project in sight, someone took away the brain-power to finish the job. That's what is happening in this case, don't you see? Firstly, after immense labour on a virus, we are on the very threshold of obtaining a vaccine for it, and you come along and swipe my right hand. Secondly, you've not only taken the brains of my outfit, you've deprived this unit of one of the most experienced specialists we have.'

'Which is why I took her,' said Marshall, with no alteration of tone, '... because she is good.'

He saw the puzzlement in the man's face. 'I'll try and explain. The situation at present is not only medical, as far as the likes of me are concerned, it's another world. Now, I'm an investigator and my aim is to find the source of contamination, which includes the carrier as well. The factors which govern the spread of viral organisms, or whatever you call them, their life-span, best conditions for growth, symptoms in illness, in short, all manner of things, are vital clues if I'm to carry out my job properly. If you think it out, this outfit has got three very capable specialists to get on with the fight from within; there are only laymen like me, who don't even know the rules, to fight outside. So, quite rightly, I'm going to seek an ally, not a medical student, or even you, but by your own admission, the best available.'

'Okay,' said the Australian, with resignation in his voice, 'I realise the CMO has backed you on this but I ask one thing.'

'And that is?'

'If this virus turns out to be either of the two we fear most then you allow her to return, because, by God, we're going to need her.'

'Promise,' said Marshall, simply.

When Dawson had left the PR man turned to Marshall: 'Which two do you think he meant?'

Without hesitation the security man replied: 'No idea. But we'll know soon enough, if my assistant leaves.'

The tour commenced with two guides instead of the planned one. A greying tweed-jacket-and-cavalry-twill-trousers type, the man in overall charge of the relief services, soon took Robins and Ferguson under his wing. Thereafter, they were completely separate from the rest of the party, lost in the logistic and administrative details that were more their world. The other party, consisting of Marshall, Anne and Gibson kept their original guide, Don.

The village was clustered about a road shaped like a reversed letter S. Along the farther side of the top curve of this stood the broad frontage of The Swan. On the nearer side of this curve lay the Village Green and, on a line parallel with the bottom curve of the S shape was the frontage of the church, as if arranged in silent confrontation, perhaps, to the wickedness of the 'demon drink'. This arrangement of the two principle buildings created the foundation of a roughly rectangular layout as the remainder, all houses, lined the longer connecting sides.

But the plan was difficult to visualise now for, as the parties walked over to the first temporary building parked on the 'green', the sky-line of tent and trailer-roofs mixed with the thatch of houses presented a confused picture. At waist height coloured tapes and, at intervals, notices proclaimed the coded identity of this sector.

'Blue area,' read Gibson, aloud.

'This is the safe-area where all meals are prepared,' Don explained. Then, having reached the first tent, he opened a canvas flap. 'Apart from the meals for the Isolation Section, red area, all meals are consumed here,' he added, nodding to the Spartan arrangement of foldable tables and chairs.

'Luxury,' concluded Marshall, 'but where does everyone sleep?'

Don dropped the flap into place and moved away before answering: 'We've managed to fit everyone in with the local people except, of course, for those nursing the patients. They have their own house within the Isolation Section.'

Moving in the direction of the church they came to a complex of two trailers which were connected by a tent. Marked with green tape and the usual notices, the latter presumably for those who were colour blind, this sprawling structure claimed almost a third of the small 'green' area. On a large painted board prominently displayed outside the entrance to the tent section were the words, Dressing Area.

'Presumably you will want to visit the isolation area,' asked Don, then hurriedly, 'that is, of course, apart from the ward.' In his manner was the inkling of tension for which Marshall's next remark provided the perfect release.

'That is, of course,' parodied Marshall, 'including the ward.'

'Absolutely no chance,' replied Don with firm conviction. 'It is against all the rules to let visitors into the isolation section, never mind the ward. We'll bend the rules, Marshall, but only so far.'

The security man might not have heard the protestations for he was busily searching his pockets for something. By the time Don had finished speaking Marshall had found pen and paper and, at the same time that he wrote, replied irritably: 'Don't bother to waste my time any longer, Doctor.' Then, looking up, said: 'I assume you do not know the phone extension for your CMO, but here it is. Ring him and see what he has to say.'

Reaction to the outburst was a uniform startled silence. In the corner of the tent two orderlies bent to suddenly remembered duties with a fervour indicating their exclusion from the argument.

As Marshall proffered the note for the second time, Don recovered sufficiently to speak. 'Even the CMO couldn't authorise this, surely?' His question echoed clearly his disbelief but the tone of his voice told Marshall that the epidemiologist was weakening.

Marshall sighed. 'Look. Who do you want? The Minister? Home Secretary? Make up your mind but make it quick.' He almost spat out these last words, before adding: 'I've wasted enough time already. Nowhere is off limits to me and my people. Understand?'

Anne knew that shouting at Don would not bring instant subservience but she realised Marshall had placed the doctor, by his pressure, in a situation where he must make a decision, one way or another.

Several seconds elapsed before Don, who hadn't once taken his eyes off his protagonist, broke the silence. When he did speak it was in the tone of one who has suddenly found an answer. 'Okay. Here's what we do. Full protection suits with closed circuit breathing system. Wash-down on completion,' he said, his tone business-like. Turning to Anne, he continued: 'No need for you to come '

'But...' she began, before he cut in.

'But, nothing, Anne. There are three very valid reasons why I don't want you along on this foolish errand. One, the structure of the suits we shall be wearing, as you know, is such that normal conversation is impracticable. Therefore, as your present role is mainly concerned with supplying medical answers where Mr Marshall requires them, your presence, muted as you will be, can only be superfluous. Secondly, the fewer people going in decreases the chances of contagion coming out. And, thirdly...'

'Thirdly, Anne is going to make a tiny little phone call to London for you,' interrupted the security man.

'Quite.' returned their guide, handing the scribbled note to Anne. 'There's just one more thing, gentlemen,' he continued. 'If the response from our CMO isn't favourable you can be sure of a stay in the isolation section for two to three weeks.'

No less than fifteen minutes had elapsed before the party re-emerged from the tent. Now the three men were almost completely clothed in white PVC suits and, in other surroundings, they might have been astronauts on their way to the launch-pad. For the moment, the zip-around clear-view face-masks lay folded on their shoulders with the integral air-supply valve switched off.

The Red Area was marked off in similar fashion to the other areas but the large Biological Hazard notices could not possibly be overlooked to allow mistaken entry. Following Don, the two visitors soon arrived at the entrance to the area. Even without their guide each man would have known the specific route they, in fact, everyone, must adhere to within the section, for Don had ensured that both the layout and route were fully understood by both.

The area bounded by the red tapes took in the whole of the church, and, pessimistically, the graveyard, as well as the nearest house with its large garden. The result was a roughly square shape of some hundred square yards. The prescribed route began at the rear door of the house, the top floor of which had been taken over as quarters for the isolation-ward nurses, through the downstairs rooms and out through the front door. From here a distance of thirty feet connected the house with the front entrance of the church. After passing through the church they would leave by a door at the other end whereupon they would pass the incineration and chemical-disposal plant on their way to the decontamination plant. Here they would, extraordinarily, be washed down with disinfectant before shedding their protective suits. Finally they would walk the few paces to the house and leave the isolation section by the same route.

'This is where we go self-contained,' said Don, as they reached the front door of the church. 'Remember that after we switch on the air we've approximately fifteen minutes before...well, before asphyxiation becomes a greater risk than infection. I'll be keeping an eye on the time and we'll pull out at minute ten. Okay?' He waited for the answering nod from Marshall and a very nervous version from the PR man. 'Right, switch on the air, test it and then zip up your facemasks. Then we'll check each other for leaks.'

A minute later they were inside the church.

Even with the afternoon heat at its greatest the interior of the church was still cool, which was one of the main reasons it was chosen as the ward. But the effect produced by the sunlight, slanting through the stained-glass windows on the activity below, created an eerie effect that disturbed the visitors in varying degrees.

After a short but loud, and sometimes indistinct, conversation between Don and a figure labelled Head Nurse, Marshall and the PR man were greeted with a distinctly icy look before the woman waved them through. The three figures shuffled on down the few shallow steps until they were in the body of the church.

The immediate impression presented by the scene was of Spartan correctness. Some eighteen-or-so white tubular-framed beds, not all of which were occupied, were arranged in conventional hospital-ward fashion. By the side of each stood white-painted lockers upon which sat a solitary glass from which poked a thermometer. Dotted here-and-there were 'drip' trolleys from some of which a bottle of fluid was suspended.

Around the beds figures dressed in long gowns, facemasks and over-shoes went about their business in practised silence as they tended their patients. For all the reaction they provoked the visitors might not have been there.

Don stopped at one bed and the eyes of the two followers strayed to the golden tresses of the young patient lying there. She was almost completely immobile, only the occasional movement of her head from side to side to show she was alive. Or almost all, for dead people don't sweat or flush with blood even, as in the girl's case, when the skin is pinched from loss of fluid and features deeply etched through pain.

After a few seconds, Don, nudged them and pointed to his facemask. Then pointing to the girl he mouthed, in exaggerated mime: 'Thirteen years.'

As Marshall looked around at the faces of those who were suffering, he could understand the extremes the medical staff had gone to contain the virus, a deadly virus that existed in this very room. Now they were in the midst of a battle. On the one hand, an undiscovered virus multiplied and destroyed the life in these bodies, gradually and painfully. On the other hand, the slim resources of medicine fought to keep the patients well while the laboratories searched for the specific killer and hoped, as they all hoped, that there was something in their arsenal with which to fight it. It seemed to the security man that they just might be holding their own. But then, he reflected, the battle had only just begun.

It happened just as they turned away and were looking further down the line of beds. Even over the noise made by the demand-valve in the self-contained breathing system there could be no doubting that the other noise was a scream. All three turned around to see the young girl sat up, fear in her eyes and a streak of blood dripped from her mouth onto the white sheet across her lap.

'Mummy!' she cried, hysterically, before calming hands came to her in the form of a couple of nurses. Gradually the crying subsided to a wimper.

Rational review of what had happened would have combined the obvious suffering with shock on waking from a troubled sleep to discover the three 'spacemen' at the foot of her bed. The blood was a symptom, possibly of the disease but also possibly, of a lip or tongue bitten in fear. Whatever it was it transfixed Gibson in horror and it required a firm nudge from Don and Marshall to move him away.

In what seemed no time at all Don was again gesturing, this time to a clock on the wall, and they moved down the ward to the rear of the church. Here a door led out into the sunshine and, although they could not possibly detect it, the feeling of cleanliness and fresh air.

It took barely three minutes to shower with disinfectant followed by another of fresh water before they were struggling out of their suits.

'Satisfied?' asked Don, quite unnecessarily washing his hands.

Gibson said nothing, his mind elsewhere.

Marshall also ignored the question but responded with another: 'Just what are they doing for them at the moment?'

'All they can. Keeping the temperature down with drugs. Giving them something for the pain. In response to dehydration due to vomiting or diarrhoea, and plain sweating we put fluid and chemicals lost through the intravenous 'drip' system. Otherwise, there is little we can do. The term for it is Supportive Measures.'

'So they must just wait, and let them die possibly, until they get something from the labs. Is that it?' This was Gibson, the pallor fast disappearing from his face.

'I'm afraid so,' replied Don. Noticing they were ready, he added: 'I'll go over to the house and wait for Anne there.'

But there was no need for them to wait. As they approached the house an unhappy looking Anne was waiting by the door. 'All clear,' she said, loudly. 'But it looks as if there might be some bad news, Paul.'

'What's that?'

'He wouldn't say on the telephone but we've just been recalled. They're organising another helicopter now and we've to be at Barton's Farm for pick-up in half-an-hour.'

As the trio of Anne, Marshall and the PR man sat in the back of the Range Rover waiting, all was peaceful. Robins and Ferguson had not been recalled because they were too involved with the situation on their 'patch'. In fact, neither of the men had been seen since the tour had commenced. Now, apart from the crying of birds, all was silent as the golden sun edged nearer to the western horizon.

Prompted by the activity of lighting a cigarette, Gibson spoke quietly: 'What a crying shame.' He suddenly seemed to realise he had spoken aloud and added, quickly: 'The girl, I mean. Crying shame.' He paused to shake his head. 'Any more news on the carrier?' he asked, turning his head towards the security man.

'You know as much as we do,' responded Marshall, blankly.

'Ah. But do we know as much as you do?' the PR man persisted, exhibiting an inquisitiveness that until now had been dormant.

Marshall ignored him.

'I suppose illness in children must always be upsetting,' said Anne, weakly. 'Perhaps it's the fear and obvious helplessness which claws ... calls out for help,' she added, the last part of the sentence coming out in a rush. 'Excuse me,' she said, then got clumsily out of her seat and climbed down from the vehicle.

'I'd no idea she was so upset,' said Gibson in hushed urgency. 'I suppose I expect doctors to be used to it. Do you think I should go out to her?' he asked.

'Leave her alone. She's better on her own for a few minutes. You must remember she's a specialist, a laboratory type who perhaps doesn't see all that much of the suffering side of life. More important, she's a woman, with her own way of dealing with stress,' said Marshall.

'But she didn't even come in with us,' argued Gibson.

'No. But she got enough of the facts from Don more than likely, when she was doing her turnover. What you said must have sparked it off,' he explained, at the same time ordering silence with his raised hand as the microbiologist returned to the Range Rover.

As Gibson turned to look at Anne's approach, and away from Marshall, the security man surreptitiously popped two pills into his mouth and swallowed. Still out of Gibson's view he closed his eyes quickly but then needed to place his hand heavily on the armrest to combat the faintness and nausea he felt.

For the next ten minutes-or-so silence once again prevailed until a tiny dot in the sky grew to the shape of a helicopter which, with an ear-shattering scream of engines and fluttering rotor blades, landed some twenty yards from the car.

Chapter Three
(Thursday: 2200-Friday 0300)

It was dark when the three returned to the Department of Health building. The corridors, now dimly lit, echoed to their footsteps as they approached the suite of offices in which the CMO and his team waited. They met the occasional uniformed security patrol, members of the permanent DOH staff, but no-one else. The building seemed almost deserted.

'Well, that's something,' remarked Anne, pointing to the site of the recent building activity outside the suite. 'We should get a little peace now.'

Marshall grunted agreement and, after ushering the PR man through the doorway, quickly glanced back over his shoulder.

At the same time, along the corridor, a man unbent from the task of checking a door lock and, for an instant, their gazes met. Marshall reflected that this was more fitting work for men with smooth hands. He stepped into the suite and closed the door.

'You look better, much better,' greeted a shirt-sleeved Sir Roland, his relief at their return barely concealed. Then, remembering why he had been unnerved into making such a human comment, he continued: 'Which is more than can be said of our problem. Please sit down.'

As Marshall took the chair he noted the others who were present. Browning and Prendle-James flanked the CMO while the three men from the department of Public and International Health, and Overseas Development, Selby, Ashton and Walsh respectively, sat in their original positions around the table.

'Now, Mr Marshall,' began Sir Roland, 'I think we have shown quite clearly that we can go well beyond the rules in order to co-operate with your investigations.' The no-nonsense tone he used was nothing if not business like. 'That you were allowed into, and most unusually out of, the isolation section at Dent should be ample proof of that.'

Aware that Sir Roland was displeased at something with which he was doubtless connected, Marshall watched as he stretched an arm towards a tape-recorder which had been placed on the table.

'This,' announced the CMO, retrieving an instantly recognisable object, 'is a recorded message I received by special-delivery just three hours ago. Perhaps when you have all heard its contents Mr Marshall will tell us what exactly is going on.' With that he handed the cassette to Browning who clicked it into the machine and pressed the tab.

'This message,' said the accentless voice which they heard after a few seconds of silence, 'is directed to the Chief Medical Officer of Health in whose hands its further dissemination rests.' A short pause followed during which the majority of those hunched around the table managed to glance at Sir Roland.

'As you are now completely aware, certain viral organisms have been liberated among the community of Dent,' continued the voice and, although it didn't detract from the clarity of speech, a loud background hum on the tape was an irritating distraction. 'We, the Power Reversion Group, hereby claim all responsibility for this infection. Furthermore, this is but the first in a series of demonstrations which will occur over the next few days.'

After two or three seconds of silence the CMO nodded to Browning, who stopped the tape.

'The rest is blank,' explained Sir Roland. 'I ran it through twice to make sure.'

Marshall responded quickly. 'Does anyone outside this room know of this tape?'

'No.' The CMO had had the best part of three hours to ready himself for the moment when Marshall would be confronted with the taped message. He had expected a different reaction to the one he was seeing in the security man, at least one of surprise, and had looked forward, even in his concerned state, to the moment when he would demand an explanation. Now, that initiative had been taken from him with Marshall's swift recovery to news, which still left the rest of them stunned.

Marshall rose. 'Excuse me a moment. I must make a phone call.'

The CMO nodded vaguely and watched as the security man left the room and entered his, Sir Roland's, office. Then his interest was drawn by the babble of excited comment from those at the table. However, as they heard Marshall begin talking, the chatter in the boardroom quickly ceased. Their unashamed eavesdropping claimed but scant reward for, apart from curtly stated pieces of innocuous sounding information, nothing was really added to what they already knew. In two minutes Marshall was back.

'Well, Mr Marshall?' prompted the CMO, as the security man regained his seat in silence.

'Well, what?' returned the security man, innocently.

'Don't be obtuse, man,' said the CMO, irritated.

'Let's hope it's a hoax,' offered Marshall, reflecting a comment he had heard expressed when on his way to the telephone.

Sir Roland's response to this was a strangled sigh followed by a tightening of the skin around his mouth. He could tolerate Marshall's diversions no more. 'Claire,' he called. 'Get me Reuters, please.'

With her acknowledgement he turned to Marshall. 'Hoax or not I refuse to stumble around in the dark any longer,' he said, hotly. 'Perhaps the investigative talents of newspaper men would be better.....'

'You know that would be a very irresponsible thing to do,' injected Marshall. 'I've already discussed the dangers such a move will... '

This time it was the CMO's turn to interrupt. 'You have a better idea?' he challenged. 'Like, for instance, telling me just what you're playing at?'

For three or four seconds the security man did not reply. Then, with a loud sigh, he said. 'All right, if I could see you in private, perhaps in your office, I will fill you in on the details.'

It had been a good try but Marshall had known even before he'd said it that the CMO would not be interested in such clandestine activities as secret meetings, in fact Marshall had hoped for such a reaction.

Sir Roland shook his head. 'What you have for my ears you can say to everyone present,' he persisted, reflecting the pattern of behaviour which had borne the stamp of all his negotiations, in that he would never settle for anything less than exactly what he wanted.

'You're certain?' queried the security man.

'Absolutely!'

'You must then realise,' began Marshall when the CMO had cancelled the telephone call, 'that what I have to say now will cut you off from the outside world for days or even weeks. There is no way that any information from this room is going to find its way beyond that door,' he pointed to the connecting door at the end of the corridor, 'except that carried by me, or possibly my assistant.'

'What about our families?' asked an indignant Walsh.

'Your families will be informed, officially, that you are employed on matters affecting the security of the nation.'

'You can order that?' put in the PR man.

'Not only can, will,' returned Marshall, who chose not to tell the whole truth: that his men were already in the process of carrying out this task. 'I'll take your mobiles too,' he added.

'You don't trust us?' This from Prendle-James.

Marshall attempted a smile but it didn't come off. 'Mobile phone traffic is insecure. People, journalists, can and do sometimes intercept such conversations. Let's avoid the possibility entirely.'

No-one moved. 'You'll get them back,' he added.

Slowly a group of phones collected in front of Marshall and he began putting them into his pockets after switching each one off. 'You will still be able to make calls via a switchboard which will be the only route for use by the telephones in this suite.' Again, he was careful with the truth. The landline phones had been intercepted by his people for some time. Now they would actively manage the telephone traffic like a manual exchange. He looked over to Claire. 'I'm sure Claire will assist you with this, at first.'

Marshall hadn't finished. 'You should know that internet access will also be disabled shortly. The internet is not secure.'

'We have internet security on all our systems,' said Gibson. 'We run scans all the time.'

Marshall sighed. 'Just as well your field is medicine,' he said, casting his eyes around the group. 'You really have no idea, have you? Between your computer and all the other computers most of your emails and search requests are sent in plain language, unencrypted. These data can and are regularly intercepted, filtered, read, and sometimes as with Pakistan, China, and other states, it is claimed, re-routed or swallowed into a 'black hole' from where the sender and recipient will never see them again.' Marshall sighed again. 'I could go on but I don't think I have time to waste explaining beginner-level security. We have more important things to do.'

The CMO, as usual, was fighting an inner turmoil but was calm when next spoke. 'So no-one leaves this suite,' he confirmed. 'Go on.'

Marshall didn't speak immediately. He was tired now. For so long it seemed he had skimped on sleep. Even the previous two days had yielded little more than the occasional catnap and he was beginning to feel it. And the transfusions, so vital but debilitating, were taking their toll. So for something like five seconds he just sat there resting, listening to the confused hum of the traffic in the streets below. Suddenly he became aware that they were all waiting.

'Three weeks ago,' he began, 'a serious fire occurred at a research laboratory in which four specialists died. With them went the records and cultures from almost two years work, which was unfortunate, for it wasn't just any lab. It carried a security grading of Top Secret and was connected with defence projects.'

'Virological research?' inquired the professor.

'Virological, bacteriological and chemical....'

'Warfare,' gasped the International Health man, making his first, and melodramatic, contribution to the meeting. 'Germ warfare,' he continued, as the others looked at him more in startled amazement at his outburst than the validity of his claim. 'The government were supposed to have halted work in that field years ago.'

'Let Mr Marshall finish!' The CMO, sensing that an argument could very easily develop and disrupt his meeting, discouraged Ashton with a glare.

'Anyway,' continued the security man, unperturbed, 'the investigation that followed discovered the blaze had started in a store room. The bodies were identified even though they were very badly charred. But further tests, in line with those carried out by the fire department, failed to reveal just why it was that, with ample time to do so, the researchers failed to get out.

'Suspicions were triggered by this and, when we found the door-lock with the mechanism in the locked position, it was obvious that what had seemed to be a simple accident was now multiple murder, and carried out in a pretty cool manner if our reconstruction is accurate.'

'Basically,' he sighed, 'the reconstruction goes something like this. A person or persons unknown evaded the security guards and entered the research wing. Once there they either overpowered the workers by force or, more simply, used a gas-gun to knock them out. Who can be sure? Fire leaves few clues. Then they took whatever they had come to get, started the fire to cover their tracks and left by the same route they had used to enter. The closed-circuit ventilation system, so necessary in such environments, prevented any sign of the fire attracting the guards until it was much too late.'

The CMO stirred. 'And when you heard of the Dent outbreak you suspected a connection with the laboratory incident,' he reasoned, reaching the natural conclusion.

'Correct. With the wide variety of cultures under test at the lab, it was quite possible a phial of some dangerous organism had been taken, injected into the carrier, and this man then transported to Dent,' replied Marshall.

'Carriers, possibly?' put in Browning, stressing the plural.

'What do you mean?' queried the security man.

The PMO tapped the tape-recorder with a pencil. 'The tape spoke of a series of demonstrations. Unless the one carrier is to infect all the sites of these demonstrations it will require more than one carrier,' he said simply. Then he added, quickly: 'You said there may have been various cultures at the lab. It may be that a number of carriers are indeed infected, and each with a different virus.'

'Good God!' exclaimed Prendle-James.

'Precisely,' sympathised Marshall. 'If the situation is as complex as Mr Browning says, then our job, yours and mine together, is made immeasurably more difficult.' He turned to face Sir Roland. 'Of course, if and when we find the Dent carrier we may be able to discover what the position is.'

'Yes,' responded a worried CMO. 'We heard about him from your friend Henderson.' For an instant it seemed he would say more. His mouth opened but nothing came out and his jaw shut, biting off what he knew was nothing more constructive than circumspection. But he didn't give up easily and the familiar fixed stare froze his expression. He was thinking deeply.

Around the table others struck similar poses as they too wrestled with the problems of the situation, each hoping to unearth an idea into which they could channel their energies.

But nothing came. All that could be done, both medically and from the security point of view, was being done. Their position at present, and until something turned up from the steps already taken, continued to be one of 'wait and see'.

It was Claire who broke the silence. She had been in her office since the CMO had cancelled the call to Reuters, a call which, incidentally, he had privately instructed her not to make under any circumstances. Now she entered the boardroom and addressed her boss. 'There's a man outside who says he's to pick up a parcel.'

'That's for me,' said Marshall, rising from his chair. 'I'm sending the tape for analysis.' After which he scooped up the cassette and headed for the door. In a matter of seconds he was back.

'All the domestic luxuries, camp-beds and blankets, et cetera, will be here in about half-an-hour,' he announced. 'They're fixing up bathing facilities at the moment.'

The interruption seemed to lift the meeting out of the doldrums for when Marshall sat down the vacant expressions he had previously noted had vanished. In this re-awakened mood it was the professor who spoke first. 'I've been thinking about the break-in you spoke of,' he began. 'I doubt if they have any relevance to the situation we face but one or two things puzzle me.'

'Hector,' said the CMO, 'I think we should leave the security aspects to Mr Marshall...'

'No, Sir Roland,' interjected Marshall. 'We need all the help we can get. So if you don't mind, I'd like to hear what your scientific officer has to say.'

The CMO shrugged.

Prendle-James looked quizzically at the security man. Then, realising he had captured everyone's attention, he continued. 'Firstly, how did they manage to get into this establishment undetected? Secondly, if the person involved in the lab break-in is the same man responsible for infecting Dent, there is only one way he could have managed it and been able to transport the disease to the village.'

Noticing Marshall's frown, he elaborated. 'I mean that he must have either been previously infected with the virus, and survived the illness long before the break-in, or he simply emptied the contents of a phial among the people of Dent. In the latter case, he is not only a blundering fool, he is most probably very ill himself.'

Marshall nodded earnestly. The gesture meant nothing, however; it merely gave him time to think. 'I think I can answer one of your questions satisfactorily, that of how they managed to get into the lab, but the other is more difficult,' he said. 'I may have misled you into believing the research lab was protected by the conventional defences of a military establishment. The fact is that this wasn't so. As you may already know, and as our International Health representative pointed out, the government was supposed to have closed down such labs in response to not only public opinion but international agreement, too. However, and I won't argue the rights or wrongs of it, it was felt the research was too important to cancel, on the basis that we needed to know them in order to defend against these agents. Porton Down, the natural site for such work, was too closely monitored and so the cover, and anonymity, of an innocuous business was used. Although guards were present, in the military sense, security didn't really exist.'

Aware that Ashton only needed an opening in the conversation in which to argue the morality of such a situation, Marshall hurried onto the other question. 'As to how the virus was transported to Dent, your guess is as good as mine. Henderson, the security man in charge of investigations at the village, has unearthed nothing to indicate that the contents of any phial, assuming one existed, were distributed there. Again, I can only say that we hope to find out when we find the carrier.'

'Always back to the carrier,' observed Selby, from the end of the table. 'Incidentally, something strikes me as odd about the tape-recording we heard.'

'Go on,' said Sir Roland, when the Public Health man hesitated. 'I have a feeling we share the same impression.'

'It's just that my experience of terrorism, purely via the media, I hasten to add, is that no incident occurs without a faction claiming responsibility,' said Selby. 'What I'm trying to say is that by sending the tape to the Chief Medical Officer, instead of the usual newspaper offices, the perpetrators of the outbreak have gone the opposite way to the norm. They seem to be courting confidentiality instead of the usual publicity. That is unless…'

'No we haven't received any indication that the press have been approached with the news,' interrupted Marshall, 'but I see your point. We don't know why they are following this unusual policy. Perhaps it suits their purpose not to have the panic which publication would provoke. For my own part I am just grateful for their reticence.'

'Hear, hear,' said the professor, with feeling. 'Let us pray that they don't change their minds on that one.'

At this point the CMO began to wrap up the meeting. It was decided that a twenty-four hour watch would be necessary on the telephones and computer email systems, in addition to the four-hourly routine calls from Dent. With the rapid escalation of the situation very possible, Sir Roland wanted quick responsiveness to incoming requests for information. Therefore, one person would be awake at all times.

In addition, it was decided that information of promising treatment at the Dent site would be stockpiled at the DOH lest it be required by some other location in the future. This task would fall to the same watch-keeper.

There were numerous questions on this subject, the last of which was aired by Marshall. 'It's quite likely that messages will arrive for me when I'm away. If the situation deteriorates as much as we think possible, it may be that I will be spending very little time here. In view of this, would it be possible to have someone keep a watching brief over the whole of the, er, information cell?'

'You mean to rapidly up-date you on the situation when required?'

Marshall nodded. 'It would help me tremendously.'

'You're in danger of having more assistants than I have, Mr Marshall. But I see that it is quite necessary,' said Sir Roland. 'We will decide exactly who shall run this… information cell in the morning. I think it can wait until then.'

The CMO turned to address the meeting generally. 'Well, that's about it. Any other questions?'

'Yes,' replied Browning, 'I would like to ask Mr Marshall how he is going to prevent news of our incarceration from becoming known. We all have our places of work and daytime commitments. Sooner or later we are going to be missed.'

'Quite true,' answered Marshall. 'It is now Thursday night. Tomorrow your departments will be informed that for various reasons you are unavailable. Also, with the building work taking place outside this section, we should be able to convince the inquisitive that this place is out of bounds due to structural alterations. Saturday and Sunday should create no problems, of course. We might even get away with Monday. However, on Monday we will review the situation. Does that answer your question?'

Browning smiled. 'You seem to have an answer for everything.'

'I'm in a game where answers are essential, whether they be right or wrong,' replied the security man, icily. Then, to the CMO only, he added: 'I shall be away for some hours tonight. I have a meeting with my superiors. I will leave you my phone number before I go.'

At this Sir Roland quickly wound-up the meeting and headed for his office. Browning and Prendle-James followed him while the remainder took the opportunity to stretch their legs before airing less formal opinions.

In a corner away from the rest Marshall and Anne spoke in low voices.

'Telephone call, Mr Marshall,' called Claire.

Excusing himself, Marshall left Anne to her own devices and made for the secretary's office. As he entered, Claire pointed to the telephone and then withdrew, shutting the door behind her.

'We've found him,' said the voice of Henderson.

'Good,' responded Marshall.

''fraid not. He's dead.'

Unusually, Marshall's face changed expression several times in the two minutes it took to complete the telephone conversation.

Then he went and told the CMO that the carrier was dead. He did not tell him everything that Henderson had said, just as he hadn't told everything at the meeting recently completed - and for similar reasons. Besides, Marshall knew that Sir Roland would have enough to worry him now that the possible source of answers to his questions was lost, without having to speculate why the man had died so unexpectedly, from a bullet blasted through the base of his skull.

An hour later, Marshall was in deep discussion with his boss. More precisely, he was drawing to the end of his report and had just paused for breath before adding, finally: 'The situation, therefore, is following the suspected pattern, sir.'

'Except that we didn't expect to find the man as we did,' corrected the man who was sitting opposite Marshall. 'It shows very careful planning to put both the body and the car in a marsh deep enough for such an operation, outside dredged and therefore frequented channels.'

At fifty-eight years of age and dressed smartly in civilian clothes, Rear-Admiral Benson at first glance may have eluded the correct estimation of his status from purely visible evidence. From his physical stature bereft of gold-braided uniform he differed little from other males of his age. But there was that certain something which qualified him for a more esoteric club of men. The straightness of spine was undoubtedly the first indicator of this, but it was more prolonged study which drew out the others; the cragginess of features blurred by too much association with the sea, although it was some years ago, and the glinting intelligence which shone from his blue eyes. It was this last which wrenched respect from any beholder, the eyes that were now levelled at Marshall. 'Any ideas on how they could get this carrier to infect the village of Dent to the exclusion of any other communities?'

Marshall shifted uncomfortably in the plump armchair. They were alone in the shabby above-the-shop room. The faintly nauseous smells of the flat were representative of its normal function as a rather undersized, though at present untenanted, family home. From the centre of the high ceiling shone a low-wattage lamp whose meagre light was further filtered by an ancient cloth lampshade. But as the cover, convenience and proximity that such premises afforded were excellent for the task, neither man objected too much in silence, and not at all aloud.

'Too many ifs and buts, sir,' replied the security man, shaking his head briefly. 'A pantechnicon perhaps, freighting both car and carrier to the area. It should be possible to run a life-support unit from the vehicle's engine to supply a plastic tent, airtight, in the back. A modified motor-home, perhaps. It's all speculation, I know, but no protective clothing was found with the car and no other cases of this virus infection have been reported.'

'Plausible, all the same,' adjudged the admiral. 'Do you think the executioner was a member of the same team who brought the carrier to Dent?'

'Most likely, sir. The carrier must have been a very dangerous person to have around, naturally. With our operatives looking for him, it was only a matter of time before he was found. He could have told us quite a lot about this operation. He had to go.'

Benson moved forward to lean his elbows on the table but changed his mind as he discerned the discoloured table-top. Instead he returned to his upright posture and looked back to Marshall. 'What then of his usefulness as a carrier?'

'There is that,' conceded the security man. 'But I would think that if the plan is to ensure localisation of the outbreak, and the bulletin seems to suggest just that, then the best guarantee of this is to destroy the infective agent, the carrier.'

Benson sighed. 'Which means that for the other promised demonstrations they need at least one more carrier, although there may be several.'

'Yes, sir. But if we are able to get word to the other carriers, don't ask me how, radio broadcast I suppose, detailing how the first carrier died, we may have something of morale-breaking value. Henderson is quite sure, from all the signs at the site of the ditched car, that we were not expected to find it....'

'Yes, I see what you mean,' interrupted Benson. 'It is unusual for fanatics - some Islamic funda-mentalists apart - to knowingly go to certain, scheduled deaths. And unless we and the Americans have missed something, it isn't Al Qaeda or their friends.'

For a few moments they were silent. Benson used the time and the subdued lighting to ad-vantage by appraising the facial features of one of his most trusted men. The advantage afforded by the lighting came from the positions of the two men in relation to the light from the street-lamps. These threw a square of sodium light onto Mar-shall, who was sat furthest from the uncurtained window. Benson, his back to the street, was sil-houetted and his expression therefore unreadable.

The admiral looked keenly at his employee. He noticed the deeply-etched lines of the security man's face and the swelling beneath the eyes. Although medically ignorant in comparison with those observers at the DOH, he mentally quanti-fied the wellbeing of the man before him, a task he had found necessary all too often in the past with other operatives. He reflected then that his agent's appearance would probably degenerate before it improved, if ever his health was to improve. True, there were factors in this operation which had not been experienced by an agent of his before. Nevertheless, he felt certain that the continuation of Marshall's symptoms would necessarily reduce his effectiveness and probably inflict permanent injury to his agent's health.

'I know what you are thinking, sir, but it is my job,' said Marshall, possessed of an intuition that had served him well in many situations in the past. His voice was barely controlled but low in key as he continued: 'I've done the donkey-work on this one. I set it up.' He stopped then, sensing that he was close to going too far, but he couldn't help adding with the trace of a smile: 'Besides, in this particular situation, who else can you use? You have to use me.'

Benson was noted for his disciplinarian attitudes in a number of circles, some in which he didn't even move, which was sure indication of the reverberative power of his displeasure. It said a great deal for the truth in Marshall's outburst, however, that the admiral's response was not only muted, it was totally absent.

'So we can begin,' said Benson, after a further pause in which Marshall had returned to his normal inscrutable self.

'Any leads on J, sir?' asked Marshall.

'We're still nibbling away,' replied Benson. 'We found J's father and he's giving us plenty of co-operation. It seems Monsieur Chaval and his son haven't seen eye-to-eye since J turned fanatic while at university. When, as you researched quite correctly, J teamed up with the mercenary character, D'rosario, and showed signs of becoming too much of an embarrassment, the billionaire father bought his son's permanent exile with the gift of one-hundred millions.'

'Dollars?'

'UK pounds,' responded Benson, flatly. 'Being a businessman Chaval wasn't going to release that much capital so he gave him stock and a few verbal conditions to adhere to. Six months ago he was alarmed to hear that eighty million pounds worth of this stock had been sold in one day. It took a lot of buying for him to stop the run on his interests the sale caused. Needless to say there is no love lost between them. They haven't met since his father threw him out five years ago.'

'Any I.D., sir?'

Benson shook his head. 'Part of the deal was a clear-out of all photographs. Everything to remind him of his son was destroyed. He really hates him. An artist's impression has been obtained from a few old photographs from his former acquaintances, but the likeness of him is, naturally, some years out of date. He could have undergone plastic surgery in the interim.' Benson pushed a cardboard folder across the table.

'Not exactly full of character is it?' commented Marshall, having selected a portrait sketch for perusal. A face, dark in the colour of the Mediterranean races, was the setting for almost petite features of nose and lips in that, with coal black eyes, they grouped close together in neat fragility. Showing only the beginnings of swarthy beard the face gave the overall impression of belonging to a man in his early twenties and one, moreover, mirrored thousands of times on the shores of the inland-sea east of Gibraltar.

'The impression,' said Benson, nodding to the sketch the security man was holding, 'takes note of the father's characteristics where possible and we think it could be a good likeness.'

'Do we know what he used these eighty million pounds for, sir?' asked Marshall, closing the folder on the photographs, the image now committed to memory.

'Not yet,' he replied, with the sureness of tone which Marshall had grown to understand to mean that the information would be available in time, and sooner rather than later.

'The mercenary?' persisted Marshall.

'Nothing to add to your own investigations. Nothing heard or seen since the middle of last year when he left London for Paris to join J. Remember, it is pure supposition that they are working together and are behind the Power Reversion Group.' Benson was tactful enough not to mention that indeed the only source of inspiration had been Marshall's hunch on the subject.

'Yes, sir. But the general trend fits, doesn't it?' He didn't wait for a reply but went on, using his fingers to illustrate the points he was raising. 'They are known to have teamed up shortly after the guerrilla group was decimated. The organisation we have seen in the fanatic's recent operations bears the hallmarks of D'rosario's methods.' He stopped and shot a glance at Benson, 'I assume we're certain, at least, that it was J who withdrew the share capital?'

'Correct,' he replied. 'Authenticated this morning.'

'So,' continued Marshall, back to finger counting, 'after a cessation of activities lasting six months we know J and D'rosario have large amounts of capital in hand.' He paused for a moment as if thinking it through before adding, confidently: 'We have the connection with the deaths of the man at Dent and the earlier episode. It all fits. I still think it is much more probable than possible.'

'I'm with you there,' agreed Benson, 'that's why I'm deploying maximum effort to finding out what this character J is doing with the money. Do you think there might be contact between this fellow and the DOH people? We're pretty well out on a limb associating with Fletcher's team. It may well be that the unprecedented liaison may alert them to the fact that we suspect a plant.'

'I think I've satisfied them that there are legitimate reasons for our collaboration but I also believe that a letter from the top, addressed personally to the CMO, would go a long way towards keeping it that way,' said Marshall.

'Agreed,' responded the admiral.

'As for contact, I've yet to discover the means but I'm almost certain some sort of communication exists otherwise how could instructions be passed to the plant,' continued the security man. 'I think the close confinement situation we have engineered there will yield results if only because there will be very little privacy. With this, and the weather, we may force the impostor into making a mistake....'

'You're assuming you'll notice it among the other displays of stress behaviour,' interrupted Benson. 'It will need no great deal of pressure to ignite the tempers of some of these people,' he added, tapping his pen against the list of names provided by Marshall.

Once again, in the short silence which followed, Marshall's intuition told him that his bosses' worries were not only directed toward those of the CMO and his staff. Marshall remained silent.

'Look, there is nothing further to discuss until a few results come in or something happens. Do your time in the back room; the nurse is already there. Then spend an hour resting. By then I should have that letter for Sir Roland,' said Benson, winding up the meeting.

Marshall left then, closing the ill-fitting door behind him. For some minutes afterwards the admiral looked vacantly into middle-space before remembering, suddenly, where he was. He then took pen to paper and began to write.

'I'm beginning to hate this bloody job', he said, quietly. 'The man should be on sick leave, not on active service.'

On Marshall's return to the DOH suite the interior was in darkness. But in darkness only so far as Marshall could see and only for two seconds for, as he moved to walk down the corridor, the door to his right opened and he was bathed in light from the utility-room.

'Come in,' whispered the silhouetted figure in the doorway. 'Coffee?'

'Yes please,' responded Marshall, gratefully, recognising Browning as he entered the room.

'Don't you ever sleep?' asked the Principal Medical Officer, over his shoulder as Marshall followed him in.

'Not if someone can possibly help it,' responded Marshall. 'I might ask the same of you.'

'You might, indeed. Sentry-go, I'm afraid,' he left off his preparation of the beverage to point at a list on the wall. Two-hour watches for all except the ladies and the CMO.'

'Thanks,' said Marshall as the PMO handed him his coffee. 'Is everybody settled in?'

The PMO sat heavily in the one armchair as Marshall leaned against a cupboard.

'No problems,' responded Browning, 'your man appeared with our bedding, as you promised, and we're allowed to use a bathroom they've fixed up on another floor.'

'Sleeping arrangements okay?' prompted the security man.

'Again, no problems. The ladies are in my office,' replied Browning. Then he checked himself:

'But, of course, you won't be familiar with the layout of the place yet, will you?'

Marshall refrained from saying he knew the layout of the whole DOH building rather better than most of those who spent their working lives there. Instead, he waited for Browning to continue.

'Well you've seen the boardroom,' said the PMO, picking his words carefully. 'In there are Gibson, Walsh, Selby, Ashton, er, Hector and myself, presently. Next door to that, on this side of the corridor, is the dutyman's beat or, more exactly, where I'm supposed to be when I'm not making coffee,' he explained, smiling in mock sheepishness.

'You mean the other side of this wall?'

'No, the lavatory is there. The office, which belongs to the secretary and young Gibson, ordinarily, is the other side of that. So it is the boardroom, secretary's office, lavatory and,' he pointed to the floor, 'utility room.'

Noticing the feigned difficulty in understanding which Marshall was demonstrating, Browning said: 'I'd show you around if it wasn't so late. I mean early. But most people are keeping duty through the night as it is and there's no sense in disturb...'

'No. That's quite alright,' injected Marshall. 'I'm just a little tired that's all. Go on.'

'All right,' continued Browning not at all sure that it was 'all right'. 'Going down the other side of the corridor towards the boardroom we have just two offices. The one opposite to this place is the one Hector and I normally share. The other is the CMO's office. For sleeping purposes the ladies, Claire and Doctor Mackenzie, have my office and the CMO and yourself are in the CMO' s office. You'll find your bed already made up.'

Marshall forced a smile: 'I should consider myself flattered to be sharing the illustrious company of your CMO, if I didn't detect his motive for such hospitality was solely to keep an eye on me.'

'You may be right there. He's nobody's fool. But he is a very good man,' said the PMO.

'There's a lot to be said for loyalty,' commented Marshall.

'Except that I mean it!' The response from Browning was quite definitely serious and effective if it was meant to warn off Marshall from further remarks of that ilk.

They fell to an awkward silence then. As Marshall sipped the hot coffee he took to surveying the room. It was all that a utility room should be. That is, a hybrid mixture of store room, cleaning cupboard and, of course, the mandatory tea and coffee making equipment.

Wanting to take the antagonism from the atmosphere that he had created with his remark, Marshall looked around for the means to do it. It was the large electric water-heater that drew his attention. The container was fed cold water via a copper pipe that erupted from a mess of shoddy and discoloured cement in the upper wall.

'Do they ever finish these buildings?' mused Marshall, aloud.

Recognising the attempt at small-talk Browning gave the question due attention. 'Planning. There's the problem,' he said, in a throwaway manner. 'If one hand could bring itself to let the other know what it was doing well, we might just do that,' he added, light-heartedly.

'Well I'll drink to that,' announced Marshall, before finishing the last of his beverage. 'I'm off to bed. Thanks for the coffee.'

'Sweet dreams,' offered Browning, the moment of tension past. 'I think I'd better be getting back to my post. Here's a torch. We don't want you walking over my boss, do we?'

They separated at the door to the CMO's office and Marshall managed to stall his entrance until the PMO had entered the opposite room. Only then did he open the door, shut it firmly behind him, and switch on the overhead lights.

The glare from the long fluorescent tubes was startling even to Marshall's eyes. Seconds later, as the security man had intended, Sir Roland was hauling himself to a sitting position from under a mountain of blankets precariously placed on a ridiculously small camp-bed. At first he made no sign of objecting to the disturbance but a glance at his watch soon changed that. As he inhaled deeply, the better to chastise the perpetrator of such a diabolical interruption of his sleep, Marshall caught his attention by making the universally understood signal of silence. Comical though the sight of the CMO was, with mouth agape, Marshall was not in the mood for laughter. He used his time more usefully, therefore. From his breast pocket he drew a large envelope and, in passing the knight's desk, grabbed a letter opener and handed both to the startled figure.

For something around three minutes the CMO read the long letter in silence. The bulk of the envelope contents originated from Benson's hand. Among these was a covering letter but if Sir Roland was impressed by the familiar signature he wasn't saying, for Marshall once again indicated silence and then pointed to the CMO's safe.

Five minutes later with the letter securely deposited, the lights were once more extinguished and Marshall fell down into the sleep of a very tired man. Across the room, by the window, the CMO's eyelids flickered in the dim light as he began some very earnest thinking.

Chapter Four
(Friday: 0600 – 1230)

It seemed to Marshall that only minutes had elapsed before he was once more awake. Yet, as he forced his eyelids apart, he was at a loss as to the reason for his sudden wakefulness, especially as he was still dog-tired and could see no-one around who might have been instrumental in forcing him from his slumbers. Then he heard what his muzzy brain told him he had heard the first time: a shout, and it was a shout in anger rather than alarm.

Marshall was having difficulty in thinking straight but, though he moved in 'automatic', his trained body responded. In no more than fifteen seconds he was out of bed, clad - somewhat shoddily - in a jumble of clothes, and closing the door of the room behind him. As he approached the source of the noise, within the office now used as the duty-man's room, he recognised Gibson's voice as being the most loudly voluble; another softer voice was more reasoning but defensive. The security man's arrival at the door of the room coincided with that of Browning, whose bleary-eyed face poked around the door-jamb a split-second before his.

'Stop that row!' barked the PMO, entering the room.

The two antagonists ceased arguing abruptly at the order but Gibson didn't wait very long before he announced his protest to the fast-growing audience. 'He was asleep!'

'I was not!' disclaimed Walsh, whose eyes didn't seem to Marshall those of one who had only just awakened.

'He was,' accused the PR man, his voice rising sharply. 'I heard the telephone.'

'Shut up, both of you,' ordered Browning, who was clearly in no mood to allow an escalation of the row.

In the brief silence which followed, Marshall checked the time on the wall-clock: six-fifteen. He groaned inwardly as he realised just how little sleep he had had. He desperately needed rest, but now, although he felt the altercation had little to do with him, he must stay - he had a duty to get to the bottom of the problem.

It was while these thoughts were mulling around his brain that he sensed that the silence had lasted for an inordinately long period. A return to clear thinking and vision provided him with the answer. Both Gibson and the PMO were staring at him.

'Good Lord!' said Browning. 'You look terrible. Are you alright?'

'I never do look beautiful when awakened in the middle of the night,' responded Marshall. Then consciously changing the subject slightly, added: 'What seems to be the matter, anyway?'

'That is exactly what I intend to find out,' answered the CMO entering the room. He turned his hard glare first to Gibson before switching to the seated Overseas Development representative. 'Right! Slowly, Walsh. What happened?'

'I was sat here doing nothing - certainly not sleeping - when your PR chap rushed in and started shouting.....'

'Why?' Sir Roland's terse question, fired at Gibson, carried a force which knocked the recipient off balance.

'I...I was washing next door when I heard the telephone ringing,' explained Gibson, subdued. 'I thought it might be someone with news. I didn't hear anyone answer it - I mean I didn't hear anyone talking - so I came here to investigate.'

He looked pointedly at Walsh, renewed strength in his stature. 'When I arrived he was rubbing his eyes. When I asked him about the telephone call he claimed there wasn't one.'

'Did anyone else hear the telephone ring?' asked Sir Roland, before the rapidly reddening face of Walsh could turn to verbal release.

The response to the question proved negative and he looked back to Gibson, saying: 'No-one else heard it. Are you sure?'

'Yes,' replied the PR man, without hesitation but his expression said that he was now puzzled, 'I'm sure I heard it.'

At this the CMO's investigative talents seemed to have been exhausted for he didn't continue. Instead, it was Marshall who spoke.

'Assuming there was a telephone call, don't you think they would have rung again by now - at least, if it was important. The fact that they haven't,' said the security man, 'suggests that it wasn't, or, that it was merely a wrong number.'

'But there wasn't any phone call,' insisted Walsh, in frustration. 'This is becoming ridiculous.....'

'Okay. But......'

'Look, can't we check somehow?' interjected Gibson loudly, drowning out Marshall's words.

'Only if it was an outside call,' responded Marshall. 'If it came through the internal network - no chance.'

'I don't know what you heard,' he continued, 'but the fact that no-one else heard it and that no subsequent call has been received to verify its existence, leaves me to conclude that it was not a telephone call.'

'Then what did I hear?' demanded the PR man, who then shrugged his shoulders when no-one answered. His frame sagged visibly. 'Oh, perhaps you're right....it's just that I've had little peace from thinking about that little girl in Dent.'

He rubbed his face with his hands then. No-one spoke; they waited expectantly for him to continue: this was their reaction to one of their number's struggle with strain. At the same time, however, he was under scrutiny from several professional viewpoints.

He looked around at the circle of faces, weariness in his face, and said: 'Here we are waiting for the same thing to happen again. It could be Ipswich or Norwich, perhaps a thousand cases, hundreds of deaths. Just waiting and not knowing why.'

His gaze had dropped to the floor as he spoke but suddenly, as if proving that he hadn't completely cracked, he looked up and added, with a smile: 'I know we shouldn't get involved but having seen the suffering of that thirteen-year-old and facing the possibility of having to stand-by helplessly while others suffer.... Well, a sleepless night is a sleepless night.'

'I think we all understand,' said the CMO in a fatherly manner. 'We are all involved in an unusual situation which has potentially disastrous consequences, Gibson,' he continued, except that his attention was now directed to all rather than solely toward the PR man.

'We may all feel the pressure upon us in the next few days or - God forbid - weeks. We must, however, remain calm for we are the people who must sort out this mess - at least, on the medical side.' The CMO looked then from Walsh to Gibson and, displaying a power no-one there would even consider to question, said: 'We will now forget this episode.'

With that he left, motioning for selected people to follow him. So it was that Marshall found himself with Browning, Prendle-James and Sir Roland in the CMO's somewhat untidy office-cum-bedroom.

'So what was all that about?' said the CMO when the door had been closed. Then, sensing he could be accused by this remark of having been asleep in the other room, he added quickly: 'I know what happened on the surface but we still haven't found out why.'

'Strain?' offered Browning, simply.

'So soon?' returned Sir Roland.

'Quite possible,' interrupted Marshall. 'Couple what he saw at Dent with the active imagination which is a prerequisite of a Public Relations operator and it is, as I say, quite possible. Add to that the loss of a night's sleep and it could well be a certainty.'

'But to the extent of hearing things?' persisted the CMO, obviously at a loss and relying totally upon the others for constructive thought. 'Hector,' he called to the professor, whose interest seemed more drawn to the traffic in the street below, 'what do you think?'

Prendle-James sighed. 'I don't pretend to understand the workings of the mind,' he said, turning from the window. 'Psychology has always seemed such an unscientific subject to me. But I spent a good deal of last night suffering from insomnia too and I haven't - I hope - heard any esoteric goings on. Of course, I didn't visit Dent and apply to what is there the imagination of an apparently unworldly young man, as Gibson appears to have done.' He paused then, looking pointedly at Marshall. 'By throwing a security blanket over this affair you cannot prevent similar occurrences of stress-behaviour happening again,' he continued, a gleam in his eyes. 'For one thing you expect a few individuals to tackle a job for which contingency plans usually exist on a national level.'

'I've given my reasons,' reminded Marshall, his tone hard.

'Yes, you certainly have.' Agitation entered the professor's manner. 'And how shrewd of you to tie the Dent outbreak to that of the laboratory incident - before the fanatics claimed responsibility and in the absence of any real evidence to support the link between the two.'

'Meaning?'

'Meaning, I spent a sleepless night too.'

'Gentlemen!' admonished the CMO. 'The object of this discussion is Gibson. Let me remind you of that.'

'I think a sedative followed by a few hours' sleep will go a long way to restoring him,' injected Browning, sensing that nothing constructive would come from such a heated exchange as was developing between the security man and Hector.

'I agree,' responded Sir Roland, grateful for positive action. 'Organise that, will you? Let us hope it does the trick.'

For some minutes the conversation covered the setting up of the Information Cell and that of the specialised medical organisation within the DOH suite. Along the way the temperature of the discussion got back to normal. It was during this period that the subject of who was to run the Cell came up, when Marshall was absent. It was the security man who raised the issue.

'It will require someone with dedication,' he said, 'for he will not have much time for anything else if things get hot.'

'Gibson!' Browning's enthusiasm was noticeable for Marshall had provided the solution to the continued employment of the PR man. 'Excellent idea,' he enthused, 'the distraction of hard work should be quite beneficial.'

Sir Roland nodded in agreement. With such recommendations he didn't need further persuasion.

After breakfast - which arrived in meals-on-wheels style - the DOH team burst into a spell of activity which persisted for almost two hours without respite.

Marshall began his work by supervising the organisation of the information cell for which the office shared by Claire and the PR man, Gibson, was used. To help in this task, Marshall enlisted the aid of Selby and Ashton. Gibson had protested strongly when informed that although he was to take charge of the 'operational' information cell, he would be spending the next few hours recouping his lost night's sleep and - with the logical argument that if he was to be in charge of its running he must be there while the information cell was being brought into existence - he won the dubious right to forgo rest and spent the time with such industry as almost to usurp Marshall's initiative.

At one end of the boardroom an odd assortment of work-surfaces had been brought together and, at Browning's direction, the Scientific Officer and Anne - aided by Walsh - were assembling the specialist system whereby all available information on the treatment of the patients in Dent could be disseminated to medical teams at the sites of fresh outbreaks.

The CMO saw nothing of this activity and, apart from an irritating crash as a collision of interests occurred outside his office, he didn't hear it either for together with his Claire he was ploughing through the mountain of administrative work he had been forced to neglect since the outbreak at Dent.

By ten-thirty, over one-and-three-quarter hours since work had commenced, some semblance of order was becoming evident in both the information cell and the specialist area. Where a confusion of charts and other papers had lain curled upon desk-tops, was now a pristine system of trays, logs and data sheets with charts pinned neatly on the walls. Some little way from completion, the system, which hopefully would provide the trends and the vital clues Marshall needed to track down the fanatics, was emerging.

Next door in the boardroom a similar transformation was taking place as desk-tops were arranged neatly with reference books and hastily scribbled case-notes in bulging files. Anne, above all, seemed extremely active and her industry drew silent - but visual - admiration from those with even the briefest interest in that room.

Then the telephone rang and abruptly all activity ceased. After the row earlier this reaction was perhaps predictable. Work didn't continue, however, when the telephone call was over or, indeed, when the package - which the phone call had heralded - arrived at the door of the suite. In fact activity to further ready the two systems did not recommence until some hours later for another activity, more frenzied, and not only involving those at the DOH, was about to take precedence in the need for attention and action.

'Russia!?' The astounded cry from Ashton might have echoed the emotional outburst of the majority of those sat around the now quiescent tape-recorder, for the same expression of disbelief was in all of their faces.

Such was the response to an almost identical message to that concerning Dent. Again, the signature of the fanatical claimants was the Power Reversion Group; again, Marshall had the tape rushed away for analysis and, again, he telephoned Benson with the news.

'UN,' he said, repeating the essence of his boss's response.

In the boardroom the assembled company strained their ears once more for intelligible sounds but were rewarded only with meaningless crackle.

'Yes, sir,' said Marshall, adding mere punctuation to the conversation before injecting, finally, 'I'll need a Fax machine as soon as possible…..' With that he replaced the receiver and returned to the boardroom.

'A Fax machine?' echoed Gibson, as if sampling some strange word from the past.

Marshall had heard him. 'I asked for a Fax machine because they don't use Telex anymore,' he replied, cryptically, returning to his seat. 'It's more difficult for those outside the government systems to intercept land-line traffic,' he added as explanation. 'The old facsimile transmission is the best thing we have for moving printed data around the world with some security.' His glance towards Gibson brooked no argument.

In response, Gibson shrugged.

'The United Nations Security Council is being informed,' said Marshall, resuming his place at the table.

'Surely this is a matter for the WHO, also?' protested the International Health man, Ashton. If he intended further comment he was firmly warned off by the glare of a very unsympathetic CMO, who saw in the remark Ashton's intention to have some effect on the conversation regarding his own interests.

'The Security Council will inform the World Health Organisation headquarters in Geneva,' responded Marshall. 'Besides, the reason for going about it this way is to ensure the preservation of security.'

'Wise thinking,' said the CMO. 'The normal response to a call for help - in more usual circumstances than these - is for Geneva to ring around the world recruiting qualified medical men to come to the aid of the country in distress. The usual barriers between nations tend to be forgotten, quite rightly, in such events.

'I should think the way your people are going about it,' he continued, 'could only occasion the loss of the expertise the 'ring-around-the-world' method brings in, Mr Marshall. However, a Security Council instruction would certainly be respected by the WHO.'

'Yes, but what about this loss of expertise?' said Anne. 'Surely security shouldn't be given such importance when people could be dying? We should be sending medical aid to... to...'

'Plomsk,' provided Marshall.

'Whatever-it-is-called,' she said, irritated.

'But you have everything you need here,' reasoned Marshall. 'Information cell, specialist knowledge and only a telephone call away from the experience that Dent provides. Surely this, together with no small ability on the part of the Russians should be quite adequate for the situation.'

'We shall obviously have to wait and see,' she responded, heatedly.

'You said something about a Fax machine on the phone,' prompted Browning.

'Yes, I did,' replied Marshall, 'I realised a flaw in our system could be communications: it may be that information might be delayed, not even arrive at the Russian site because of the complications security cut-outs would create, but most importantly using the alternative of email would make interception by the media too easy. Security would likely be compromised.

'So I've arranged for a Fax machine, hooked-up to a phone-line to put us in direct communication with Geneva. Apart from interpreter problems we need to keep people thinking that the Russian outbreak, should they find out it exists, is the only one. A direct link to Plomsk would just be asking for trouble.'

'So your security remains secure,' said the CMO.

'Basically, yes,' confirmed Marshall. 'It's true that lots more people know about it but I think we may avoid the panic public knowledge would surely cause.'

'It's fantastic!' said Prendle-James, a scientific officer not given to using such a word in its modern idiom. 'Who,' he continued, 'would want to create such havoc as this?'

'Why is the more important question,' offered Marshall.

'We are already working on a short list of the possible perpetrators but we've yet to find a motive. It could be money or power - the usual form of ransom demand - but, well...that's my job.' He smiled weakly. 'You've got enough on your plates as it is,' he added, in defence of his reticence

'I agree entirely with that,' said Prendle-James, 'but one thing intrigues me. How the devil did they 'carry' this thing into the obscure Russian....village named in the tape?'

'Wish I knew,' replied Marshall, having to raise his voice above the strident ringing of the telephone.

The telephone call was from Dent and, while Anne answered it, most, of the company fell into voluble speculation over the incident in Russia. Those who chose to forgo participation in this fruitless exercise in preference for eavesdropping were rewarded with more than the normal telephonic activity from that direction: albeit merely the four-hourly situation report from the site that they were witnessing, and even though the jargon may have had little meaning to some, that things were happening beyond the normal was not in doubt.

When she had completed her conversation Anne replaced the receiver slowly before returning to the table. She then occasioned one of those esoteric discussions that only those of privileged qualification may be privy to. And she, the CMO, Browning and Hector, huddled into private debate.

'Gentlemen,' called Fletcher, to the assembled company, at the end of several minutes of discussion, 'your attention, please.'

The laymen's chatter ceased.

'We have just received the latest sitrep from Dent, as you may have gathered,' he began. 'The news is that certain indications, provided for us through close monitoring of our patients, have made it likely that a diagnosis of the illness may be made within the next twenty-four hours. In short, symptoms are beginning to appear which will provide the identity - and therefore specific treatment - of this disease.' He looked quickly around the circle of faces. 'In a situation like this, where all the news seems to be bad, it is perhaps the best news we are likely to receive. At least if we know what it is we can attack it.'

No-one said anything. There was nothing to say. After a second or two of silence the CMO began to wrap-up the meeting, adding: 'We have no time to put the final touches to our organisation. We must begin feeding information into Geneva as soon as possible. Let's get cracking.'

Shortly afterwards the Fax machine arrived and then a telephone call from Benson summoned Marshall and his assistant to the admiral's office.

Barraclough stood at the bridge window and looked aft through the rain. As Chief Officer his job, when the ship was alongside, entailed the supervision of cargo-loading and checking the trim of the ship as a whole. Aboard the LASH Vessel *Baccarat* the cargo consisted of up to sixty eighty-ton barges or lighters as the ship's type, Lighter Aboard SHip, indicated. It was the operation of embarking these lighters which filled a portion of Barraclough's view.

Baccarat's existence was based upon the purely commercial need of many shipping companies to get dry cargo from one point of land to that of another. However, she and her sister ships were an example of ultra-efficiency in that - operating from large ports - they could almost totally ignore delays in normal shore-loading through the use of on-board loading gear. Principally this took the form of a five-hundred tonne gantry crane which lifted pre-loaded barges out of the water from a cut-out in the *Baccarat*'s stern. The money-saving aspect was further reinforced by the fact that the barges' cargo did not have to be touched from the time of its loading by the manufacturer - on a site as remote as the upper reaches of a canal until sometime after it was re-floated in the estuary of the river of destination. To maximise this efficient trade *Baccarat* operated on the Sheerness to New Orleans run.

Barraclough had witnessed the loading operation many times in the three years he had been with the ship. The embarkation of the present cargo hardly took up any of his concentration as by now his subconscious compared the action his eye noticed with a mental template of the correct actions leaving him free to think of other things. So it was that he withdrew his gaze some two hundred feet and surveyed the six shapes which shouldn't have been there.

He was a tidy man, of appearance and action. He was proud of the way he had managed to combine a love of the sea with love of efficiency, of neatness and getting things right. The *Baccarat* had never before sailed with less than a full cargo of sixty barges. This time would be different: only fifty-four barges would be carried, six more left by the quayside for a later voyage. It was this, to him waste of profitable space which niggled his sensitivities together with the untidiness which the six replacement vessels created with the ship's lines.

The six replacement vessels were smaller than the barges and special cradles had been built to support them in their stowage. Close to the bow of each rose a stubby superstructure which dropped away abruptly to leave just over half of their length with a low free-board. Even out of water the tugs could not be mistaken for any other craft: the power in their lines boasted the fact that - small as they might be - they could push or pull anything which floated.

Again with his sensitivities linked to the balance-sheet, Barraclough wondered just what had induced his company to go to the expense which had obviously been incurred in shipping the small tugs by this means. 'Some powerful persuasion at the top, I shouldn't wonder,' he reflected, a thought underlined when he remembered what had been embarked with them.

Some forty people had joined as the tiny craft were hoisted aboard. Two of them were at Barraclough's side now as he continued to gaze through the window. 'Rough lot,' he thought.

He had already queried the reason for taking both the craft and the full crews on the voyage, pointing out that it was more usual for the personnel to fly to the destination. The answer had been quite reasonable, he had to admit. 'Full maintenance checks,' the Swede had replied, and Barraclough had noticed that the Swede seemed to be the spokesman for the officers he had met. There had followed a rather complicated story which told of the transfer of the little fleet to another company and, due to early delivery made possible by the *Baccarat* sailing, the postponement of vital maintenance checks.

As the crane delivered the last barge to its cradle position, Barraclough turned away from the window. 'Well, that's it. All ready to go,' he said to the two men.

'And calm waters, I hope,' added the Swede. 'I don't want my men manoeuvring heavy weights with the deck heaving beneath them.'

Barraclough murmured agreement, impatient to get below. Then a thought struck him. 'At least the gimbal effect of the cradles will minimise ship motion,' he announced.

'That is what we thought,' nodded the Swede.

For Barraclough the comment, combined with those he had previously heard from the Swede, appealed to his sensitivities. Now he could see that it all made sense: the special cradles would facilitate maintenance in what was normally a dangerous environment for such activity. He saw the efficacy of carrying out costly maintenance *en route* for the buyer, cutting down the time and overheads which other methods would demand. Having managed to reconcile in his mind the upset created in his own sphere of influence, with the obvious efficiency of the newcomers, his suspicions were allayed.

Unfortunately for Barraclough his estimation of their motive fell very far short of the truth.

Chapter Five

(Friday: 1230 – Midnight)

Benson's office was situated amid the jumble of government buildings which line the western side of Whitehall. In his outer office Marshall met the admiral's middle-aged personal assistant, Frank Jenkins, with whom Marshall had often worked in the days when Jenkins had been on the active list. Also in the room was Benson's secretary and it was in her care that he placed Anne.

'Take a well-earned breather,' he advised, as he and Jenkins filed into the inner room.

Although Benson had heard their knock on the door he waited until the person with him had finished speaking before he acknowledged their presence.

Benson had lived in this room for many years of his working life and, because it was used solely by him, its decor had gradually been influenced by his taste until now it reflected not the starkness of the usual government colour-plan but, instead, an air of quiet opulence perfectly blended in a room built when grandeur was inherent in building design for the government buildings around Whitehall.

In those few seconds Marshall had at his disposal before he was formally noticed by his boss,

he took in the figure of the stranger. In naval uniform with the two-thick-and-one-thin gold rings
which indicated a rank of Lieutenant-Commander,
the man was moving toward middle-age with his
crop of steel-grey hair and weather-beaten face, the
greatest indication of this progression.

When at last Benson 'saw' them, he introduced
the man as an expert in the field of underwater
acoustics who was at that moment attached to an
Admiralty underwater research establishment at
Portsmouth. 'Lieutenant-Commander Grey is with
us in connection with the tape you sent for analysis,' explained Benson.

'Yes,' confirmed the seaman. 'It was passed to
my department by your own analysts with a view
to our discovering the source of the loud background noise you heard on the tape.'

With that he left his seat and switched on a
small portable cassette-player placed on a
side-table. Once again Marshall heard the flat
speech of the fanatic and, though only a second or
two of the tape was played this time, it was
enough for him to discern the loud machinery
noise.

'Quite simply,' resumed Grey, 'the source of
that noise is a certain type of ventilation-fan motor.' He consulted a sheet of paper before adding:
'Specifically, it is a product manufactured by the
Honshu Electrics Company of Kure, Japan.'

'Quite simply,' responded Marshall in the
politest tone of mimicry.

'You seem sceptical,' said Benson, misreading his employee's meaning.

'Not at all, sir. But I am interested to know just how you can tell all of that from such a perfectly innocuous noise.'

The navy man smiled. 'Perhaps it isn't quite as simple as I made out,' he said. Then, with a note of warning in his voice, he added: 'Naturally, I cannot go into the reasons why we take such an interest in this type of thing very much beyond the general statement that we catalogue sounds for a variety of military purposes. But perhaps I can explain something of these things without breaking any rules.'

Marshall nodded.

'You see,' began Grey, 'noises that we hear are made up of one or more tones, or frequencies as we call them. The human ear can detect a whole range of frequencies between about eighteen cycles-per-second - hertz, that is - and eighteen thousand hertz. Within this range lies a good deal of the frequencies generated by machinery of all types. In the navy we train operators to intercept these sounds by listening with the aid of hydrophones. As operators have been doing since the early days of submarines, they can differentiate between the thumping noise of a tanker in ballast and, say, the fast-revving engines of a trawler. This he can do by ear. If we need to discover which type of tanker - motor, steam, single- or multi-screw, large or small - we require a high degree of expertise, expertise which is costly and which takes many years of training to acquire. So now we use machines which are becoming more and more sophisticated. These machines have leap-frogged their designed potential, have had to, for now the question isn't 'what type of ship?' but 'which specific ship?''

'But how does that explain the apparent need to know exact units of machinery from the noises they make?' queried Marshall

'Because by breaking down the mass of machinery noises a ship makes, as she passes through the water, we discover just what types of machinery she carries. Possibly it is better to say that we find out the noises made by items of marine machinery and when we hear a certain type of ship passing by we look at it through the periscope - or discover its name by other means - and tally the noise signature, as it is called, with the identity of the ship.'

'Like putting together a jig-saw in the dark,' mused Jenkins aloud.

'True,' confirmed the seaman, 'but that implies a hit and miss situation. I think our revelation of the source of your tape noise should persuade you that it is anything but that.'

'So the tape was recorded aboard a ship,' decided Benson. 'Do your records run to providing the exact ship?'

Grey shook his head. 'Not enough information, unfortunately, sir. It would require the measured frequencies from a large number of items carried by the ship to pinpoint it exactly.' He paused then as he picked up his piece of paper again and, after a brief perusal, said: 'However, we have got it down to the shipyard which fits this particular motor in its vessels, the Kinashu yard at Hisane.'

'The second tape,' said Marshall. 'Anything on that?'

'Not enough time,' said Benson. 'Lieutenant-Commander Grey has heard it and he thinks it is probably the same source.' The admiral's serious countenance relaxed then. 'His evidence for this is based upon the calculated distance from noise source, the fan, to the microphone - around thirty feet in both cases.'

He turned his head to address the navy man. 'I've got to hand it to you. I had no idea so much information could be obtained from, to my ears, a single noise.'

There followed a short discussion on similar lines but as it began to cover the same ground Benson terminated the meeting. As the naval officer left, Benson motioned for Marshall to stay. 'I think a chat with a shipping specialist is our next step,' he said. 'I'm hoping we can get something out of this.'

'Assuming he uses half his wealth on this plan of his, what sort of ship can you get for fifty million pounds? I wonder,' thought Marshall, aloud.

'Possibly, seventy million,' corrected the admiral. 'His father has revealed further evidence of selling of his son's quota of shares. But let us leave the question of ship prices until we have someone around who knows what he is talking about.'

Having been stopped in one direction of inquiry, Marshall switched back again to the tape analysis. 'What news from our own analysts, sir?'

Benson selected a sheet of paper from those which littered his desk. After a brief perusal of this he looked across to Marshall. 'We naturally haven't allowed the father to hear the tape but, from his reaction to the description we gave him of the voice, we are ninety per cent certain it is J who spoke on the tape. Corroborating evidence in support of this is provided by comparing his environmental and ethnic voice traits.'

'Well that is certainly something,' sighed Marshall, with feeling. For weeks he had been out on a limb as he pushed the theory that J was somehow connected with this operation. Now, as he noticed the faint smile that Benson was expressing, he could feel some of the heavy weight of responsibility evaporating.

'You want the pressure brought on now?' asked Benson and, with the question - and its subtle transfer of initiative - Marshall knew he was firmly back in the saddle. It was Marshall's show.

'I think it might be premature to do so at the moment, sir,' replied Marshall. 'I think we need to wait until we find out just exactly what it is that J wants.'

'Yes, I agree, but the standing committee of the Security Council are watching the situation as closely as they can from New York. They're all ready to press the button for a full meeting at short notice. We'll need to keep a very light finger on the pulse,' said Benson.

Just then the door opened and Jenkins walked in. 'Miss Mackenzie is waiting in the outer office,' he reminded them.

Benson sighed. 'You had better wheel her in then,' he said, nodding to Jenkins.

The news, that the USA had joined the select but seemingly fast-growing fraternity specially chosen to accommodate the same viral particles assailing Dent, reached Marshall and Anne as they arrived back in the DOH suite. Once again it was the small, secluded, community which suffered. This time it was the turn of Randall's Halt, a one-time staging-post that had long since forgotten its original function, but which still provided a location for a hundred-or-so people to scrape a livelihood, however, as the cluster of weatherboard houses clinging to the side of a hill above the Colorado River testified.

It seemed to Marshall that the fanatics were determined to demonstrate their ability to take the virus to the most remote areas of the civilised world. He was ruminating on this point as he gazed, alone, at the bustle which had overtaken the boardroom, when he was joined by the CMO.

'You brought our girl back safely, I see,' said the CMO, nodding in the direction of Anne who was now seated at a cleared space among the littered desk-tops of the specialist's section. 'I had the distressing thought that you may have abducted our expert permanently. God knows why. Perhaps I'm becoming paranoid.'

Marshall smiled grimly. 'I think I understand what you mean,' he said. 'This could be only the beginning.'

They looked upon the scene before them for some moments in silence. The activity they saw, of orderly plodding at the desks marked by the appearance of more and more charts and diagrams upon the wall, of growing desk-top files, of in-trays supplied by Ashton, Selby and Williams whose occupations were now that of go-betweens, providing information from the information cell to the specialists and vice versa, of the more frequent ring of a telephone or the chatter of the telex machine, registered on the experienced minds of both men.

What they saw drove them both to the same conclusion: if this was the level of activity three outbreaks could cause, what would be the effect of ten such outbreaks, of ten, twenty or more? Sooner or later they knew they must rely upon other countries to provide their own control units. Perhaps they would have to despatch Browning, Prendle-James or Anne to setup such nerve centres. Whatever they did, such dissemination of information would eventually overburden the security-cover they were trying to maintain. Eventually the word would get out, the news spread rapidly and panic would ensue with all the chaos and breakdown in communications that could cause.

'It's been like this since you left,' said Browning, who had just joined them. 'Geneva, ex-Plomsk, is exhibiting a voracious appetite for information.'

'It can only worsen with the US outbreak,' warned Marshall.

'You said it,' agreed Browning, already moving away to his place in the paper-chase.

A shout drew Marshall's attention toward the information cell. It wasn't the shout of argument this time, though it was mouthed by Gibson. It was the serious tone of advice or command and only a shout because the noise created by the Fax machine made it necessary.

Sir Roland smiled. 'Gibson renewed,' he said.

And so he appeared to be for, when Marshall caught sight of the PR man, he was sat at the only available desk space and his appearance, of shirt-sleeves and harassed expression, was reminiscent of an overworked editor in the midst of a busy session at the City desk.

'There we are,' he pronounced, to no-one in particular but aware of the presence of his two visitors. 'We are now fully operational.' With that he threw down his pencil and leaned back into his chair.

'Well, there's one person who is enjoying himself,' joked Marshall to the CMO, loud enough for Gibson to hear.

Gibson chuckled.

Marshall moved over to the wall which sported a large map of the world. His first appraisal took in the three plastic-headed pins whose yellow brightness formed a straight line across the centre of the northern hemisphere land-masses.

'Do you think that is significant?' asked Marshall, pointing out the linearity of the line.

'Who can say?' responded the PR man. 'It is a Mercator's Projection,' he added. 'With the vast differences between map and actual disposition of the continents, well, it is possibly just a coincidence.'

'Looks neat, anyway,' quipped the security man, before he turned away from the map. 'The UK - Russia - United States,' he recounted. 'Where's the significance in that, then?'

The PR man shrugged his shoulders. 'As they are the three most powerful nations, military-wise, anyway, it could be that they have most say about things.'

Marshall did not argue this point with the obvious answer that, with France, China, North Korea, Pakistan, India, Israel having joined the nuclear 'club', and probably Iran shortly to join, Gibson's historic view of military power was somewhat at odds with reality. Furthermore, in conventional warfare it was likely China could overrun all the rest put together. But he said none of this, wishing to draw out Gibson on his views.

'And that if the fanatics convince the heavies that they mean business the rest will follow?' provided Marshall. 'That is a possibility, or they might be only the first three of a string of outbreaks meant to create panic and confusion, one of the most common goals of fanatical anarchists.'

'They don't seem to have courted publicity so far,' argued Sir Roland.

'Unless they are waiting until they have more ammunition - more outbreaks - perhaps one in every country. To suddenly break the news to the world at that point would cause immediate chaos.' Marshall paused for a moment, seemingly deep in thought.

'Any ideas, Mr Information?' he asked eventually.

'Well, one or two thoughts,' said the PR man. 'They're not fully formed, really. Just things that have been mulling about at the back of my mind.'

'Go on,' encouraged his boss.

'I keep getting the idea that fanatics tend to be idealists,' he said. 'Following that through I get the notion that these people want to change the system - they're political. So, putting together what we have, three outbreaks, deep concern among the medical fraternity of three countries, United Nations involvement - at least as high as the World Health Organisation - and the prospect of more incidents. That is a hell of a lot of pressure. And I should think they hope to bring this pressure to bear to change the system.'

'You didn't come to these conclusions by consulting a few maps on these walls and the information we have so far received,' said the CMO.

'No sir, I didn't. As I say, they're just thoughts that came to me, er, earlier.'

'Like last night, for instance?' prompted Marshall.

'Yes,' confirmed the PR man, self-consciously.

'What then is their goal?' asked Marshall, a new respect discernable in his voice.

'Well,' resumed the PR man, enthusiastically, 'I tried to put myself in their shoes. Here I am with what amounts to a pretty lethal weapon which has unfortunately one drawback. Being biological it is extremely dangerous. Not only to those I wish infect but also my own people. With that in mind I should use this weapon to secure quick changes in the system. But what changes? What changes would occur quickly enough - and give the best return - using this power? If I demand the world recognise my faction, whatever it is, and provide me with, say, a seat at the UN and a country of my own, my regime would only last as long as I was able to control this dangerously unstable virus.'

'Come to the point,' demanded Sir Roland.

'I'm just saying that if I was to demand nuclear disarmament instead, of which those three countries,' he pointed to the map, 'are still the principle stock-holders, I would put the whole world back into the melting pot. In that one action I would achieve a levelling of military potency to the point of conventional warfare where everyone could fight on more equal terms. For fanatics, that would mean better terms.

'Can you imagine the effect on the balance of power?' he asked, 'China would rank as the world's number-one power through the pre-nuclear principle that the warring nation with the greatest population was most likely to dominate others, especially as that particular country has been ramping up conventional weapons for years. Within twenty years the world economy as we know it today will have disappeared. Through the smoke and confusion would rise a new wave of leaders and factions. Perhaps the fanatic we heard on the tape wants to be one of them.'

Although the Fax machine made its stuttering sound and the telephone rang as he finished speaking there might have been complete silence in that room for neither the CMO nor Marshall was hearing anything now.

Deep in thought, both minds were wondering whether they had been wrong to bow to Gibson's insistence and forgo the treatment and rest that Browning had earlier prescribed for him. But such was the fantastical quality of the plan the PR man had outlined that they didn't wonder he had lain awake all night in thinking it out. They mentally moved to the next step, tacit appraisal of his ideas, and it came as a shock to realise they were actually entertaining the notion that the plan could work.

Then they thought of the practicalities of nuclear disarmament and saw the great differences between the theory and the practice of carrying out such a formidable task, of the need for extensive supervision in the countries concerned - requiring the participation of hundreds of thousands of people - and, with the numbers involved, the treachery so possible.

However, Marshall did attach some credibility to the scheme. Wasn't the professionalism of J's involvement, so far, proof that they were planning for nothing less than world-scale terrorism. The flaw in Gibson's idea was in the physical execution of nuclear disarmament but the rest, Marshall knew, was chillingly plausible. Marshall explained his doubts about such a theory, though he didn't confess to the fact that, outside of implementing nuclear disarmament, he felt it to be a possibility.

'It was only a jumble of thoughts,' said Gibson, apologetically.

'Don't get me wrong,' returned Marshall, quickly. 'We need all the help we can get. All the ideas you may have on the subject. It all helps. And, if what we have just heard is an example of the quality of thought that will come out of this room, I shall be happy to listen to anything you say.'

The next communication to reach the DOH was not of the type which was becoming routine in that it was not a package, was not a tape, and made no reference to any new outbreak. To say it had nothing to do with the situation would be to go one step too far: it had everything to do with the situation and the latest moves the fanatics had taken. Addressed specifically to Marshall it was a heavily-sealed buff envelope and was brought by a courier whom the security man knew personally.

The enclosures Marshall drew from the envelope, as he sat alone in the utility room, numbered ten-or-so pages and were collectively, as the covering letter indicated, a transcript of a tape-recording received at the UN building in New York. The covering letter went on to state that an immediate meeting of the Security Council had been called to discuss and act upon the contents of the tape.

Marshall read the whole thing twice through before he leaned back in his chair and stared vacantly into middle-space. When he rose from his seat it was to leave the utility room, papers in hand, in search of the CMO.

Within a few minutes, and with an absence of commotion, he had assembled all the people in the CMO's office: Sir Roland, Browning, Prendle-James, Anne, Ashton, Selby, Walsh, the PR man, Claire - all were there. When all had found seats and the noise had ceased, he began.

'Two hours ago a package, similar to the ones we have been receiving here, arrived at the reception desk of the United Nations building in New York. The contents of that package were three cassettes and on them were approximately ten pages of talking. I know it was that much because I have a transcript here.' He held the papers aloft.

'At this moment an emergency meeting of the Security Council is in session. When you hear why, such an action will not surprise you. And you will know why - and to hell with security - because it is becoming clear to me that only you and the microbiologists behind you can stop this madman. No-one else can do it. It isn't sufficient for you to simply nurse the victims back to health, you must find a substance to neutralise the virus and therefore nullify the power of these fanatics.'

This was a new Marshall to all in that room for in his voice was a passion he hadn't shown before. Slowly his gaze fell to the papers in his hand.

'"To the Secretary General of the United Nations,"' he read. '"We, the Power Reversion Group, feel we have amply demonstrated our ability to control a viral disease. Moreover, one which is capable of decimating the population of the area concerned. Our boast is that no settlement on Earth is too remote for our treatment. But we have, you will note, tempered our actions in the three demonstrations to date with some compassion, in that the situations were remote, the communities small, and therefore the risk of spread to other areas minimised."' Marshall stopped reading to allow the voiced indignation of those present to subside.

'"We find it necessary, however,"' he continued, when all was again quiet, '"to charge a fee for our continued commitment to a humanitarian policy. In fact the all-in price includes complete cessation of this regrettable activity. But how much, you may ask? The answer is simply an amount of money, gold bullion to be exact, from each nation listed in Annex One of this message which is contained on tape number two. All the figures have been researched most carefully and there will be no appeal against them."'

Marshall looked up from reading, again. 'I've looked at Annex One and it is full of technicalities based upon population and wealth. Basically, it means the richer the nation the more you pay out. It would take an accountant to make any sense of it.'

'Could I see it?' asked the Scientific Officer.

Marshall handed him the relevant portion before continuing with his reading. '"We realise there will be those nations who consider the price excessive to the point of prohibition. Rest assured we are not racists and would not persecute one nation because of its beliefs. This is a whole-world situation and we would apply our punishment for non-payment on a world basis."

'"But what are these punishments? Sufficient to say that if the full payment is not agreed upon, and we do not get word of agreement within the stated time-limit, we will take the following action: one, within twenty-four hours of the time limit expiring, twenty-or-more incidents will occur; two, within twenty-four hours following the expiry of this first deadline fifty-or-more outbreaks will occur. No further action will be taken after this latter period because the disease will have assumed pandemic proportions, anyway. Targets for these infections would in all cases be large cities or towns."'

'I think we can safely say that their interpretation of the word 'pandemic' is literally an infectious disease affecting the whole world,' interrupted Browning.

Marshall nodded slowly, then bent his head to the papers once more. '"But, of course, we hope no nation would be stupid enough to allow such action and therefore my last instruction is to tell you to load your allotted amounts of gold bullion onto trucks ready for shipment. Delivery instructions will be detailed in a later message."'

The security man put the sheaf of papers onto the table behind him. 'They have given the UN until eight tomorrow morning – our time, that is - to communicate their acceptance.'

'How so?' asked Gibson.

'Pardon?'

'How do they inform them?'

'British World Service and the Voice of America. A code word in both cases,' he replied. 'Incidentally, the last tape contains their political manifesto. I shan't read it out because it is so thin. Their main aim, they say, is the re-distribution of wealth - a latter-day Robin Hood mission of giving to the poor what they took from the rich. The ring of truth is markedly absent, unfortunately, and the tone and composition of the tirade indicates a motive nothing higher than the selfish acquisition of money and power.'

'Excuse me if I pinch myself,' said Selby. 'I cannot really believe this happening.'

'Nor can anyone,' consoled Marshall, 'but if they pull this one off you may spend the rest of your life in a society where you will need to pinch yourself daily as you wonder if your existence is real.'

'That bad?'

'That bad.'

Marshall turned to Gibson. 'Seems you were closer than I imagined.'

'I wish now that I hadn't even been that close,' he replied. 'But at least it wasn't nuclear disarmament. Surely nothing can be as dangerous as that?'

'The objective here is clearer than it first appears,' said Prendle-James loudly, tapping the paper in front of him. 'It equates to 50% of the gold reserves. It even lists the tonnages.'

'Do we still have any gold after Brown sold it off in a fire-sale around 2000?' said Ashton, surprise in his voice.

'I hope so. They want a hundred-and-sixty tonnes of it,' replied Prendle-James. 'That's bad enough, but they're demanding 50% of the gold reserves of the twenty wealthiest nations. Fifty per cent of the USA's reserves, according to their demands, is about four-thousand tonnes. I've totted them all up and it comes to 11,000 tonnes.'

'A tad greedy?' suggested Browning.

'If my suspicions are correct,' said Prendle-James, 'this isn't about greed for gold. It's more about flattening the global economy.'

'Really?' Browning was sceptical. 'Couldn't the UN give this bullion to the fanatics and just freeze the gold reserve figures. Couldn't they just say we will assume the gold is still in our bank vaults and carry on as normal. They could cover it with 'paper' just like they do with quantitative easing. Like QE it's just printing virtual banknotes, so they've had the practice.'

Prendle-James gave Browning a look that could be loosely interpreted as: 'better stick to your day-job,' but when he spoke he was diplomatic.

'I wish I could believe that,' he said. 'In a perfect world it would work but then this situation would not occur in a perfect world. We have to look first at the psychological result of losing so much gold. Business is based upon capital and part of that capital is gold. The rest of capital is paper money and shares and bonds and...whatever. Paper money—more often digital money nowadays— is not 'covered' by gold: the world moved off the Gold Standard many years ago, as you've intimated. Now a banknote is as likely to be 'covered' by a Treasury or Gilt or some other IOU or whatever with little or no connection to the precious metal.'

Marshall looked over to the CMO, his expression indicating that he sensed Prendle-James was 'on a roll' and this could become tiresome. In response, the CMO allowed a frightened smile to grace his lips but that was all. He was listening intently to his Scientific Officer.

'Gold's role in the economy is not as a pretty metal that does not rust,' continued Prendle-James. 'It is the commodity most used as a hedge against the vicissitudes of a sinking stock market, of nations in recession or depression. Not that the stock-market *seems* to be sinking at the moment; due to quantitative easing, or 'monetisation' as the US call it, the economy has been flooded with devalued money which makes the stock exchange indices grow higher and higher.'

He seemed to think about this for a while, toying with the notion of explaining further but thought better of it. 'No, gold is the rainy-day stuff. For some nations, their holding of gold could be the only thing a creditor will accept when he calls in the debt.'

He checked around the table with a glance. His audience were still with him, he decided. 'It's only my opinion of course, but this is where I believe the terrorists have been canny. The world economy is extremely fragile at the moment. The price of gold is already very high and rising, and that is an indicator of fear among everyone, stock-market players, businessmen, individuals. Gold is the main thing people buy when they do not trust or do not understand what is going on in the economy. That's why purchasing gold in this situation is called a 'flight to safety.'

'Now, take half the reserves of the twenty wealthiest nations out of the equation and the gold price will skyrocket, attracting more and more money and further weakening the money available to trade on the stock market and available for all kinds of investment. All the money will be locked-up in the money-box that is gold and business, trade, investment, life as we know it would start to dry up. '

'A bit strong, Hector,' said Browning.

'Not a bit of it,' he responded. 'You see, you have to consider the background to this heist. The western nations are in severe debt. If they were businesses, most would be bankrupt many times over. Fortunately, governments do not go bankrupt, but their credit rating with other countries – who buy their debt – is measured mostly by the strength or otherwise of the currency. This strength, or weakness, is a strong indicator of a country's economy and its debt.'

He saw the frowns that this brought to the faces of his audience and looked a little bemused for a moment. Then he brightened. 'Let me give you an example of how serious things are. Take the US government. It is currently 14 trillion dollars in the red on its equivalent of a credit card. It's getting on for 1.5 trillion in the red just on this year's budget. It's an unimaginable 140 trillion in the red on its unfunded liabilities - things that it is committed to paying for but does not have the wherewithal to do so. The US dollar has been devaluing steeply for the past two years and the cost of living there has risen to hysterical highs over the same period in comparison with what they were used to before.'

He could see that people's eyes were beginning to glaze over. 'You can find all this on the internet,' he said.

'If we still had access to the internet,' quipped Gibson, with feeling. He looked to Marshall but the security man did not react.

'And this perfect storm, if I can call it that, is coming about because they remove half the world's gold reserves,' mused Browning. 'From what you've been saying, that was pretty much the case before this caper came along.'

'This 'caper' simply expedites the collapse by removing the time and a large amount of reserves that may have been used to turn around the global economy.'

'Imagine if the press got a hold of this?' It was Gibson. 'Can you imagine the panic that would follow?'

'The idea is that the press won't get hold of it,' said Marshall, firmly. 'Not without a lot of mas-saging of the story first.'

'I haven't finished,' said Prendle-James. 'It gets worse. As I say, if you pull the rug from beneath the feet of the markets – in this case, the gold con-tent - the whole thing collapses. Speculation is as much part of any business as the people who spe-cifically devote their lives to it. You can be certain that for all the people worrying just what they will lose by this theft, there will be an equal or greater number speculating as to what they can gain.

'Relative stability may follow the news, how-ever you dress it up,' he continued, looking di-rectly at Marshall, 'but not for long. There will be a run on the stock markets of the world. Commodities will become the market, that and land, things you can touch. Finance and the invisibles will suffer, possibly greatly. The pensions relying on banking stocks and municipal debt will be wiped out. In the end, of course, we should all suffer. Resources will run out and public order will break down and civil war will breakout as a prelude to international war.'

Around the room several faces looked to Prendle-James with some scepticism.

In response, Prendle-James shrugged. 'We're at the tipping point and this caper, as you call it, will push the world economy over the edge.' He looked around him but none of the expressions had changed. He took this to mean that they didn't believe him instead of what their faces were really registering: shock.

'Don't believe anything I say,' he said, dismissively. 'Do your own homework. A look at history over the past 100 years should be enough. We've been here before. Well, almost. It's all on the internet.'

Again Gibson looked pointedly at Marshall but he was wasting his time.

'But if the UN kept it secret?' persisted Ashton.

Prendle-James just shrugged.

'No point,' replied Marshall. 'The authorities must tell the world and quickly, before the fanatics can present their own version.'

'Eleven thousand tonnes of gold,' reflected the CMO, who had been unusually silent since the meeting began. 'It will take some effort to move that lot. As for what they will do with thousands of tonnes of gold once they've got it, I've no idea.'

'They don't need to do anything,' said Prendle-James. 'Just sit on it and watch the world economy go down the drain. Then again, if they were somehow able to begin leaking it back onto the market they would destabilise the gold market too!'

'Charming people,' decided Browning.

'We don't know if they intend moving it, yet,' cautioned Marshall. 'In fact, we don't know what any of their intentions are.'

'Still, the choice is clear,' continued Browning. 'Human annihilation or economic meltdown.'

'It's the same thing,' said Prendle-James, to no-one in particular. 'The result, that is.'

Marshall looked around the room, watching their faces carefully in response to his next words. 'We do know who they are, however. At least, we know their leader. His name is Chaval, but he goes under the name of J. His chief henchman is a mercenary called D'rosario.'

Chapter Six
(Saturday: 0030 – 0900)

On entering Benson's office Marshall found it more crowded than on the occasion of his last visit. Now, in addition to Benson and Jenkins, Marshall saw four other men, two of whom he recognised as being from the local branch of the CIA and with whom he had a working relationship. Both were predictably stocky of frame and had the friendly look of people normally employed on less than friendly duties. The other two were strangers to all, a fact made obvious by their unease, and Marshall knew they must be the shipping experts loaned by the marine underwriting company.

'I assume you know Winkleman and Reynolds,' said Benson, indicating the CIA men.

'Trust the Americans to get in on the act,' responded Marshall with humour, to which they returned a smile.

'We also have Mr White, an underwriter, and Chief Officer Taylor who has vast experience of the more illegal aspects of running commercial ships,' continued Benson, who then waited in silence while the nods of introduction were exchanged.

'The purpose of our meeting is to discuss certain happenings of late. The two Americans are with us to carry back to their superiors a report of our conclusions, whereas our friends from the shipping world are here to avail us of their experience. Marshall is our liaison officer with the Department of Health, who are also closely involved in this matter,' he said, and Marshall noted the way Benson had given nothing away by ambiguously referring to him as 'liaison officer'.

For the next few minutes Benson gave an outline of the situation, missing out details where they would not be of benefit to the civilians. Marshall watched dispassionately as the two men's expression changed from polite interest to utmost seriousness while the normal colour of their faces changed to a grey pallor. Finally, the admiral referred to the meeting he and Marshall had attended with the navy man, at which the latter had revealed the source of the background noise heard on the tapes. 'So that is the story so far,' he concluded. 'I will now hand you over to Marshall who will direct your attention to where our thoughts lie.'

Marshall rose from his chair.

'The points we can deal with most effectively here concern their leader's new-found wealth, between eighty and one-hundred-million pounds sterling; the fact that the motor was aboard a ship which was built in the *Kinashu* shipyard; and, lastly, that the fanatics have a lot of gold to move,' he said.

'Do we know just how much gold they require to move?' asked the Chief Officer.

'Around eleven thousand tonnes,' said Jenkins.

The underwriter gasped.

The Chief Officer, however, was too involved with the practicalities of the matter to react emotionally. 'Imperial or metric?' he asked.

'Metric.'

'Now our thoughts are these,' said Marshall, after the interruption. 'Their plan must be to move the gold because the nations concerned have been instructed to load the bullion aboard trucks. Together with the information I've just outlined we think it obvious that shipping is involved for transport to destination or destinations as yet unknown. What we must know primarily, is what he will need to carry the bullion. What type of ships?'

'You are certain it will be more than one ship?' queried the underwriter.

'I would think so. The gold reserves are scattered around the world. Unless he contemplated a protracted voyage, picking up the bullion at the nearest ports - which seems highly improbable - he must use more than one ship.'

The underwriter thought for a moment. 'Well, if that is the case, let me say there are few ships of one-thousand tonnes which couldn't manage to carry one tenth of the total you have just quoted. Conversely, though you doubt the possibility of such an occurrence, there are many large ships which could accommodate the whole eleven-thousand tonnes and still have ninety per cent, of their optimum cargo-carrying capacity available.'

'Let's say the man has, say, fifty millions-or-so to spend,' he continued. 'Have you given any thought to the possibility of his hijacking the ships rather than paying for them.'

'Hi-jack must be ruled out if only that this operation bears the marks of much better organisation than the uncertainty piracy would achieve,' responded Benson, 'and – a word of caution regarding your presumed budget - we don't know if all fifty millions are available for buying ships. He must have other expenses to sort out: spares, fuel, et cetera....'

'He certainly won't *buy* a lot of new or recent second-hand hulls with fifty millions, never mind what he is left with after the items you mentioned, say thirty million. A couple or three general cargo liners of a meagre ten-thousand tonnes would dent that very badly. No, more likely he's hiring his vessels,' decided the underwriter.

'Yes,' he continued, thinking aloud. 'That would be a different situation altogether. Once he has taken the gold he couldn't return the ships anyway. The insurance would certainly be invalidated as soon as the underwriters heard what he was using them for, especially as he would have put them into the danger a world-retaliation might cause. Why buy them, indeed?'

Benson coughed then, preparatory to interrupting the underwriter's increasing movement towards inaudible thought. 'So what of the link with the Kinashu yard?'

White was back with them now and in response to the question, delved into a commodious brief-case - one of the two he had brought with him - and selected a buff-coloured cardboard folder.

'Kinashu,' he said, after a few moments study, 'specialize in the larger vessel: tankers and OBOs, from around the sixty-thousand to the hundred-thousand tonnes gross.' He turned specifically to Benson. 'These would appear excessively large for the job.'

'Nevertheless,' persisted Marshall, like his boss trying to maintain initiative, 'we know one of their ships is involved.' He sighed then, masking his irritation at the slow progress. 'Look,' he said, 'I have ten-thousand tonnes of gold-bullion which is made up of various amounts in different parts of the world. I want ten ships to move them to - say for argument, the Antarctic. What type of ships can I hire for the amount of money I have available?'

'I see,' replied the underwriter. 'Let me give you an appraisal on the state of shipping as it affects this situation. Then we can discuss any relevant points it may raise.'

'If a person wishes to hire a ship he can normally do it at two broad levels dependent upon his needs. The first one is full charter, in which case he pays for the hire of the ship and a crew picked by the owners. The second is called 'bareboat charter' where you hire the ship and provide the crew yourself. Your link-man with the owners is a broker who, just like an insurance broker, will arrange the contract for you.

'The market for ships - those laid-up around the world - is quite large at present,' he continued, consulting another folder. 'In all there are some five-hundred-and-seventy-three ships available, most of which are sea-worthy. Of these, Greece has two-hundred-and-thirty-two distributed about the three ports of Piraeus, Chalkis and Itea. Norway comes next in numbers with exactly ninety ships scattered along the fjords of her western coast. Then there is Denmark: twenty-five, UK: twenty-two,' he was reading straight from the folder now,' Sweden: twenty - rest of Europe share about the same, Singapore and Malay peninsula have fifteen, as with Brunei Bay and Hong Kong. Mauritania has the largest ship graveyard in the world, but they are rust-buckets. No. The rest are dotted, in ones and twos, around the world.'

'Well you're right about choice, but what type would you say?' queried Benson.

The Chief Officer came in here. 'The preference would be cargo-liner at about ten-thousand tonnes gross but, with the crew you are likely to be employing, this might not be a good idea. The next best would be the bulk-carrier, a good strong back which wouldn't be worried about the incorrect stowage of the amounts you have in mind.'

'Do you have a breakdown of types for this laid-up fleet?' asked Marshall.

'We certainly do,' said White, selecting another folder. 'Let me see. Same period - that is, last month. Tankers: two-hundred-and-seventy-five, general cargo - which covers anything from 'reefers', refrigerator ships, to cruise-liners by way of a motley collection of ships which carry anything dry - one-hundred-and-seventy-nine, bulk-carriers: thirty-four, bulk and oil: twenty-seven, ore-carriers: ten, ore and oil: twenty-five, container-ships: two, gas-tankers - of all types - eighteen. These figures do not take account of age or tonnage, both of which are very variable and go right across the board.'

'You said the most probable vessel they would use is the bulk-carrier, but I don't remember this being included in the types of ship Mr White says *Kinashu* build..'

Before Benson could finish White was once more delving into his brief-case in search of the *Kinashu* folder. 'I agree I didn't say bulk,' admitted a perspiring underwriter, rapidly flicking through the pages. 'Ah, here it is. *Kinashu*. Tankers and OBOs.'

'OBO means, ore, bulk or oil,' supplied the Chief Officer, 'but we are talking in the region of eighty-thousand gross tonnes when we speak of the products of that yard - much too large for such a small cargo. That refers to just one of them and as I've already said, if you were to split the bullion into ten equal parts one of these parcels would be lost in such a ship's holds.'

For a few moments there was silence. It seemed to Marshall that there was something missing, a part of the jig-saw yet to emerge before they could speculate further. But Marshall was not prepared to wait for more information to help them. He would use the assembled expertise to its limit in other directions and, if nothing had come to light by that stage, then - and only then - would he postpone the meeting until the elusive 'piece' arrived naturally in the course of events.

'Okay, we'll leave it at that for the moment,' he announced, then re-adopting his earlier stance continued: 'But assuming I've got my ships, how do I go about crewing them and generally getting them ready for sea?'

The underwriter relaxed then, as the interest switched to his colleague.

'As Mr White has said, you approach a broker and tell him what your requirements are,' said the Chief Officer. 'He will arrange the charter with the owners. You've said that the fanatic's father was involved to a great extent in shipping. That being the case, it is highly probable that their leader knows the ropes pretty well himself.

'The next step is to get a crew together. Not all at once, but you will need to start with a Chief Officer, Chief Engineer, Bosun and possibly three or four able seamen. Their job is to carry-out a thorough inspection of the ship. They then arrange full trials of all her machinery at a shipyard. At about this time her new Captain joins and the rest of the crew arrive in dribs and drabs right up to the time when she begins storing in preparation for sea.'

'In this specific situation,' interrupted Marshall, 'where could a crew be found - knowing as they must just what is required of them?'

'That depends mainly upon the government under whose flag - and safety regulations - the vessel will sail. It is most unlikely that any but those ships sailing under a so-called 'flag of convenience', or the crews they sometimes attract, would be the target for recruitment by this particular operator.

The 'flag of convenience' countries, of which there are several, exist - as far as shipping is concerned - for the lucrative darker side of life where unsafe ships are operated by crews of dubious competency. Perhaps that is putting it at its blackest because in recent years a lot of pressure has been brought to bear on these countries to raise their standards, with some success. But it is in the shade of this darker side that your crews will certainly be found.

'Your officers,' he continued, 'will most probably be naughty boys - you find plenty in the 'Inquiries' section of Lloyd's newspaper during the course of a year. Not all those who lose their tickets are criminals, I hasten to add. But for the type you require for this kind of operation a search of such ports as Dakar, Macao and Laurenco Marques - Maputo as it now is - should supply all the officers needed. And, for your seamen or firemen, the bars of the ports of the world offer a constant supply.'

'But surely there are regulations to prevent disqualified personnel from taking ships to sea,' argued the security man.

'Of course,' agreed Taylor, 'but we're talking about the seamier side of shipping. We're talking about the increased profit margin an operator can achieve by ensuring only the minimum - least expensive - safety procedures are observed; even new ships are run less expensively by employing personnel with 'bought' tickets who, naturally, cannot command the salary of *bone fide* officers.

'Money corrupts in shipping just as much as it does elsewhere. The main reason such a system exists, in spite of tough legislation, is our old friend the 'flag of convenience' country. Let me give you an example. We'll pretend a country is short of money. As a means of raising cash she decides to become a sea-faring nation but makes it known that her standards are not quite as high as those expected by the more respected maritime countries. As she has lower safety standards it follows that she must allow lower standards of competency in the seaman who hold her credentials. Incidentally up until recently it was possible for a person holding a First Mate's ticket to swap it for a Master's ticket of one of these countries. Naturally, this Master's ticket would only be valid for use in ships sailing under this flag as the rest of the world would not tolerate such flaunting of their regulations.

'But we wish to employ disqualified officers - that is, those who have lost their tickets through some misdemeanour who subsequently cannot find employment because they are effectively struck off. All I need do in this situation, is to take the documents of my potential crew to the embassy of the 'flag of convenience' nation. I inform them that I will be bringing money to their country by operating one or more of their ships and I would like to employ the personnel listed. Whereupon money changes hands and I receive 'clean' documents on the strength of the old. The only condition with this plan is that they are valid for the ships of that nation only but, as there **is** no going back when you have reached this level, it is hardly a surprise to anyone.'

'So we must look to the 'flag of convenience' countries for the crews of these ships,' confirmed Marshall.

'That is correct,' replied the Chief Officer. 'And you can look to the same countries, of course, for the types of ship you are seeking because, as I say, an officer with this country's ticket would only be allowed near ships operating under that flag.'

'Yes. We could short-list the possibilities,' put in White, enthusiastically. 'I could get you a list, in under a few minutes, of all the ships of such nations which are or have been laid-up recently.'

In fact it took just eight minutes from the time White accessed his firm's web-site from Benson's laptop to list the required information.

As White was working, Marshall asked for a detailed brief on the layout of the possible ship-types they had discussed. The Chief Officer considered that all types covered would be of 'all-aft' configuration where propulsion machinery, accommodation and steering position would all be right aft allowing an unbroken run of holds between it and the forepart of the vessel. Marshall discovered, much to his surprise, that there was little difference in the general layout of the after sections of such ships, be they eight- or eighty-thousand tonnes, a feature of design which made the job of memorising the information so much easier.

Presently, as Marshall and Taylor exhausted the subject, talk shifted to the reasons for the trend towards specialist design in modern shipping.

'You must realise that a cargo-ship is just a means of transporting cargo across the oceans,' said Taylor. 'Simple though this seems, it is not always apparent in the minds of many people I speak with. If you build any ship - barring cruise-liners - above fifteen thousand tonnes you are moving into the specialist fields of Crude Oil, Bulk or Ore. Those are the three main types. And their existence is merely an indication of the trend throughout the commercial world: the greatest amount from one place to another - in one load -equals maximum profits through minimum running costs.

'Incidentally, the OBO - Ore, Bulk and Oil - is a specialist load-carrier whose existence came about in order to further cut-out the dead-legs in cargo carrying; the problem with oil-tankers has always been the same - the need to spend the return leg of its voyage, after it has delivered the oil, 'in ballast' as the tanks were cleaned in readiness for the embarkation of the next load. In other words the tanker was only profitable on one leg of the journey as it delivered its specialised cargo. By taking a bulk-carrier and building tanks around and underneath its holds, a vessel which could be used for both legs of its voyage - and therefore more profitably - was invented. The oil would form the outward cargo while bulk could be loaded for the return trip - allowing the very necessary tank cleaning to be carried out at the same time. They never carry both types of cargo at the same time, of course.'

It was difficult for those who cared to listen to him to share the mariner's enthusiasm for the subject, concerned as they undoubtedly were with their own problems, but this didn't seem to slow him down.

'Even turn-around times are becoming shorter and shorter,' he was now saying, 'and they don't rely too much on stevedores nowadays. A pair of Stülcken cranes can load and off-load from the ship so cutting down on the involvement of sensitive dockyard workers. Mechanically-operated hatch-covers contribute to the same theme. There's also a purpose-built vessel of some thirty-thousand tonnes which operates between the Mississippi and the rivers on the European sea-board. It's called the LASH-vessel - Lighter Aboard Ship – and does nothing but ferry barges which it loads and unloads using a ship-borne crane rated at an incredible five-hundred tonnes. The interesting thing is that it requires no dock-yard participation whatsoever in its operation.'

He would have continued further but was halted by a signal from his colleague who quickly got the attention of them all.

'Well,' said the underwriter, after rapid con-sultation of the printout from his computer search, 'our task has been lessened a great deal even in the broad term, gentlemen. The total ships laid-up under such flags is one-hundred-and-thirty. Of these, nine are purely bulk-carriers and six are OBOs.'

He looked about him then, a gleam of humour in his eyes. 'It is interesting to see that two of the OBOs are in the seventy-thousand tonnes and above class.'

'This is more like it,' said Jenkins, revealing an interest that all of them now shared.

White continued. 'Of those fifteen ships, eleven are now in commission,' he said, moving unbid-den to the telephone on Benson's desk.

After instructing Benson's secretary he ex-plained his action to them. 'What I have in mind could take some hours to sort out – it's more of a data collection than I'm qualified   to do in a sim-ple computer search - but I hope to discover just what those ships are doing at present. The fact that it is now the early hours of Saturday will not help, of course, but....'

'We have the intelligence services of every country on the fanatic's list at our disposal,' said Benson. 'I'm sure we can uncover the information you...we, require.'

'Thank you, sir. I will get a list of the ship's names and......Hullo? Martin? Yes, quite helpful but we need something more...' For two minutes White rattled off a list of instructions over the telephone while the security men looked on.

'He'll get the list of ship's names to us as soon as possible, together with their statistics,' he announced as he replaced the receiver, 'then it will be mostly up to your people.'

Marshall did not stay to hear the result of White's telephone call. Instead he left after a short and private discussion with Benson and headed for the DOH. On arrival at the suite he displayed only passing interest in the nocturnal vigil maintained by Ashton, before turning into the darkness of the CMO's office. Then, at a time when representatives of the world's nations were discussing the demise of civilisation in a more hurried way than usual, he silently lay on his camp-bed and lapsed into unconsciousness.

Such behaviour didn't indicate disrespect for the seriousness of the situation: quite the opposite was nearer the truth as Marshall was under the strictest orders to rest. He and Benson realised that, whatever the decision reached by the Security Council, the next twenty-four hours could demand a level of activity from Marshall - mental and physical - that his present state of health would find extremely taxing. Benson had therefore sent him to bed. With him he took just two instructions, both of which would begin to take effect from 08.00 - the time of the dead-line - by which time the world must decide whether to accept J's terms or suffer an epidemic a thousand times more devastating than the Black Death.

'Marburg or Ebola!' announced the CMO.

It was seven-fifteen and only ten minutes since the slumber of the DOH suite had been interrupted with a telephone call. Anne had been the intended recipient but five-minutes later the CMO had also been wakened and three-minutes after that all of the company were assembled in the boardroom. In a more-or-less conscious state, their bedraggled figures further eroding any formality the hastily called meeting possessed by lounging or leaning in postures of the waking dead. Or so it had been until the CMO had spoken, then the news brought the erectness of spine among them that a grenadier-guardsman would have been proud of.

Marshall showed no emotion at the news but watched, instead, the reactions of the others. Why such a response from the others? Surely Marburg and Ebola had been among the list of possibilities from the start. So why the surprise? Was it the fact that at last they had seen their enemy identified, or was it more likely the response of people who knew they were up against the very virus which scared them most?

'Marburg and Ebola,' repeated the CMO, more quietly, 'After lengthy discussions between Dent and Porton Down it has been established beyond reasonable doubt - and sooner than anticipated - that the Marburg or Ebola viruses are responsible for the infection at Dent.'

Sir Roland leaned heavily on his forearms as he gazed at his team. 'Be in no doubt that these are the most dangerous of the viruses we had suspected. However, we do at least know what we have to tackle and, although we have little to combat these diseases, we do have the concerted effort of the world's leading brains looking at them,' he said. He knew it was rather thin, that they had little hope of destroying the virus, but he needed to maintain some semblance of optimism if he were to motivate his team sufficiently for them to continue their role of information exchange for the outbreak sites with some enthusiasm.

'As it is essential that we all understand exactly what we are up against with this virus,' he continued, 'I have asked Doctor MacKenzie - who is something of an authority on these particular diseases - to give you a briefing on the subject.'

Anne rose from her seat next to Marshall. Having had a little more time than the others since rising she had managed to effect an appearance little less stunning than normal. What was more, she bore the confidence in her eyes of one who is about to speak on the things she knows.

'It first became apparent that a completely new virus was around when, in nineteen-sixty-seven, three simultaneous outbreaks occurred in Europe. One of these was in Belgrade, Yugoslavia, while the others were both in West Germany at Frankfurt-am-Main and, the university town which later gave its name to the disease, Marburg. All infections occurred in laboratories which had recently received Green Monkeys - *Cercopitheceus aethiops* - from the same batch captured on the shores of Lake Kyoga, Uganda.

'In all, there were twenty-five primary cases - infections where there has been direct contact between the monkeys and the patient - and seven secondary cases - where those infected have passed it on to others. Of the primary infections seven died. None of the secondary cases resulted in a fatality. An estimation of the robustness of this virus can be made when you consider that a secondary infection occurred no less than eighty-three days after one particular patient had recovered from the disease.

'Eight years later another, smaller, outbreak was reported when a young Australian hitch-hiker was admitted to hospital in Johannesburg, South Africa. Acutely ill at the time of admission, he never recovered and died shortly afterwards. A few days later his girl-friend, who had accompanied him on his trek through Uganda and Zambia, became ill. A nursing sister who had attended both patients also went down with the illness at about the same time. Conclusive proof that Marburg was the infecting agent came when the virus was isolated in the anterior chamber of the nurse's right eye. Both the girl-friend and the nurse made painful recoveries.'

Anne paused then and Marshall knew this was no hasty collection of thought being delivered by a microbiologist; it was a narrative that she had delivered many times, made fluid but unemotional by repetition.

'Other than those outbreaks Marburg has been out of sight to all attempts to find it or its natural reservoir,' she continued.

'As a matter of interest,' interrupted Gibson, 'what were these monkeys used for?'

'To supply tissue for primary cell cultures...'

'Another case of carving-up animals for cosmetics research and such-like?' he retorted.

'Not at all,' she answered calmly, 'Rhesus-monkey kidney tissue is used to isolate a whole range of viruses. For example, polio virus, influenza and para-influenza viruses can all be isolated using this medium. The Green or Vervet-monkey is used for a very similar purpose. Definitely not cosmetic, would you say?'

But Gibson said nothing.

'Go on, Mackenzie,' instructed Sir Roland.

The track record in combating Marburg would, on the surface appear to be very good: only eight fatalities from a total of thirty-five known cases -

and an unknown virus at that. But you must set against this record the fact that the most experienced microbiologists in the world had a hand in beating it, which, together with the application of good nursing practices were entirely responsible for the low death-toll.

'But what if such expertise is not available? What would be the outcome of an outbreak in a remote area where medical help even of the most basic kind is perhaps hundreds of miles away? The story of Marburg's sister virus, Ebola, should give you some indication of just what can happen.

'Ebola - whose name is taken from that of a river in Zaire - appeared first in nineteen-seventy-six in Sudan. It was July of that year when a storekeeper in a cotton-factory at Nzara fell ill, followed a fortnight later by the illness of another employee of the same company. This was the start of a chain of events which was to spread the disease to Maridi, some distance to the south, and, possibly through the many infections occurring there, to Yambuku - later in the year -which took the virus into Zaire.

'This disease approached epidemic proportions between July and November of nineteen-seventy-six in that some three-hundred cases are documented - with one-hundred-and-fifty-one deaths - in the Sudan outbreaks, and two-hundred-and-thirty-seven cases - with two-hundred-and-eleven deaths - from those in Zaire. Throughout the major part of this epidemic the death-rate was about ninety per cent. It was only when good nursing techniques and the use of protective clothing were applied that this staggering statistic was altered for the better.'

'You mean there was something fundamentally wrong with the hygiene policy before?' said Marshall.

'Most certainly,' she responded. 'Instances where the same syringe was used more than once without sterilisation were quite common. Quarantine and containment rules were not stringent enough and people who had had contact with confirmed cases were not traced. It is a notable fact that many of the hospital infections were among nursing staff: of seventy-or-so staff infected in one Sudanese hospital, forty died.'

'How was it that they suddenly got wise and instituted better nursing techniques?' queried Selby.

'Not just by luck, I can tell you,' she replied. 'As soon as the WHO heard of the outbreaks - or rather epidemic as it had become by then - they phoned the specialists on their list, despatched them and medical supplies to Sudan and Zaire and, split into teams and allocated to various hospitals, the long slow fight to get the disease under control, institution of the precautions I have mentioned was only part of a whole list of services - laboratories included - to which, admittedly, the affected countries had not had access in the beginning.'

'So if the tragically high proportion of deaths were due primarily to the inability to contain the disease, the fact that the recent outbreaks are being

accorded the best treatment we have should severely lessen the serious consequences,' decided
Marshall, aloud.

'True. But you must realise that we are not
speaking of remote areas when we mention Dent,
Plomsk or Randall's Halt. We are speaking of
communities whose countries possess the highest
degree of expertise in the treatment of tropical
diseases,' she replied. 'If these horrible people do
infect twenty or fifty cities with the virus, two
things will happen. First, specialised knowledge
will rapidly be exhausted as the need for teams to
be sent to the outbreak sites first discovered uses
up the pool of world-class specialists. Secondly,
the majority of these sites will be, I presume, in
countries which do not have the expertise anyway
and, without the WHO support, would display a
similar but much more devastating situation to
that demonstrated in the Ebola outbreaks

'Which elevates the importance of the role you
will play,' cut in the CMO, addressing them all. 'If
the situation develops that way, information - telephonic expertise - will be required in vast
amounts. I have no doubts. We must deliver!'

He took the time then for a long slow look
around his team. 'Go on, Doctor MacKenzie,' he
said finally. 'We've had the history of Marburg and
Ebola, now tell us what we have with which to
destroy this disease,' and it was noticeable to all
that a hint of scorn was in his voice as he said this.

Unperturbed, Anne swung back into the flat,
unemotional, narrative that she had adopted in the

beginning. 'Marburg and Ebola,' she began, 'look identical under the electron microscope. There is however a difference between them - apart from the obvious one of name - which is fundamental: the antigen of the Marburg virus is different to that of Ebola. To understand the difference and its significance it is necessary to know what happens when a viral particle invades the body.

'In this event, the body's defences react according to the flavour of the virus. If we think of this flavour as the antigen and the specific defence substance as the antibody, we have the antigen-antibody reaction when the two meet. It isn't fully understood how only a specific antibody will attack a viral particle with a specific antigen but the sequence of events is. Simply, as the virus enters the system details of its specific flavour are transmitted to the antibody producing factory which then produces exactly the right antibody to combat the virus. The problem, and the reason why viruses can continue to destroy cells, is that the antibody producing factory will only begin to manufacture specific antibodies when the virus is detected and so does not have a ready-made stock of them. Therefore, if the virus is powerful there may be insufficient time for enough antibody to be produced before the virus destroys a sufficient number of cells to kill the patient.'

'But what about the person who has had the disease before? Wouldn't he have built up resistance to the bug?' injected Marshall.

'Yes,' she returned. 'But we are assuming here - and with relevance considering Marburg and Ebola are new diseases - that this is a first infection.'

'Incidentally,' she continued, to the room generally now, 'the result of a viral illness in which the patient survives is convalescent plasma, the fluid part of the blood which still contains circulating antibody. By transfusing this into a patient suffering from that specific disease we can considerably augment his resistance to the virus and, hopefully, destroy the virus. We managed to obtain convalescent plasma in the earlier outbreaks of both Marburg and Ebola.

'Another substance we can use to combat viral infection is interferon. Again, not very much is known about how it works or why. It is known that it is the substance created from the battle between antigen and antibody and that it is not specific in its action. That is to say, it is possible that the interferon produced in one viral infection would have an effect on a completely different viral infection. Interferon does not destroy the viral particle but seems to stop it multiplying and therefore halts its destructive behaviour. To date, unfortunately little success has been obtained in using interferon with patients suffering from Marburg or Ebola.

'So there you are, three lines of defence,' she said tiredly: 'the production of specific antibodies to fight the virus: convalescent plasma, if available, from patients who have survived an infection of that specific virus: and interferon, which is produced as a result of the antigen-antibody reaction which then provides, possibly, a broad-spectrum 'brake' on the progress of a variety of viruses, giving the body's defences time to destroy them.'

'Thank you,' said the CMO, indicating for Anne to resume her seat.

'Which one do you think it is?' queried Marshall, still directing his questions at Anne.

'Pardon?'

'Which? Marburg or Ebola?'

'We must wait for confirmation, Mr Marshall,' interjected the CMO. 'I can say that we hope it will be Ebola - and most determinedly so - for although we were able to obtain over one-hundred litres of convalescent plasma from the Ebola outbreak which must give us a better chance of combating this situation, only a few litres of the Marburg variety have been secured.'

'And prevention?' put in Selby. 'I assume no work has been done on a vaccine?'

The CMO looked quickly at the representative from the Public Health Department. 'You assume correctly, Selby,' he said. 'No vaccine for either disease exists.'

'Perhaps there won't be an epidemic,' blurted Ashton. 'The UN will pay, won't they? Then the fanatics will not need to use their carriers.'

'Perhaps and perhaps not,' responded the CMO, 'but our job is to assume the worst. What may or may not be is not for us to worry over. At most it is a problem for the security organisation. We are busy enough as it is.'

Sir Roland glanced at the clock. 'We will find out one way or the other shortly: it's now twenty-minutes-to-eight and the dead-line for the UN's decision is on the hour. In half-an-hour or so we should receive the news.'

Chapter Seven
(Saturday: 0900 – 1100)

'They're going to pay,' called Marshall to those assembled in the boardroom of the DOH suite.

The deliverer of this news was the telephone receiver he held, whose mouthpiece he temporarily cupped with his hand, muffled against the raised voice of his announcement. At the other end of the line was his boss, Benson, who continued the conversation with an almost non-stop monologue to which Marshall merely added punctuation. Behind him the CMO's team lent practiced ears to the telephone call now that, apparently, their worst fears of an epidemic were unlikely to be realised.

At one stage Marshall snatched up a piece of paper, turned it over to present the blank side, drew a pencil from his pocket and began scribbling frantically.

'All nine?' he repeated, when his jottings were complete. Then: 'Both built at the *Kinashu* yard? Yes, sir.'

The conversation followed for some time in the same vein, which set the eavesdroppers something of a task in deciphering the probable drift of a one-sided story that was all they could hear. Their conclusions were not helped when finally, and without warning, Marshall slammed down the receiver onto its cradle. 'Damn!' he said, explosively, turning to face the bewildered audience at the same time.

'Bad news?' queried Browning.

'Could be,' replied the security man, with a sigh. 'We've been fortunate in that our enquiries into the organisation J controls are beginning to show results,' he explained. 'Working on the theories that J would not be prepared to allow the gold he obtained to remain in the countries in which it was legally deposited, we reasoned he would prefer to stockpile it in one place - where it would be more convenient to keep an eye on it - and for this he would require ships. The theory doesn't run to a conclusion as to where he might choose as his destination, indeed we have no ideas at all on this subject, but to collect and deliver the gold from the nations he has selected he has to cross water and for that he must have ships.

'The problem we have just come up against is that, after narrowing down the field of possible ships to less than a dozen, we are having difficulty in locating their present positions, Apparently, the so-called ship-location expertise we require grinds but slowly on weekends,' he said, with more than a trace of sarcasm in his voice. 'Now we must wait god-knows-how-long for these ships to be traced. What makes it worse is that it is only a hunch: we may be on the wrong track altogether. In any case, it looks as though we will be too late for an interception.'

'Do you think that is wise?' asked Gibson, who had jolted upright in his seat. 'To interfere with this operation? Surely we must avoid the deal back-firing and being faced with the wrath of the fanatics - and possibly the epidemic we hope to avoid.'

'Wise or not; epidemic or economic ruin,' returned Marshall. 'These are decisions for the UN. My department's job is to uncover and provide as much information on the fanatics as possible and furnish the Security Council with the results.'

Marshall's tone had become quite tense as he replied to the PR man's question, now he changed both the direction and his tone as he spoke to Anne. 'Incidentally, they agree and will get the word to us just when you're to go, Anne. Be prepared to leave at any time.'

Anne responded with a nod.

'Now where was I........'

'Wait a minute!' It was Sir Roland, whose frame had suddenly tensed, his eyes glinting with suspicion. 'What is this about one of my staff leaving?' he demanded.

'My staff, Sir Roland. My assistant, remember. You loaned her to me yourself,' reminded Marshall breezily.

The CMO's complexion turned puce. In that moment the pent-up frustrations of three days under constant pressure glowed in his rigid expression. But, almost out of control as he had been for an instant, he rapidly drew back from the brink of an anger which mentally cowed those about him.

'Mr Marshall,' he began with a fiercely controlled voice, 'you were accorded the temporary privilege of the services of one of my staff. However, that was before we knew the identity of the disease and just how vitally important was Doctor MacKenzie's role in effecting a solution to...'

'I assure you,' broke in Marshall, 'that she will not deviate one degree from her chosen work.'

The CMO, mouth open ready to pitch a vitriolic attack, stopped in his tracks as he realised what Marshall had said. 'Explain yourself,' he demanded, guardedly.

'We didn't - don't - want to raise anyone's hopes,' Marshall began, with obvious regret that he should be forced to reveal the reason being plain in his face. 'Believe me when I say that. But, at a meeting Anne - Doctor MacKenzie - had with my boss, she explained a few things. Notably these were about her past work. I wasn't privy to this meeting but apparently over the last two years she has been carrying out research, privately, with a view to obtaining a vaccine for this disease.'

'Why didn't you inform us of this?' demanded Sir Roland, of Anne. 'This is the first I have heard of it.'

'It hasn't been tested sufficiently,' she shrieked, feeling the pressure of her domineering boss.

'What hasn't?'

'The vaccine and equine interferon,' she said.

The CMO sat very erect, completely awake and very surprised. But no more than the rest of his staff.

'The vaccine?' he said at last, looking stupidly toward the girl. 'And interferon? You mean, you have successfully treated a patient with the interferon from a horse as opposed to the normal human source of it?'

'We did try to keep it quiet...,' began Marshall, only to be silenced by the raised hand of Sir Roland.

The CMO nodded towards Anne indicating that it should be she who next spoke.

'We've already tested it in primates with some success but no experiments involving humans have yet been carried out. Obviously, no one would sanction deliberate infection with this disease and, as no natural outbreaks occurred during my research, it is therefore of questionable usefulness,' she said. 'Porton Down have taken over my project - and the antiserum - and, if I read Mr Marshall's message correctly, not only have they been reproducing the interferon like mad, but they have already sent the first batch to Dent.'

'Even though we're not sure if it is Marburg?' he put in.

'Yes,' she answered. 'At worst, the substances can do no harm. I understand a patient has already been selected in view of the rapid deterioration they have been experiencing.' She looked directly at Gibson. 'The little girl? She's to be the first.'

'My God!' exclaimed the CMO. 'Am I to be told nothing?'

The Scientific Officer stirred. 'I think I'm……'

Again the CMO raised his arm to silence the speaker.

Prendle-James, confident of his position in Sir Roland's hierarchy, made the mistake of ignoring the sign. 'But this is preposterous… '

'Prendle-James,' snarled the CMO. 'Shut up!' At the same time, as if to re-enforce his statement, a not inconsiderable palm slammed down on the table with such force that both furniture and limb seemed likely to crack.

Instantly, all was still. The Scientific Officer's expression said nothing other than that he was completely stunned by the power of anger the CMO had naturally never even hinted in his direction before. In the several seconds of complete silence which ensued, Prendle-James' expression remained fixed.

'Now, young lady. And you too, Mr Marshall,' said the CMO with the studied diction of one who is about to exact full and utter retribution. 'You are going to tell me everything. In my office, please.'

The three rose as one before the CMO led the way. As they filed out, with Marshall taking up the rear, the security man beckoned the PR man.

'Look after this,' whispered Marshall, as Gibson very rapidly caught up with him. 'Not a word of what is written on this paper to any of the others. Understand?'

The PR man nodded, a grave expression on his young face.

'It is in your custody,' continued Marshall, 'because I expect a phone call referring to it, shortly. As the man in charge of the info' cell, you will be responsible for taking that call in, er, my absence.'

With that and a last sight of a still nodding PR man, the security man moved quickly into the CMO's office and the sure-fire roasting the dazed audience knew would certainly ensue. As the door shut behind him they heard the cacophony of one of the portable fans being started-up, an event which merely confirmed what they already knew; that the words the CMO intended to use were not intended for their ears and the fan's noise was just a means of guaranteeing such.

Only three of the people left in the boardroom fell into speculation at the turn of events: Ashton, Selby and Walsh. Browning and Claire could not have been tempted into such disloyalty although shocked by their boss's action. Prendle-James similarly would not have even allowed others to talk freely on the subject but would surely have quashed such speculation with a cutting remark, had he been of normal mind, that is. But the Scientific Officer at that time was deep in thought and not completely recovered from the shock he had just experienced.

Another in deep cogitation was the PR man. He was also nervous, an emotion which turned to the beginnings of fear as he studied the list that Marshall had lodged with him. Standing alone he read through the twelve ships names - alongside which were a number of peculiar squiggles - and then folded the sheet and placed it in his trouser pocket.

When they had emerged from the CMO's office both Anne and Marshall headed straight for the utility-room. Already there was Browning, sat in the only comfortable chair, sipping coffee and smoking his pipe.

'Teach you to upset my boss,' he remarked with a grin. 'I have to admit he reacted a little more violently than I've known him do before.'

'I don't know if I shouldn't feel flattered at such treatment if that is the case,' returned the security man, above the clatter of crockery as they, both he and Anne, sought to prepare their deserved refreshment.

'It isn't funny,' said Anne, and one look at her face convinced Browning that this was an opinion she expressed seriously.

'Come on, Annie,' encouraged the PMO. 'Cheer up. Here we are with the promise of an end to the spread of this terrible disease - albeit at the cost of the world economy - and you couldn't look more glum.'

Marshall refrained from pointing out that Browning's statement was, as far as it concerned world affairs, somewhat naive. But then he didn't really believe this was what the PMO really thought, it being simply used as a soothing balm to the girl's feelings.

But the PMO hadn't finished. He turned to Marshall. 'I've never known such a pretty girl with such a dour expression,' he continued. 'Must be the company she keeps!'

'Doubtless,' affirmed Marshall.

Anne responded then with a smile which unfortunately clashed with her concentration on other things. The urn from which she was gingerly coaxing a modicum of very hot water suddenly gushed far too rapidly for her needs and she stepped back in alarm.

Browning, showing unexpected nimbleness, was first to intercept the potentially dangerous development as - with practised ease - he cut off the vaporous stream of water. It said something for the pressure behind the unruly tap that in the brief period of three seconds half of the spillage-bucket placed beneath had been filled.

'Dodgy things these contraptions,' said Browning after a sigh of relief.

'I did try to turn it off,' claimed a worried Anne, 'but it just stuck!'

Browning took her cup and deftly filled it with hot water. As he handed it back to her, he said: 'You must try to concentrate, my girl. You've a lot on your plate at the moment, I know. But then, we all have.'

'What were you doing in here on your own?' asked Marshall, abruptly. He realised such emotive talk as Browning had adopted could only do harm to Anne.

'Private relaxation and meditation,' answered the PMO, smoothly. 'The herd-instinct is a trait of the human race which has never really appealed to me.'

'Same here. What have you been meditating about?' continued Marshall.

The PMO looked directly at the security man, with a humorous countenance which didn't conceal the suspicion in his eye. 'Though I suspect the third degree in your manner,' he accused, 'I am sufficiently interested in any answers you can supply to my questions to ignore the slur of your interrogation.'

'None intended, I'm sure,' responded Marshall.

'One or two things keep rattling around my head,' said Browning, regaining his seat. 'For instance, where is this madman going to keep his bullion? Surely there is no place on this earth which would be immune from the attack the UN forces are likely to mount.'

'Unless he intends that a protective barrier of this virus should be his defence?' offered Marshall.

'A few bombs - conventional would do, I suppose - and both virus and the fanatics would be dead....'

'....and the gold spread over some acres in the process,' put in the security man, carrying through Browning's reasoning.

171

'Hm. Something there,' conceded the PMO. 'Though for a fraction of the price they paid in the first place, much of the gold could be recovered by sifting the surrounding countryside.'

'True,' responded Marshall. 'There is, however, one protection we should find difficult to combat.'

'And that is?'

'The same measures we are facing at present: carriers in a multitude of towns or cities around the world who are ready to strike anytime J wants them to,' said Marshall. 'Although he has said that in payment of the gold he will stop the outbreaks going ahead, he will certainly use the virus as protection when he goes in to pick up the stuff and perhaps for some time after it reaches its destination.'

'That theory assumes J's carriers have a useful life of months or years,' returned the PMO.

'Why not?'

'We know that one patient in the initial Marburg outbreak passed on the disease some eighty days after he himself had been infected,' explained the PMO. 'Such longevity in a virus is not common in the case of a convalescent carrier - as this patient was - where it isn't totally eliminated by the time of the patient's clinical recovery. Disregarding the convalescent carrier, therefore, we are left with the possibilities of temporary or chronic varieties. The difference between the two types is one of duration only. Both are the result of a person's contact with an infected patient. Although the person may acquire the virus from the patient, he merely harbours it or, at worst, suffers a mild form of the illness. Temporary carriers are those persons in whom the virus is active for up to a year; chronic carriers can endure in this state for upwards of two years.'

'Doesn't that fit in with the theory?' asked Marshall.

'Perfectly,' responded the PMO, quickly. 'But not for Marburg. You see, we have been discussing carrier characteristics generally - apart from the convalescent carrier - and what has been observed over many years. Not all viruses exist for long in the human carrier environment; some last for the remainder of the carrier's life. So you see, there must be uncertainty with a new disease because we haven't had the years as a yardstick to measure its tenure as an infective agent.

'Following this reasoning a little further,' continued the PMO, 'we can safely say that J's medical experts - whoever they be - cannot possibly predict just how long the carriers will be effective.'

'So it could be weeks, months or years before J will have lost the protection his carriers afford him?'

'Exactly!'

'If that is the case and I were J, I should want to accomplish my plans in as short a time as possible to minimise the risk of losing this lever prematurely. Not that this helps us very much, we are just as incapable of judging when the danger is past,' continued Marshall, meditatively sipping his coffee. 'We do know one thing from this piece of information: he will waste little time in converting or hiding the gold.'

'You think he might trickle the gold into the international market, then?'

'Not really,' sighed Marshall, an air of despondency about him now, 'because he will be the subject of the greatest surveillance exercise the world has seen. He won't be able to breathe faster without the world knowing by how many breaths per minute.'

'Well, that just about exhausts my inventiveness on the subject,' concluded Browning.

But Marshall ignored the remark. 'And anyway, if time is vital to J he couldn't possibly trickle the gold. It would need to resemble something like a flood. No, he must have a pet country somewhere. Coastal, of course. Which will provide him with sanctuary for long enough for disruption of the world's economy to materialise,' he said.

All the time they had been speaking Anne had remained silent, occasionally drinking her coffee but otherwise motionless. Now she rose quickly, drawing the attention of the two men.

'I can't stand anymore of this,' she said with a frown. Then, adding a quick nervous, smile: 'I think I'll join the others. Surely they have happier things to talk about?'

With that she left, gently closing the door behind her.

'Quite jittery, wouldn't you say?' said Browning, nodding towards the door.

'Aren't you?' countered Marshall.

'Of course, and I suppose I should make allowances for Anne.'

'Especially so,' insisted Marshall. 'She is the most knowledgeable person we have on the subject of Marburg, isn't she? Anne has a lot on her mind and the test at Dent isn't calculated to soothe her nerves.'

During the time Marshall was speaking the PMO's attention wandered somewhat. That Marshall was sincere in what he said Browning had no doubt and - had he heard all that was said - he would most certainly have agreed. It was no great tragedy that he failed to listen but it was for his own good that he saw what Marshall was saying to him by signs.

So it was that moments later without a noticeable halt in conversation, which now moved onto matters both domestic and mundane, that both men consulted the notebook which became the medium for a written conversation very different in content from that which was audible.

The first indication that the UN had received the fanatic's instructions for the movement of the gold came at ten-fifteen when Benson rang the information through. Several brief telephone calls followed as the full details became available, but sufficient information arrived to keep Marshall and Gibson busy plotting the news.

When all the information was in, consultation of the wall maps provided a general picture of the first stage in the transfer of wealth to the fanatics. Certain ports in selected countries had been earmarked as the destinations for the convoys of trucks which would carry the bullion from the gold stores. There were four such ports in the North American Continent alone: Vancouver, Baltimore, Boston and Norfolk, the last three seeming to cater for any of the routes from the vaults of the Federal Gold Reserve at Fort Knox. Another port was Leningrad, situated as it was on the Russian Baltic coast. Six more ports: Tokyo, Brest, Cape Town, Southampton, Wilhelmshaven and Naples, completed the list.

'Again the step-by-step planning,' mused Marshall, as he surveyed the map with the ports picked out in red-coloured tabs. 'He tells us where we should take the gold. But which wharf? Which berth?'

'One other point,' said Gibson. 'You have twelve ships-names on this list,' he proffered the piece of paper given to him by Marshall, 'but there are only eleven ports marked on the map.'

'I'm hoping our friends in the shipping world may help us on that one, before it is too late,' responded the security man.

'Yes, it is the weekend as you've already said,' remembered Gibson.

Marshall turned back to look at the map. 'Twelve ships and eleven ports. That means one ship in all of them, except one,' he reasoned. 'I see

Russia has been mentioned only once,' he continued, tapping the map where Leningrad was
marked,' so it could be that he has two ships
alongside in the same place.'

The security man thought back to one of the
brief, informative, conversations he had had with
Benson earlier. The Lloyd's List would normally
give a guide to the whereabouts of every
ocean-going ship in the world but the particular
vessels named are still down as being in
moth-balls. He would inquire further, the admiral
had said. Although Marshall did not believe such a
respected firm of underwriters as Lloyds could
possibly be involved in this situation, he did pon-
der further the question of why the positions of
these ships hadn't yet been traced. They had already sifted through the list of ships berthed in
these ports, hadn't they?

He reached then for the telephone and dialled
Benson's number.

'How long did I say they had given the UN to
get the gold to the assembly ports?' he asked Gibson, who was still peering at the map.

'Until ten o'clock tonight,' responded the PR
man, without turning round. 'The exact delivery
points - the ships - are to be given later,'

Marshall returned his attention to the telephone
and the ringing tone it emitted.

'Benson,' replied the voice, on Benson's private
line.

'Marshall, sir. I've been thinking over the
ship-location problem.'

'Yes?'

'Two possibilities, sir. One; that they aren't yet in port but arriving before midnight tonight, our time or, two; that they have changed their names.'

A faint muttering told Marshall that Benson was in conference and he suspected the other participants to be White and Taylor.

'The possibility is being looked into,' replied Benson, shortly, 'and we will get the news to you as soon as we get it ourselves.'

'Roger, sir.'

'Incidentally,' put in Benson, hurriedly, 'we have one for you. Perhaps you can sort it out. White has been very busy and has come up with the interesting information that every single one of those OBOs has embarked a heavy load of fuel oil. Apparently this is unusual because it is usually crude oil which these ships carry in their tanks. As with everything else, we're working on it.'

In the normally unused passenger-accommodation located on the Lower Bridge Deck of the motor-driven OBO *Orico,* two men sat in the deep, comfortable, armchairs and listened with palling interest to the loudspeaker's clear tones. That this suite of rooms was the passenger-accommodation was a belief valid only to those who gazed on the original fitting-out specification of the ships drawings or to the uninitiated passer-by who noted, from the lettering on the door, that this was *Private - Passenger Accommodation Only.*

But, in truth, there was no-one aboard the *Orico* who would be considered uninitiated, who bothered with such things as those 'correct on the day' blue-prints, or in fact could be called a passenger, especially the two men who were earning their wages there at that moment.

Over the preceding week, ever since they had become operational, one or other of the men had been on watch. In the daytime period between nine in the morning and nine in the evening, both could generally be found there. Now, at ten-fifty-three, they were both listening - and watching, for, filling the length of the walls to port and starboard were impressive, purpose-built consoles. The array which sprawled across the entire length of the port-side wall incorporated not only the high-power radio receiver - whose output they were monitoring by ear - but a transmitter capable of radiating three-kilowatts power, more than ample for world-wide communications. A bank of three large-spool tape-recorders, with racks beneath for the stowage of a considerable number of tapes, filled the remaining space.

Lining the other wall was a computer, a digital clock and a large illuminated tote board which had some forty one-line spaces in a list. Half of the spaces were displaying information in computer-style script. Picked out in this fashion the lowest entry read: *Tapes 5 and 6. Delivery Instructions,* and, alongside: *Delivered.* Following along the line a number of cryptic symbols -were illuminated together with four-figure times.

Presently, the next step in the operation was signalled by the appearance of another entry on the next line of the tote; a step entitled: *Tape 7. Delivery Instructions*. Only one word followed this headline: *Issue*.

'Your turn,' said the older of the two men as he noticed the new entry flash onto the board.

The other man said nothing; merely reached for the telephone. 'Tape 7 delivery instructions to issue,' he said, without emotion.

A grunt emitted from the other end and then the connection was broken.

The man replaced the telephone. 'That's getting to be the most tiring part of this job,' he sighed. 'Beats me why they can't have a repeater in their eagle's nest.'

'You know why,' accused the older man. 'Low-profile....' He stopped abruptly as he realised the contradiction of his statement and the two of them fell into the laughter of men too easily bored.

'But you know what I mean, huh?' he persisted, shortly. 'We've got to maintain appearances. Don't want this kinda gear claiming attention if any legits come aboard.'

'He's got his little black box up there, hasn't he?' argued the other man. 'That would raise suspicions......'

'Carefully camouflaged though,' interrupted the older man. 'Has to be. I don't even know what it looks like now and I'm the specialist around here.'

'Not that it would matter very much if anyone were to make an inspection of the ship. They'd soon discover this place. That,' he nodded to the door, 'wouldn't stop anyone.'

This was the truth because the entrance door was nothing more solid than a ply-and-softwood composite.

'Look you here, sonny,' replied the older man and there was a more serious tone in his voice now, 'if anyone chances on this little lot he won't be leaving the ship. Ever. The stakes are just too high for that.'

Chapter Eight
(Saturday: 1100 – 1245)

The last incoming telephone call of that hectic Saturday morning marked the beginning of a rather confused period in the otherwise orderly organisation of the DOH suite. Predictably, it was Marshall whose attention was required for the telephone, but this time it was Dent calling.

'Marshall speaking,' he announced, tiredly.

'Remember your promise, Mr Marshall,' said the owner of a decidedly Australian voice which was loud enough for those relatively close to the telephone to hear quite clearly.

'Promise?' parried the security man, 'I don't remember making any promises...'

'As I thought,' returned the voice, who Marshall now recognised as belonging to Bryant, 'but let me remind you. I told you when you toured this place that we would require the services of Anne, er.. Doctor MacKenzie, if it was discovered that this virus was of a certain type. Well, Mr security-man, it is that certain type and I'm holding you to your promise...'

'Alright, Bryant,' calmed Marshall, 'you shall have your saviour. But you haven't told me which of the two suspected viruses you think it is.'

'We don't have any doubts about it now. It's Marburg; just been confirmed by Porton Down,' replied Bryant. Then: 'I don't know what you may have been told about the virus but mention the news to Anne and I think you will find she will be suitably impressed.'

'I will do just that,' said Marshall,' and you can expect her presence at the site around..,' he looked quickly at his watch, 'around fifteen-hundred hours, arriving by chopper.'

'Thanks a lot,' said Bryant, relief in his voice. 'I'll be waiting at the helicopter's door, tell her.' But he didn't wait for confirmation that she would indeed be told for he had replaced the receiver and the line went quiet.

On his way to the CMO's office with the news, Marshall almost bumped into Anne in the corridor.

'They want you over there now,' he told her, with unnecessary loudness of voice. 'Are you all ready?'

'All ready,' she confirmed, calmly. 'Coffee?' she asked.

He looked at the crockery on the tray she was carrying. 'Yes, please,' he said, then entered the CMO's office as she turned towards the utility room.

The CMO was at his desk dictating notes to his secretary as Marshall entered. Sir Roland noticed him immediately and paused in silence for a moment, staring over the upper rims of his glasses as the security man approached. 'What news?' he asked.

'Phone call from Dent. It's Marburg. Confirmed by Porton Down,' said Marshall. 'They want MacKenzie now.'

The CMO leant back in his chair and sighed deeply. 'Well, we knew it might be Marburg so I can't say I'm surprised, can I?' he asked, the question directed at no-one but himself. 'But I do wish it had been Ebola.'

He paused then, getting to his feet. 'Nevertheless,' he added, rather loudly, 'with what you've been telling me about our Annie and the bouquets from Dent, we may yet win the battle. Have you told her?'

'Yes. I'm about to arrange for the helicopter.....' replied Marshall, but he didn't finish the sentence for he was interrupted by a piercing scream. It was the scream of a woman in great pain and it came from the direction of the utility room.

First on the scene was Browning, closely followed - to the point where they almost tripped over each other - by Gibson and Marshall.

Looking over Gibson's shoulder in the narrow corridor-like room, Marshall saw a very white-faced Anne with Browning coaxing her into the comfortable arm-chair. Then he glanced down to where Browning gently supported Anne's right arm. And there he saw the cause of the girl's pain, a lower arm whose skin was now as pink as a boiled lobster where large blisters were already beginning to form.

A queer little noise drew the security man's attention nearer and he was aware that it was Gibson who made it.

'Get the first-aid box,' instructed Browning, which gave Gibson the only excuse he needed to leave the scene and the PR man quickly made a dash for the PMO's office.

It took minutes only to place the 'cage' of bandages around the arm but away from the skin - and to dose Anne with a sedative. Still white, she was strong enough after this time to tell what happened.

'I got a shock,' she complained.

'I'll bet you did,' said Marshall, sympathetically. 'Scalding hot water tends to...'

'No. I mean an electric-shock,' she insisted. 'It was quite definitely an electric-shock which caused me to open the tap too wide.'

'Okay, we'll have a look at it later,' soothed the PMO.

Quite correctly the girl took this remark as appeasement and candid disregard for her claim. 'Look, believe me! Would I do the same stupid thing I did earlier?' she argued. 'There is something wrong with that urn.   I got an electric shock from the tap!'

The PMO looked quickly at Marshall, the latter framed by a gathering crowd now assembled in the corridor. The look merely conveyed interest which replaced scepticism. Then he leaned over to the socket where the urn was connected to the wall and he removed the plug. 'Ashton,' he called, noticing the man's face in the doorway, 'call the duty electrician and ask him to step up here.' He turned to Marshall again: 'We can't suffer the loss of our refreshments at such a critical time, can we?'

'Certainly not, Doctor,' said Marshall, which though in the same mock serious tone Browning had used did not manage to convey the humour intended.

'Right, I think we can arrange for the experts to look at that arm,' said Browning. 'Gibson,' he called,' in my desk diary you'll find the number of the Burns Unit. Ring them, inform them who we are - may as well use the few perks which go with this job - and tell them we have a patient on the way over. Ask them to send an ambulance....'

'No ambulance,' announced Marshall, quietly.

'What?' said Browning's frown, but it didn't get as far as his vocal chords. Already in motion, the PR man halted mid-stride at the clash of orders.

'Miss Mackenzie is too important to be lost in the labyrinth of a large hospital for hours on end - especially at this time,' explained Marshall. 'She must be in Dent at three this afternoon.'

'What then do you suggest?' challenged the CMO who had arrived silently at Marshall's side.

'Someone takes her over there - my car is down below - and he ensures she is treated quickly without delay. Then he brings her back here,' offered Marshall. 'A letter from you, Sir Roland?' Marshall shrugged.

'We are at a pretty low ebb in the tides of morale in the NHS but the point has still not been reached when the CMO needs to personally smooth the path of ambulant patients, or any other patients for that matter,' fumed Sir Roland.

'A suggestion only,' placated Marshall. 'I merely wish to prevent the bolshie attitude an overworked casualty doctor may apply to an underpowered request for preferential treatment.'

'I see,' said the CMO, who then turned about and strode down the corridor to his office.

People do the strangest things under stress and such impressions as Marshall conveyed, to those whose tasks allowed periodic perusal of their surroundings, would undoubtedly have endorsed this truth. In the twenty-or-so minutes since Anne had left for the hospital Marshall had positively breezed around the suite checking on everyone's job, striking up conversations bordering on small-talk and culminating, as the clock clicked over to twelve-thirty, with his encumbered appearance in the boardroom half-dragging one of the portable electric fans. More quizzical looks greeted this last action but he merely explained that it was a little stuffy.

A keener observer than those present would have noticed that his change of behaviour was more accurately connected with the departure of Gibson.

The PR man, who had answered the call for a volunteer as Anne's escort with an offer which was more a demand - and Marshall would have been very surprised if he hadn't - would have been very interested to witness the flicker of expressions which crept over the security man's face as he had closed the door behind them. Relief was certainly one of the emotions Marshall felt difficulty in stifling but there was also an apprehension which bordered on fear; fear of a type he had only recently come to know, fear for someone else's safety.

However his behaviour may have seemed to his observers, he was not reacting in the zany way of overstress. Instead, his antics were in accordance with a fairly strict plan, as had almost all his actions in this operation since long before they had come to know of him.

At twelve-thirty-one he was joined by the CMO in the boardroom. 'It never rains but it pours, hmm?' commented Sir Roland, and Marshall noticed the stilted speech-projection of a bad actor. 'Have Dent been informed of the accident?'

Marshall nodded. 'Your PMO is on the line to them now,' he said.

'Yes, it is a little stuffy in here,' confirmed the CMO, looking at the newly-positioned fan. 'In fact, it's getting to be like an old 'pea-souper'.'

'Just what I thought, Sir Roland,' agreed the security man carrying on the banter. 'Running the fan for a few minutes will do us all a lot of good.'

'If you are hoping it will blow away our bad luck,' put in Prendle-James, breaking the injured silence which had existed since he had earned the

CMO's rebuke, 'remember it is only a machine - and a rather noisy one at that.'

'We can but try,' answered Marshall, good-humouredly, before switching on the fan.

As before, and as the Scientific Officer had just confirmed, the noise from the fan was quite noticeable, sounding as if a metal rod were being drawn across metal railings but with less regularity and in a higher-pitched note. But the operation of switching on the fan had more effect than just causing a draught through the room, it also seemed that Marshall - and to a lesser extent the CMO - was instantly transformed in manner.

'Could you get everyone in here,' said Sir Roland to the PMO who, having just entered the room, was closing the door behind him.

At the same time Marshall was circuiting the boardroom scanning the walls and ceiling with an electronic device he had taken from his pocket.

'No changes,' he said when he had returned to the CMO's side.

Seconds later the scene was similar to that on numerous occasions before as everyone sat around the long table except that now the chairs normally occupied by Anne and the PR man were, of course, empty.

'It is not I who summoned this meeting,' announced Sir Roland, when all were seated. 'It was Mr Marshall's idea to get you all together to hear something important.'

Automatically, the eyes of the others - Browning, Prendle-James, Claire, Ashton, Selby and Walsh - swung in Marshall's direction.

'Your PMO, Mr Browning,' began the security man, 'has just made three telephone calls. Before I go any further with this meeting it is important I should hear the outcome of his conversations. One was to Dent reporting the accident but it is another - the one to the burns unit where Doctor Mackenzie and Gibson are visiting which interests me most.'

'Yes, of course. How is she?' asked Selby, of the PMO.

The PMO addressed the whole meeting. 'They arrived there at twelve minutes past,' he announced. 'Mackenzie was treated immediately, of course, and they both left for here ten minutes ago. They certainly worked quickly.'

'Good,' said Marshall. 'I will now hazard the guess that our two youngsters will not be returning as planned. I have to tell you that the situation has become one of kidnap, gentlemen, with Anne as the hostage.'

'Kidnap!' exclaimed the Scientific Officer, in a mixture of surprise and tired resignation - a blend of emotions which had become commonplace through the events of the past three days. If he was seriously off-balance this state did not last long for he quickly fell into a voice which caught his earlier mood. 'Well at least sound as if you're regretting the incident when you say it,' he insisted.

'Perhaps you'd explain,' asked a nervous Walsh.

'You will get a full explanation in due course,' replied Marshall, 'but I can say that Doctor Mac-Kenzie has just been abducted by our friend Gibson and the two are most certainly some miles distant by now.'

The security man then turned to face Prendle-James squarely. 'If I seem less than unhappy at the turn of events it is with due reason. For the last few weeks my main objective has been to arrange such an occurrence,' he said. 'A trap has been engineered here with great patience and sensitivity. Sensitivity because we always knew that if we got it wrong there would be no time for a second chance. Thankfully it has worked. The pressure has been applied by just the right amount and Gibson reacted as we had intended. He ran.'

It was unfortunate for the puzzled brains of those who heard Marshall's revelations that at that moment they should hear a knock on the board-room door. The security man, with frozen expression, looked at the still unopened door and his gaze was followed by those who could do so without turning in their seats. The remainder watched Marshall closely. All were silent.

'Come in,' invited Sir Roland, having difficulty with the stability of his vocal chords.

Almost silently, the first of two people walked through the open doorway.

'Perhaps I should have mentioned,' said Marshall in half-apology. 'The third call was to my boss - inviting him to attend this meeting.'

Chapter Nine
(Saturday: 1245 – 1400)

There were nine people around the table as the CMO looked across to where the newcomers sat. In addition to the normal DOH contingent - Sir Roland, Browning and Prendle-James - and the temporary inhabitants, Selby, Ashton, Walsh and Marshall, the ring of faces now included those of Benson and Jenkins who took the places of the recently departed couple, Gibson and Anne. Claire, note-pad in hand, sat away from the table to the left of and slightly to the rear of her boss.

The CMO's eyes levelled on Benson. 'I think the time is ripe for an explanation,' he said calmly. 'I would remind you we are medical men unused to the startling events which have apparently,' and his gaze switched to Marshall, 'been perpetrated by your department.'

'Which is precisely why I am here: to explain.'

'Again according to plan?'

'Again according to plan,' replied the admiral.

As he spoke the door had opened and one of his men crossed to where the fan was still revolving noisily. He switched it off and simply nodded in Benson's direction before retracing his steps to leave the room.

'Ah, that's better,' said Benson. 'Could hardly hear meself think.'

In response, Sir Roland looked up sharply but said nothing.

'Explanations. Yes, that is why I'm here - and I agree there are a lot outstanding,' continued Benson. 'Perhaps it would be better if Marshall told you the whole story. That is, as much as he is able to tell before he must leave us. Thereafter, I shall have to manage on my own. No doubt we shall cover everything.'

'Please do, Mr Marshall,' encouraged the CMO.

'The story really began last July,' said Marshall. 'You may remember the climate of public opinion around that time. There was a lot of stuff about violations in animal welfare, particularly in the area of vivisection. July marked the crisis point in an anti-vivisection campaign which sought to expose the cruelty - real and imagined - which occurred behind the doors of laboratories engaged in cosmetics research. Cases appeared, notably in the Sunday newspapers, where evidence was gained through nothing less than burglary of such premises.

'In mid-July one of these establishments suffered an accident where two of its research workers died. At first no foul play was suspected due to lack of evidence. In fact the truth of the matter did not emerge until recently. However, it wasn't an accident - nor was it a cosmetics-testing laboratory.'

The burglar, he went on to say, had been a middle-aged freelance journalist looking for a scoop. In one of the laboratories the man had found a number of small phials racked for safety at the rear of a glass-fronted refrigerator. The lights in the lab were still on and indeed the room showed signs that work was in progress as a clump of odd-looking glass containers bore witness. He had been fortunate that his visit had found the laboratory temporarily unoccupied.

Pocketing one of the metal phials from the refrigerator he had moved over to a work area for a closer look. His interest was little more than non-technical but the markings and notations he could see amongst the paper-work had managed to convey one fact to him. It told him he was not in the cosmetics laboratory that all outward signs had indicated, instead a growing suspicion pointed to an identity more connected with the Ministry of Defence.

It was as these thoughts matured that he had become suddenly aware of someone's approach. Realizing the possibility of detection before he had entered the building he had worried to some degree on the matter. But things were different now. The situation had changed to the big league. He was out of his depth and his racing brain imagined the wrath of the authorities when they discovered a journalist in their top-secret germ-warfare factory, for that was what he knew it must be.

At the sound of the footsteps in the distance, accompanied by those of voices, he had made one last reflexive grab for information, an instinctive gesture born of years which even terror could not fully quell.

His hand had alighted on the first piece of paper within reach after he had placed the test-tube he had been inspecting on the flat surface. His hand came away with a single sheet of paper almost worthless to him but his action was to cause tragedy. As he had scuttled away to a door outside the lab marked store-room he had seen just two lucid images, the large key in the lab door and, when he had turned to back into the store, the work-top in the lab with a shiny glass test-tube rolling backwards and forwards on the flat surface as it inched its way towards the edge.

The possible consequences of a smashed test-tube had been somewhat limited in his vision as he huddled behind the closed door. His thoughts were totally taken up with the chances of discovery and he had visualized the test-tube as nothing more than an audible alarm indicating his presence in the area. Carefully he had inched open the door just in time to see two white-coated figures enter the lab.

He had wasted no time. He had leapt out of the store-room, slammed the lab door shut and turned the key. In seconds he was making his escape the way he had come. Somewhere in his subconscious he had heard the tiny tinkle of breaking glass but his brain was not in a responsive mood.

It was odd that some fifty yards down the lane he should halt for some seconds - waver uncertainly – and then slowly trudge back in the direction from which he had so recently come. Possibly it was the reinstatement of reason which had spurred him into returning to the lab. He hadn't known for certain himself. He had known that his criminal tendencies weren't sufficiently marked for him to enforce, gladly, the incarceration of the two technicians. So he would free them and face the music.

Feeling that he must get at least something out of his evening's work he had paused by the lighted but unattended entrance to the building and dug into his pockets for the piece of paper. His hand had emerged holding both the paper and the metal phial and after a brief perusal of the esoteric, to him meaningless writing, he had sought better luck with the phial. A study of the writing on the label was to produce almost the same result as that with the paper, but only almost, for somewhere in the back of his mind a bell had rung, causing a frown to appear on his face. He had gone further and opened the container. The light was too dim for him to make out the contents and his instinctive inquisitive sniff produced a nil result.

He had given up. Pocketing both the paper and the phial he had made his way around the building to the shadows and the window, which had yielded to his expertise once before. Paradoxically, his short pause had both prolonged and shortened his life.

It was when he had opened the lab door that he received his greatest shock when he saw both men lying on the floor, quite still, their facial features contorted to a degree almost impossible to assume in life. Both were dead.

The journalist had fled in real panic.

As Marshall's narrative drew to a natural, tempo-rary, conclusion at the point where the reporter had run from the building, he became aware of a change in the formerly interested features of the CMO. Now the expression was quickly changing to another, quizzical, almost sceptical.

'I fancy we have heard this story before except that there were slight differences,' he challenged. 'For instance, the story we heard some days ago contained a little more premeditation, I recall, and a fire was involved. Most notable difference, however, was that the incident was reported as happening weeks rather than months ago.'

'A different episode, nevertheless,' injected the admiral, unabashed by the insinuation that Mar-shall was telling stories to fit the facts rather than vice versa. He looked toward his employee. 'Con-tinue,' he said.

'As I said to begin with,' continued Marshall, 'the incident was mistaken for a straight-forward accident - if any accident is straight-forward. The cause of death was inhalation of toxic fumes from the substance released by the broken test tube. Ul-timately, asphyxiation took place.'

'But how could they be so careless? All the rules forbid such practice!' protested Selby.

'I don't believe you are that naive, Selby,' put in Browning. 'There is a long way between stringent safety standards and carelessness. Most people employed in such situations use common sense in applying unwieldy rules and are still safe. Occasionally, we all slip below the dividing line of safe and unsafe.' He sighed. 'I think I can imagine the situation here. A slightly more robust phial than Mr Marshall has pictured was correctly racked but left unattended for a few minutes while the lab workers went for a break - they weren't expecting anyone to go anywhere near the thing, naturally, and the phial didn't break when it fell but most likely ruptured a seal. Just a group of little details and strokes of bad luck which could occur in a million situations. You call it carelessness, Selby. I agree, but only to a point.'

'Though I say it was a glass phial,' offered Marshall, 'I am merely repeating the journalist's own story and the results of my minimal involvement with the incident in the subsequent investigation.'

'How was it the poison didn't affect the journalist when he returned to the lab?' queried Ashton.

'The air-conditioning system,' responded Marshall. 'A system of filters - standard equipment in high-containment laboratories, I believe - absorbs stale air at a fast rate and replenishes with clean air. By the time the journalist had returned to the lab the air was clean.'

'The story, Marshall,' prompted Benson.

'Yes, sir,' he returned, 'the story.'

The journalist had returned by car to his bedsit where he lived alone. His desperation was acute by the time he had arrived, to the point where he could see almost immediate arrest. However, he had been in the business a long time and although no longer the top flight operator he had once been, he still had a little black book full of contacts.

Sat by the telephone in the early hours of the morning, he short-listed the possible helpers for he had but one simple plan. Checking through the entries, many going back several years, he struck out all but half-a-dozen names. Even as he began to study these he knew there was only one name that could possibly provide the key to his escape.

And escape was what he planned. He was possessed of the instinct to run and he had decided he wouldn't be able to stop running until he was out of the country and, more importantly, into a territory so remote as to afford physical conceal-ment as well as legal disregard to extradition - places he knew were becoming fewer every year. Hence his automatic choice of the person who had to help him, a mercenary leader called D'rosario.

Even in his haste to ring the telephone number accompanying the mercenaries name the fright-ened man took time to remember his acquaint-anceship with D'rosario. He had met the merce-nary, an ex-Army major, when he had worked on one of the London newspapers. In the beginning he had believed the man to be the idealist brand of mercenary and, at a time when the 'soldier of for-tune' suffered some severe image-bashing, the re-porter had written on the virtues of the 'idealist'. The mercenary had been most grateful at the time -

just how grateful would now be tested by the telephone call.

As it turned out his fears were unfounded because within twenty-four hours of his call for help the reporter had driven down to embark on an aircraft bound with provisions for central Africa, the latest in the mercenary's sphere of operations. During the journey none of the authorities *en route* were to be troubled by being made aware of his presence.

The battered DC-3, stopping only to re-fuel, broke the last leg of its outward journey to put down on a makeshift airstrip less than a mile from where the major part of a guerrilla force of almost a thousand men were encamped. The aircraft stayed for just ten minutes, for that was all that was required to empty the cargo compartment of stores and one slightly unwell journalist, replace the same number of crates with transferred stamps, and, with engines already revving hard, shut the doors and rumble off into the clear sky, bound for its legal destination.

It had been an uncomfortable trip wedged between boxes of stores, the journalist had reflected, as they drove him to the camp. Perhaps that was why he now felt unwell with the heat almost stifling and an intensity of sunlight which made his eyes hurt badly. But he also felt quite 'grotty' as if he had caught a chill. Therefore, as soon as he had been shown his primitive quarters he had turned in.

He had brought little luggage with him. Such had been his haste that he wore the same clothes as on the night of the break-in and, apart from the 'third arm' of his portable tape-recorder, his kit was crammed into a small airline-bag. It was not a lot and even his mobile phone had been left behind lest it give his position away.

The journalist never really left his sickbed from the first time he had lain down to recover from the journey. Just before he drifted into sleep with the sound of engine noise still in his ears, he felt guilty that he hadn't told D'rosario the reason for his escape. Instead, the journalist had been very brief in his plea for help and left the rest to the mercenary's imagination. This was a mistake for not only was the journalist to die from his illness but he was to decimate the guerrilla force through infection which his 'nurse' was to transmit to those outside his hut.

Within three weeks the encampment was little more than a ghost-town with only forty of the eight hundred inhabitants still alive - and some of these barely so. It was this scene of tragedy that D'rosario was later to witness for he had been disturbed at reports of non-effectiveness in the guerrilla war in which his 'troops' were involved.

'How do you know all this? How can you be so certain of the journalist's movements interrupted Selby, at this point, 'You appear to know not only what happened but also his very thoughts on the matter. Yet he died - you say - a long time before you knew anything of the matter.'

'Quite simply because he told us,' said Marshall. 'He left a tape upon which he related the incident. It is not a pleasant experience to listen to because he made the tape when he was in the last stages of his illness, Towards the end his words weren't very intelligible.'

'The phial contained Marburg virus,' reasoned Prendle-James aloud, for it was not a question.

'Yes,' answered Marshall unnecessarily.

The CMO shifted in his seat, a quizzical expression on his face. 'I'm not sure I understand the time-scale - the chronology - of the situation,' he said. 'When did you get to hear of this?'

'We first made the connection with the journalist in January,' replied Marshall, 'You may call it luck but in fact it was the dull, boring, routine plodding of the agencies from several European countries which made the connection possible. We had been investigating the operations of a terrorist group for around six months by that time. Our inquiries enabled us to establish a link between a string of blackmailing operations, always meticulously planned and with several cut-outs to avoid connection with the regular members of the terrorist gang. It still led us to D'rosario.

'Even then, this connection had occurred by accident but it was to pave the way - by surveillance of the movements of both himself and his cronies - to a link with the real boss, Chaval. You probably recognise this name better as J.

'Checking further into the past we discovered D'rosario's visit to the guerrilla camp and the link with the journalist was made. I visited both the camp and D'rosario's flat in London. At the latter I found the tape, recorded it on the spot and spent some time studying its contents.'

'If you know it is J who is behind this, why haven't you arrested him? Or is it all part of your scheme?' queried Ashton.

'No, it isn't our policy to allow a crime of such magnitude to go unchecked, even at the outset,' replied the security-man, with feeling. 'We should very much like to prevent such goings-on. The simple fact is that J hasn't been seen, by us or anyone else, for the last eight years. We simply can't find him and, after he gave our men the slip in March, the same can now be said of D'rosario.

'Again the reason is simple. One word would suffice in general explanation: electronics. J spent his time at university among the fanatic set. He got to know a lot of people who have since left Paris for the four corners of the world. With his degree in electronics and these contacts, J has put together a world-wide organisation dedicated to terrorism. It took him several years to perfect his system: our meagre knowledge of his operations is based solely, however, upon his successes.

'His operations to the end of last year concerned the organisation of urban terrorism, blackmail and kidnapping of government officials mainly in France. Each operation was meticulously planned, as I have already said, with taped instructions being despatched to both the terrorist in the field and, where appropriate, blackmailed.'

'As in this situation,' said Selby.

'Correct,' responded Marshall. 'As in this one. There were problems, however. Although the use of such taped instructions safeguarded the identity and whereabouts of J, they couldn't possibly include contingency plans for every possible hiccup in an operation.

'That is to say, if J assumed that his operation was going according to plan and he released the next tape in the sequence of instructions - but, in fact, something had gone wrong – he would then be blind and lose control of the situation. It was obvious that all his meticulous planning would go out of the window in any operation beyond the simplest plan because he had no communications with his fanatics - in either direction - except for the very restricted instruction tapes. He needed at least one man - a capable person - on the scene. This man wouldn't just be an observer either, he would need to be part of the action - planted into the area of operations some time before the event - and possessed of the ability to 'steer' events. J certainly realised this, too: he used such a man on this job. His name - as you know him - was Gibson.'

'Gibson!' It was almost a sneer of shocked scepticism and it came from Walsh.

'But he was just a…,' began Prendle-James, who faltered as he realised what all of them now realised, that the best camouflage for such an operator as Marshall had described was the character Gibson had portrayed.

'It's a bit of a shock to realise our PR man was.. was...' The CMO didn't finish the sentence but changed his train of thought. 'How did he communicate? You said the man would need to communicate with J and vice versa. Gibson never left the suite except to go to the shower-room above. He never even used the telephone without...'

'An intricate system of bugging devices repeated everything said,' interrupted Marshall, 'We've known about it for some weeks, since it became evident what J's plans might be, when we naturally screened the place. We also installed our own system of listening devices at the same time.'

As one, seven pairs of eyes consciously dissected the decor in a futile search for the devices.

'Gibson,' he continued, 'could pass any essential information in the small hours via the transmitter when he was on watch...'

'Transmitter?' Plainly the CMO considered that Marshall was going too far - but again several pairs of eyes surveyed the room in the hope of spotting a gleaming console twinkling lights shaped into letters spelling TRANSMITTER.

'Yes, transmitter,' reiterated the security man. 'You only had the coffee urn installed three months ago, didn't you? It is such a large object but most of it is a transmitter. Its aerials are the metal frames of these top windows.' Marshall indicated the window frames whose upper panes were shut.

'Of course!' cried Browning. 'You remember, Sir Roland. When Gibson first arrived he managed to open all the top windows. On a windy day too, I seem to remember.'

'How could I forget. It took the best part of the afternoon to sort out the documents which flew about in the gale force winds,' said the CMO with feeling. 'If I remember correctly, I dictated that they should from then on be closed permanently.'

'At Gibson's suggestion, no doubt,' urged Marshall.

'You're probably right there,' said Browning.

'Just a case of 'engineering' the situation properly,' explained Marshall. 'Incidentally, Walsh, that fracas you were involved in?'

'Yes?'

'Engineered by Gibson for two reasons. Firstly, he was expecting the first tape to arrive at seven in the morning. Possibly, he was feeling the pressure a little, particularly as we had purposely delayed delivery of the package at the door below, but he needed to find out what had happened and let J know that there had been a delay. He also used the situation to try to pump me as to whether the phone was being tapped by us. I told him not but it was – and it still is.'

'Cunning blighter,' decided Prendle-James, but he went no further for the telephone had begun its strident call.

'I still don't fully understand what is going on,' protested Selby.

'You're not alone,' concurred Ashton.

Only seconds had passed since Marshall had left the suite. In response to the phone call he had intrigued his observers by disappearing into the CMO's vacant office with the suitcase Jenkins had brought in only to reappear shortly afterwards dressed in what should have been a capacious raincoat. The garment was, however, straining about a bulk that wasn't all Marshall. No-one voiced their curiosity as to why this was - nor indeed had the opportunity to do so - for after short conversation with his boss and without even a parting glance in the direction of the others, he was gone.

'It is this matter of conflicting stories that I don't understand,' said Walsh, adding thoughts to those of Selby and Ashton. He looked across to where Benson sat. 'Mr Marshall spoke of a fire before, in what I feel sure is the same laboratory he has referred to this afternoon.'

'Of course, you are right,' replied Benson. 'But if you are to grasp the full significance of recent developments I should carry on with the story from where Marshall left off.'

'Let us take up the story from where D'rosario, worried about his troops, flew into the guerrilla encampment,' he began. 'He didn't stay long. He soon realised that with the major part of his force wiped out he was finished in Africa, at least until he could re-build his army. Therefore, he pulled out the survivors of the epidemic together with the more valuable items of weaponry. But first he called by the grave of the man who had unwittingly brought such tragedy to his men and, afterwards, he visited the hut where the journalist had lain until death. He knew the man had a family though he wasn't certain just how many members there had been. He seemed to remember there was a child and with this in mind he scooped up the meagre pile of belongings, hoping to return them when he himself returned to the UK.'

Benson had been talking in the flat tones of one reciting facts from memory but then he suddenly jerked back to the present. 'Incidentally,' he said, 'we know that part of the story from the very child he returned those belongings to. We interviewed her some months ago after D'rosario had sent her father's belongings to her, and an account of what had happened, by courier,'

Then his eyes faded again as he slipped into his recital. 'From then on things aren't so clear. We depend totally upon the jigsaw of information - rumour in some instances - for our evidence. A lot of 'cause and effect' reasoning has been required to establish a story-line which fits the possibilities. It goes something like this.

'It was D'rosario's idea from the start. It was his imagination, for which he was renowned by his circle of acquaintances, which had thought to couple the journalist's taped story with J's organisation and style. Together with the special immunity that the remnants of his guerrilla force now possessed he required but a very special bond - a top-flight microbiologist - to carry out his plan.'

D'rosario had approached J, at that time little more than an acquaintance, knowing that his plan would receive instant approval - as would any scheme which involved the procurement of power which, to J, was a drug.

The object of their scheme was nothing less than world disruption as its minimum requirement but their eyes were also on the very real possibility of total economic power. J would provide from among his friends at university, and with promises of vast rewards, a microbiologist of world-class. J would also procure - ostensibly for short-hire only - a number of bulk carriers which he would deploy at ports adjacent to the bullion depots of the major gold reserves. It also fell to J - or rather to his fanatic cells around the world - to provide the 'volunteer' to spread the disease. Finally, J would provide the electronic control of the operation, deploy his man in the DOH staff, and, understandably, pick up the tab for these arrangements.

D'rosario's task was more in line with his old occupation. Using the journalist's tape as his guide, he would plan and execute another raid on the laboratory. The aim of the raid was simply to obtain fresh Marburg virus - that stolen by the journalist long having been de-activated naturally. He also was to provide the couriers who would distribute it to the fanatic cells around the world - the freshly cultivated quantities of virus the microbiologist had prepared from that which had been stolen. D'rosario picked these men from those who had survived infection from the virus and who, therefore, were immune to its effects. Their job also entailed 'minding' the potential carrier and keeping him out of circulation until he was required to carry the virus into the community. Lastly, these mercenaries provided the first link in the long chain of 'cut-outs' which would ultimately safe-guard the security of both the operation and its controllers; as soon as a carrier had done his work it was up to the mercenary to dispose of him before he could be interviewed by the authorities.

'But do the facts support our theories?' posed the admiral. 'As they said of our sailor's uniforms during the war: it fits where it touches, at least. We have the proof. The tape, the fire at the laboratory where, incidentally, we were to suffer an infection in one of my own men. We have the murdered black African who had carried the infection into Dent ...'

'What?' The CMO's face registered alarm. 'Marshall didn't tell me about that.'

'No. Of course he didn't,' censured Benson. 'There was enough to be worrying about without that as well. But the plain truth is that the black African was murdered by his 'minder' who, no doubt, has long since escaped by a pre-determined route.'

Benson paused for a second-or-so to collect his thoughts.

'So you see, gentlemen,' he said, 'the story does fit our theory in parts. Which is all well and good except - as in all situations where information is scarce - it is difficult, if not impossible, to forecast events. For instance, we know they have ships ready to embark gold - that much we have learned in the last twenty-four hours. We even know the names of those ships. We don't, however know from where they are controlled and, if we don't know this, we dare not try to interfere with the execution of the ransom payment.'

'For fear of retribution via the Marburg virus,' supplied Browning.

'Precisely,' confirmed Benson. 'But we could hear the noises they were making some weeks ago - just after the second laboratory raid. It was then that Marshall, who was getting closer than most to their shennanigans, instigated our present operation. He simply realised the possibility of a plant existing in the DOH and decided whoever the impostor was he was the only way to short-circuit the system in order to get at J.'

'So he wandered in here, told us a pack of lies about the virtues of liaisons with the security branch, and set about fixing his beady eye on Gibson,' said Browning, continuing his tendency to supplement Benson's commentary.

'No,' returned the admiral. 'Or, not exactly. Everything he told you was the truth....but perhaps he did withhold a certain amount of information. And his beady eye wasn't just on the PR man, either. It fell on everyone.'

'Bloody cheek!' spluttered the CMO, forgetting himself in his anger.

'The stakes were too high - are too high - to take any chances,' said Benson, loudly, as if stifling further dissention. 'But don't worry, everyone else was cleared,' he said, with a smile.

'Once he was certain who the imposter was,' he continued, 'Marshall could begin to work on him. First, he lulled him into thinking he was trusted: his advice was sought, he was put in charge of the information cell, even the Chief Medical Officer of Health listened to him when it came to discussing shipping. Then Marshall - only a matter of hours ago - began to apply the pressure. He scared him when he handed him the names of all the ships under J's control some time before Gibson could possibly have expected us to have discovered such information. As it was, we came by these names only after prolonged investigations with the aid of some top people in the mercantile marine.

'Marshall continued to apply the pressure in numerous ways with snippets of information spoken into the telephone or apparently repeated by him from the person on the other end of the line. But this morning was the time to move into high gear and it was then that Marshall, who had already enrolled the CMO once in his schemes, further enrolled both the CMO and the PMO for a nifty little sketch which proves that both of them had at least one alternative career fit for their talents - as actors.'

Sir Roland and Browning said nothing in response, being too careful to present stone-faces to the inquiring glances of their staff. Most baffled was Prendle-James, at least for a second, then his features relaxed as he realised - if only in part - the reason for his earlier rebuke.

But Benson was speaking. 'After taking pains to convince everyone that treatment was being tested at Dent which was a break-through in the fight against Marburg, we naturally upgraded Miss MacKenzie's value a thousand-fold when we revealed that it was all due to her efforts. Alas, gentlemen, there is absolutely no truth in that particular story. I'm afraid there is no such treatment for Marburg - as our professor would have told you - had the CMO not intervened. The simple fact is that it was just part of the plan, the pressure, with which we hoped to force Gibson to kidnap Miss Mackenzie and lead us to J.'

'You mean you used Doctor MacKenzie as bait?' snarled Selby, startled by the revelation but having difficulty maintaining his expression of shock after so much recent use.

'If you put it that way, yes,' responded Benson, calmly. 'But you've got it wrong; it isn't Doctor. It's Miss.'

'Miss?' repeated Selby, confused. 'What do you mean by that?'

'Exactly what I say,' returned the admiral, a touch annoyed that he should have to explain simple English, 'MacKenzie isn't and never has been, a doctor. She probably couldn't even find her way round a lab. But don't get me wrong, I think she is a sterling woman. A courageous woman.'

'But the people on the telephone from Dent who wanted her back,' said a confused Ashton. 'She gave us a brief, she knew her stuff..' He looked for help to the head of the table but he got little help and Prendle-James had joined the other two with stone-faced expressions.

'A week's concentrated study with a little guidance,' explained Benson. 'But let's face it, she was in little danger of discovery from within these walls with the exception of the professor who, after a period of doubt, became convinced she was not what she claimed to be. Fortunately, he didn't air his doubts until it was too late - or rather - the CMO could discourage him. But as for the rest, well, you know that virology is a fairly recent branch of medical science. When the CMO and the PMO were in medical school it was in its infancy and of course - we checked - your specialist fields are physiology and cardiac surgery respectively.

'We checked out *your* past experience as well, gentlemen,' he continued looking at the three younger men, 'with almost the same result. No danger there. But before you begin to believe this whole thing is a hoax I must tell you that some people are very poorly in Dent. Fortunately, we haven't had any deaths yet. There is a full team of doctors and nurses at the scene - only an Australian posing as a microbiologist and another security man posing as the senior epidemiologist have had any part in our operation.'

'Poor girl,' said Selby.

'What?' asked Benson, forgetting himself as he was mentally thrown off-balance.

'The girl: Miss Mackenzie,' he explained. 'I was just thinking what she has had to go through. It must have been very painful. And then to be dragged off to God-knows-where.'

'Yes, she's a brave girl, all right,' said Prendle-James, realizing the real merit of the person he had, with' good reason, distrusted. 'One of your agents?'

'No, not really. She came to us some months ago,' he replied, introspectively. 'Dedicated though. Understandable when you think about it.'

'Think about what,' asked Selby.

'Never mind,' dismissed the admiral, mentally with them again. 'You may have no worries as to the accident this morning. Your PMO was much involved in the incident. He will tell you that the scald marks you may have seen on Miss MacKenzie's arm were in fact nothing of the sort but just theatrical make-up in the form of a plastic stick-on coating.'

'Well, that is something,' sighed Selby. 'I suppose this was more of the pressure.'

'You suppose correctly,' agreed the admiral. 'It was just a few more turns of the screw to incite Gibson to flee. By Anne - Miss MacKenzie - insisting she had received a shock from the urn we could reasonably expect to check it out without him suspecting our motives. The urn, of course, would not bear investigation. Gibson must see that discovery of the transmitter would cause a fuss and the least that would happen would be the discovery of the bugging system. As the aerial must also come under scrutiny it wouldn't take long to implicate him. He had to get out.

'We gave him an opportunity he couldn't ignore. His task at the DOH must have been drawing to a close as far as his usefulness was concerned. He needed to either silence the girl or take her with him; he was close to discovery and we needed someone to take the girl to the hospital. Naturally, he jumped at it.'

'So you've accomplished everything you set out to do?' asked the CMO, but he didn't expect an answer for he continued in the same vein, 'You've finished using my office as a stage for your subterfuge - with me as one of your actors? Well, perhaps we can get back to our real jobs.'

'You can, indeed,' said Benson.

But Selby hadn't finished exercising his curiosity. 'Where do you go from here?'

'We are going to try to stop these people,' said Benson, with feeling. 'At the moment we are depending far too much on Marshall.'

'I don't understand,' said Ashton. 'Mr Marshall does not appear to me to be in any state to go chasing criminals. I know he looks a lot better than he did when he arrived, but the man is ill.'

'Not ill,' replied Benson, 'not in the traditional sense, anyway. You see, Marshall was the security man who contracted an infection while investigating the second incident at the laboratory. The infection was Marburg. He has scarcely recovered - if that is the term I should use - for he certainly hasn't had time to convalesce. On top of that he is supplying Dent with convalescent plasma - admittedly only in tiny amounts when you think of the volume of the stuff required.'

'Convalescent plasma?' repeated Sir Roland, loudly. 'So that was it. That explains the sunken cheeks, the eyes.'

'I'm afraid so,' continued Benson. 'Together with the lack of sleep. Well, that just about made him the number one candidate for redundancy in his occupation. I had people to take his place. Still have.' Benson smiled then, but it wasn't of the humorous variety. 'But he blackmailed his own boss.'

'Blackmail?'

'Blackmail. He knew the situation might demand a strike into the enemy's camp where active Marburg virus was present. As he had, like D'rosario's surviving mercenaries, suffered the infection he was perfect for the job. He was immune and that put him in a strong position.'

'Is he mad?' queried Sir Roland. 'If he's in such a sorry state surely he must realise….,' he added, but the CMO was lost for words to continue.

'No, not mad. Dedicated, yes,' said Benson, reflectively. 'One of my best men. He certainly has the mental resilience for the job.'

'He's still only one man,' censured Browning. 'He's also ill.'

Benson shrugged. 'It's not the sort of mission to go in mob-handed.' As he spoke, it seemed to his audience that he was wresting with his thoughts, trying to conceal his concern for Marshall. 'As for his, er, physical condition, he'll not give up....'

'But you're worried,' prompted Browning.

Benson nodded slowly. 'I'm worried because this is his likely to be his last job and, moreover, he is emotionally involved.'

Chapter Ten
(Saturday: 1400 – 2130)

As the helicopter climbed above the London sky-line, Marshall reflected upon the information he had received by telephone in the DOH suite only minutes earlier. At first he had viewed the news 'sector seven, close' as very good, indeed. And it was good news. But it did little to relieve the anxieties of his job as he realised the news was primarily of interest to those whose task it was to ferry him to the area indicated in the phone conversation, Gibson's predicted destination. However, the inference that his journey would be much shorter than anticipated gave him some satisfaction as it meant the long awaited final phase of a mission which had lasted for so many months would soon begin.

'It's Southampton,' confirmed the voice in the headset Marshall wore. 'Our man's helicopter contacted the tower there two minutes ago.'

'Good,' said Marshall, into the microphone of his headset. 'Good.'

Twenty minutes later as the military helicopter battled south through the rain the earphones boomed into life again. 'Directing you to sector seven, map reference…'

Marshall looked at the moving map display on the aircraft control panel and noted the point where the reference lines intersected.

But the voice hadn't finished. 'Gibson and hostage,' he continued, and Marshall looked automatically, security-minded, to the little box of tricks which contained the scrambler system, 'are embarked in saloon car, predicted destination now Fawley.'

Again the security man noted the position on the 'map' aided this time by the prodding finger of the pilot. Marshall acknowledged the transmission curtly and resumed his ponderous gaze into the blank wall of rain ahead.

Minutes later they touched down on the small airfield alongside the Hamble.

The view across Southampton Water was tinged with a murky haze as Marshall gazed at the long low profile of the ship berthed on the opposite side. The water, carrying a slight ripple, reflected the black stormy clouds above which prematurely brought the dusk nearer. Up and down the waterway ships of all sizes moved with an air of bustle which ill-befitted the normally peaceful conception of a Saturday evening. But this was a large port serving a branch of commerce which paid heed primarily to tide and current as limiting factors: not that tides were an overwhelming cause for concern in this port - the second largest in the

United Kingdom for trade - as Southampton is a deep-water port from which the world's largest passenger ships have operated.

Marshall raised the binoculars to his eyes as he had done many times in the past hour. Again he inspected the ship as he raked the 'glasses from for'ard to aft, looking for signs of movement. Two minutes later he lowered the instrument and looked briefly, and with scarcely opened eyes, into the heavens, the rain, and the gathering dusk. He was thankful for the rain; had been waiting for the dusk; and was grateful for the loan of the foul-weather clothing without which his raincoat would have been no match against the weather.

Remembering his attire reminded him of the skipper of the pilot launch, who had loaned the clothing, and whose craft lay patiently alongside the Hamble jetty not twenty feet from his vantage. Feeling into his pocket he withdrew a piece of chamois leather and proceeded to wipe the rain from the eyepieces and lenses of the binoculars before, once more, returning to gaze across the water.

The ship's present berth was some miles south of the Port of Southampton proper being among the jetties attached by pipe-line to the oil refinery at Fawley. Of the refinery Marshall could see nothing more than a blurred outline but the much closer complex of jetties were easier to discern. The particular jetty to which the ship was secured was much the same as the rest except for one rather prominent difference in that there was a large crane at the point nearest the ship. At the foot of the crane Marshall made out the sight of building materials. With the size of the crane being too large for the transfer of hoses and such-like he assumed the ship had been berthed at a jetty which was undergoing enlargement or other alteration.

Shifting his scrutiny back to the ship he began again by slowly traversing her length, starting from the bold letters on her stern.

The *Orico* was berthed no less than one thousand yards from where Marshall watched but it still seemed huge. With the stern and after-castle nearest to him the ship's side seemed almost un-ending as it stretched away to be barely seen in the haze. But then, this was no 'tramp' nor was it a specimen of the general-type of freight carrier. The *Orico* was a larger vessel of eighty-thousand tonnes dead-weight. She was able to carry either oil, bulk or ore as the OBO tag indicated but, now that she had embarked a substantial cargo of oil, her ship's sides dipped at the lowest point along her two-hundred-and-fifty metre length - to within ten or twelve feet of the water.

The *Orico* was different from almost all other ocean-goers in one visual respect and the sight of this difference puzzled Marshall as no mention of such design characteristic had been mentioned by Chief Officer Taylor. The difference lay in the structure of the after-castle in that, where other ships stopped growing in height, the *Orico* carried on with a vaguely pyramidal structure which rose hugely before the single tall funnel, On top of the pyramid was a box-like structure and the whole triggered a recollection of what Marshall had seen in old naval photographs; it was a flying-bridge. Marshall shrugged mentally, when he first thought of this, and wondered if such an unusual characteristic hadn't been a contributory factor in forcing a five-year old ship into premature retirement at Piraeus.

The tiny crackle of an electronic voice spoke to Marshall from the small radio transceiver slung around his neck. 'From Benson,' the voice said. 'White advises LASH vessel *Baccarat* sailed Sheerness midday Friday with six tugs aboard and reported not heard of since. Considers possibility exists of link with present situation. Message ends.'

Marshall acknowledged the transmission and again lifted the binoculars to his eyes. Apart from reflecting that Benson had obviously deemed the information important - his having had it transmitted in plain language - the security man merely tucked the information in the back of his mind: he had more urgent problems to attend to, the most immediate of which was the rather large one across the water from him.

As he trained the binoculars left to view the thin line of the ship's hull Marshall checked once more that the barely discernable insurance-lines were still in place. The lines, in reality very thick wires, were placed as a safety requirement lest an emergency situation should demand the vessel be towed away. One of these was attached to the 'bits' at the ship's stern and stretched - dipping with the weight to within a few feet of the water - almost a third of the ship's length forward. Here a lighter line secured the end of the hawser to the deck. The other line was arranged in the same way but from for'ard stretching aft.

Marshall checked his watch. The arrangements had been finalised only minutes ago, shortly after Gibson and the girl had been seen to board the ship from the jetty side. With one more glance at the blackening sky and the twinkling of lights on the opposite shore the security man picked up the small radio-transceiver and uttered a few words into the microphone. Then he walked calmly down the steps to the launch. He was ready.

They had moved quickly north initially, the little launch frothing white at the stern. Two miles up-river from the jetty she turned abruptly south bucketing as she crossed over the wake of a small coaster on its way to the open sea. Keeping close into this ship the launch slowed down to match the more sedate speed of the merchantman using its cover not only to obscure the view of any observer on the *Orico* as they drew near but also to confuse the OBO's radar picture into identifying just one blip where there were two 'contacts', should such a watch be being kept on-board.

With five hundred yards to go and with a pre-dicted closest point of approach of twenty-five yards on its present course the coaster stopped rotating its radar. The functioning scanner was now, briefly, rotated in an arc by hand in the direction of the *Orico*'s after-castle, the effect of which would be to distort the picture aboard the OBO as the radar of the coaster transmitted on *Orico*'s radar frequency.

At the same time the pilot launch, responding to the same call to action, slowed momentarily to clear the coaster's stern before a short high-powered dash brought it nippily along the *Orico*'s side. A foam of white water indicated the great power of reverse drive as the launch stopped in the water alongside the point where the after tow-rope connected with the ship's deck. Marshall, poised for the short climb, leapt for the rope at the very second the launch was in position and with two or three heaves on the lighter securing line fetched up to instant stillness on the OBO's deck. Already the reverse gear of the launch had begun to move it slowly back from the side of the ship when, now clear, it surged forward under full power. Thirty seconds later and only two minutes since the coaster had begun its esoteric radar operations it ceased them and, again obscured from view, the launch was close in by its starboard beam.

Aboard the *Orico*, Marshall spent two full minutes surveying the scene from a crouched position where only his eyes moved. He was facing the after-castle, flat against the raised lip of the aft-most hatch cover on the seaward side and some thirty yards from the next point of cover, the black shadow of the *Orico's* for'ard bulkhead. Satisfied that he was unobserved he crept cautiously for the shadows from which, after another pause, he made for a safer haven.

At about the time Marshall moved on to a less exposed hiding-place the scene in the Captain's Stateroom was one almost devoid of animation. The well-appointed compartment had only the low hum of a ventilation system to offset a deaf-ening silence among those present.

There were five people in the room and it was a mixture of moods having a common base in con-frontation which was responsible for the silence. After almost a minute's pause the one man who could break the silence with impunity did so.

'Run through it again,' said the man behind the captain's desk, 'but slow it down a little.'

He was a small man, standing no taller than five-and-a-half feet from the thick-pile blue carpet which abutted onto all four bulkheads. His suit was of Italian cut which emphasised his slight build and lent a chic impression to his diminutive but well-proportioned shape. His face did not echo the warmth of his clothes, however. Ruthless, the expression was cold and set in a more deep-ly-etched likeness of that which Marshall had first seen in Benson's temporary office. He was the man they knew as Chaval - as J.

Absently, J picked up a letter opener from the desk and began pricking the large, green blotter

with the point. This was the only outward mani-
festation of his emotions but there were two others
in the room who recognised when J was angry.
The cold eyes lifted then to meet those of the man
responsible for his anger.

Dishevelled after his dash from the DOH suite,
Gibson stood barely in control of himself. With the
sweat standing out on his face he began again the
story he had previously blurted out to those present. Whereas, on the first occasion, there had been
confidence even arrogance in his every breath as
he recounted how he alone had dealt with a situation which promised serious damage to their
scheme, there was now only uncertainty and suspicion. 'Marshall handed me a list with about a
dozen ship's names on it, together with their re-
spective tonnages,' he began, tentatively. 'The
names corresponded with the names our ships
used to have before we changed them.'

Gibson looked around the faces for reaction to
the news but found none, which didn't do anything for his nerves. 'It was only a question of time,
don't you see?' he reasoned, his voice a little higher
in pitch.

Another erratic glance from face to face followed, with the same result as before. Even Anne
standing away to his right, ignored him for she
had only eyes for J and they would have killed had
it been within their power.

Gibson exhaled heavily and brushed the sweat
from his eyes. For an instant he looked vacantly

into the middle-distance as he sought to remember another reason for his actions.

'We're waiting,' advised a thickset man, from the comfort of a cane chair. The voice belonged to D'rosario and though his tone was outwardly conversational it contained a certain quality, a hardness, which made every statement an instruction, every question a demand. Further, the blue eyes lent added impetus to his speech as much as the cragginess of his tanned face and close-cropped steel grey hair lent menace.

'The interferon... convalescent plasma .. antibody,' offered Gibson, suddenly grasping mentally for alibis but with the vague feeling that there was something wrong. 'They had success with substances prepared by Doctor MacKenzie here.'

Gibson jerked his thumb at the girl whose only response was an unconnected movement of her bandaged arm which she shifted in its sling. In his confusion he smiled a triumphant smile to reflect his achievement in kidnapping Anne. 'The signs were all there for the neutralization of our very weapon. She was preparing to leave for Dent when the accident allowed me to steal her away. If I hadn't..,' he shrugged an ending to the hurriedly spoken words as if that were the best way of indicating the logical conclusion.

'In the process of leaving,' growled D'rosario, 'you deprived us of our listening post and the limited control we could bring to bear on the situation. You, our very eyes if not ears, have plunged us into the dark.'

'But what of the threat to our weapon, the virus?' retorted a marginally more confident Gibson. 'What of their evidence of the identity of our ships, only a step away from the truth. What of that?'

'If I expected such from anyone, it wasn't from you,' said J tiredly. 'We checked with our own microbiologist when we heard the same news. He has categorically refuted the possibility that such treatment exists for Marburg which would be both effective and available in large enough amounts to neutralize our operations,' he said. 'As for their knowledge of the precise details of our vessels - so what? In the communiqués issued eight hours ago they were given that information, anyway. They have to know: they need to have a destination for their gold, don't they?'

Gibson remained silent as he had done through J's words. He hadn't intended to remain silent but, though he opened his mouth and affected to speak, nothing came out. Nor did he have time to recover for it was D'rosario's turn to speak.

'And, by leaving your post, we are deprived of all contact with London,' repeated the mercenary.

Perhaps aware for the first time that the situation was worsening to a degree that could affect him also, the fifth person present, a short rubicund man, whose function was to drive the ship as Captain, turned from his interested gaze through the port-hole to the proceedings he had heard within the room. As he turned to face the others he could do nothing to prevent the quick action of a nerve as it jumped at the corner of his left eye.

Gibson, overloaded as he was with so many thoughts at that moment, was still able to detect D'rosario's emphasis as he had spoken. 'What do you mean, all contact?' he queried, and the alarm bells he had begun to hear as a faint tinkle became even louder in his brain.

'Nothing heard. Microphones dead,' responded D'rosario. 'We are back to a blind situation which we suspect was caused by your departure. Simply, they realised you had kidnapped the girl and the balloon went up. We assume one of the consequences of this was a thorough search of the rooms you occupied.'

'Something doesn't add up.....'

'The lad's fast,' exclaimed D'rosario to J. But he turned quickly back to face Gibson. 'You bet there's something which doesn't add up. There's lots that doesn't add up.'

Gibson noticed the direction of D'rosario's quick gaze then saw the recipient was Anne. It was the life-supporting log of a drowning man to Gibson as he found he had a convenient scapegoat on which to dump at least some of the blame for his mistakes. 'For instance,' he said, switching his attention to Anne, 'if there was no possibility of a cure of the sort being claimed, why say there was?'

He was full of hate now and it was obvious he should take it out on the girl. 'Why?' he demanded loudly, moving towards her.

Anne said nothing, didn't even acknowledge his presence, which only served to further infuriate him. 'Why?' he repeated, but he also shook her by the shoulders to underline the question.

'Steady on,' called the captain, but though he took two paces in Gibson's direction his voice had faltered and he stopped, completely ineffectual in his attempt to intervene.

J, on the contrary, stopped Gibson's heavy hand with one word: 'Quite.' He looked over to his henchman, D'rosario, ignoring the others as if they didn't exist as he spoke in an aside. 'It is becoming plain from what we have overheard by interception that there could only be one reason for such a ploy,' he said.

'To induce her removal?' offered D'rosario.

'Quite. An objective they have accomplished,' he said, flatly, 'and, even if they didn't suspect him before, they gained certain knowledge that one of their number was an impostor.'

Again he played his cool stare onto the set features of Gibson, noting dispassionately his visible discomfort.

'Fooled,' continued J. 'But of course you searched the girl to make sure she was clean of electronic devices, and that you weren't followed, didn't you.' It was a statement, not a question: just something to be ticked off a list when looking for the flaw in any system, any plan.

Within seconds they knew they need investigate no further; Gibson's silence, more significantly his look of horror, was sufficient indication of where the system's defect lay.

But it was Anne's turn to feel the pressure. Even though Marshall's instructions had been very explicit she couldn't fully dispense with the nagging fear she now felt. Stoically, she mustered all her determination not to show her feelings.

'You didn't even search her,' continued J, and again it was a statement. And again Gibson said nothing for this time he was frantically searching his brain to discover just why he had made this most basic mistake.

Then he had the answer. He logically traced their flight from the Burns Unit as they zigzagged their way through several cut-outs on the Underground before he had contacted with the escape line and the helicopter trip south. He remembered now how the girl had behaved. His use of the concealed gun as an incentive to obedience had not been needed beyond making her aware of its presence. And, being so wrapped up with his mission, together with the excellent performance by the girl in nursing her painful arm, he had suspected nothing. Now, as he realised how expertly he had been deceived, he finally lost his temper and it was obvious who was going to receive the full weight of his wrath.

So obvious was his intention that, without a sound, D'rosario was out of his seat in one second and cuffing the aggrieved man in the next. As Gibson took receipt of the blow and the terse words of the mercenary, D'rosario swung round on the girl.

'Now, lady,' he began, and the very tone of his voice scared Anne more than Gibson could ever intimidate with blows. 'There's a hard and an easy way. The hard way is uncomfortable and just a little embarrassing for you. The easy way allows you to hand over the goods without a hand laid on you. Which is it to be?'

For ten second's there was silence during which Anne's features displayed a coolness which didn't reflect her emotional state.

'Suit yourself,' said D'rosario, tiring of the wait and he quickly lifted his hands to the neck of the dress she was wearing.

'Wait!' she cried. She had done her job as instructed by Marshall. He had told her to resist a search until they began to use force - and no further.

It took almost three minutes after D'rosario had stood back from her before she managed to remove the bandages of her arm completely. The skin she revealed was perfect, or almost, for there was one blemish - a small metal object the shape of a small matchbox stuck to her skin with two strips of adhesive tape.

'So they know where you are?' said J to Anne. 'What does that prove? My last bulletin informed them of the positions of all the ships. They also know that if they try to board these ships they will suffer the same consequences as for non-payment: liberation of the virus. Therefore what is your purpose? Why this charade?' Significantly he waved his hand in the direction of Gibson.

Anne said nothing. Again her instructions were quite explicit: say nothing until forced.

'I think I might have the answer,' offered D'rosario.' Or a few ideas, anyhow.'

'The floor - I should say deck - is yours.'

'Gibson, foolish boy, was pressured into leaving with the girl so that he would lead them here. But Gibson left them at something after midday and half-an-hour later the 'bugs' went dead. Assuming they left on his trail at about that time and used the same sort of transport, they should have arrived in this area at around the same time that he did,' said D'rosario, darting a glance in Gibson's direction.

J was inwardly surprised at his right-hand man. 'I thought we had already arrived at that conclusion,' he said, disguising his irritability with difficulty. 'Which doesn't alter the fact that no-one would dare come after her - wouldn't be allowed to - for fear of our reprisals.'

'True. Except that you miss the part played by time,' countered the mercenary. 'You see, allowing your bulletin the normal delay for delivery means that even the UN wouldn't get the message much before one this afternoon....'

'And the London end much later than that,' finished J, some expression flickering in his eyes for the first time.

'You've got it,' agreed D'rosario. 'Whoever is following milady left before the bulleting was received. He hasn't even heard of the bulletin.' He turned to look directly at his boss. 'He could be on board now,' he said softly.

'Marshall.' supplied Gibson.

And J's face wasn't quite as expressionless as it had recently been.

The first Marshall knew of the 'hue and cry' raised to search him out was the sound made by many feet shuffling on the fabric of the deck above his head. He had been waiting in the spare cabin of the lowest deck of the superstructure amongst the crew's sleeping quarters for some time. Presently, he heard the sounds of the approaching search as footsteps on ladders changed to the rattle of door-handles becoming louder by the second. Above him he could hear continued activity from what Taylor's brief informed him must be the crew's mess room complex. It seemed that the whole crew were being used to seek him out.

Judging his time nicely, noting that the nearest searchers could not be more than four doors away, he acted positively. Grabbing the door-handle quite firmly he twisted it and pulled open the door before quickly stepping out into the path of his pursuers. On his face was an expression of great surprise which, perhaps understandably, was little more pronounced than that shown by the four men who confronted him.

The search party recovered very quickly, however, and as two of their number entered on a search of the cabin Marshall had just left, one other checked him for weapons while the last of the four, the largest, operated the sound-powered telephone on the bulkhead a mere ten feet from them.

'We've found him. Lower accommodation deck,' he said in the flat monotone of one whose attention is divided. We'll bring him along in a couple of minutes.'

The man replaced the receiver with the clank of metal on metal as he misjudged the move by a fraction of an inch. Marshall watched as he slotted the receiver into its stowage on the second attempt and was faintly flattered that they considered him so dangerous as to warrant this level of surveillance in custody. This, in turn, prompted another, less rewarding, conclusion. The depletion of strength following his illness, the unsociable hours and the giving of blood, the effect of the rain which had found its way down the back of his neck, the short climb over the ship's side and, finally, his short but hectic efforts he had made since entering the after-castle structure, had all contributed to his present state and the sensation of nausea now advancing and receding in waves. Marshall began to worry to an extent greater than he had so far because his physical strength, a minor problem until now, was diminishing to the point where he wondered if it wouldn't jeopardise the mission.

Chapter Eleven
(Saturday: 2130 – 2300)

The scene which confronted Marshall as he entered the Captain's Stateroom was little changed from that of half-an-hour previously. Now, as then, Gibson and Anne stood to the right and D'rosario was again seated midway between them and J's desk. Resuming his non-participatory role, the captain had returned to face the window as if his whole concentration were focussed on the scene beyond.

Reaction to his appearance was understandably more pronounced in the people who knew him: both Gibson and Anne registered surprise to some degree. In the ex-PR man this surprise responded to his notion that he couldn't possibly have been followed on his flight from London, a notion at last dispelled. Anne, most affected, as indicated by a gasp, saw more the change in Marshall's physical stature which seemed to have undergone some subtle treatment rendering him less substantial. The sparse clothing he wore - T-shirt, jeans and sneakers - leant itself to this conclusion as much as his now bare arms confirmed the pallor of his complexion and his state of health.

'Ilianov,' said J flatly, beckoning with the letter opener.

Quickly the large-man crossed to J's desk carrying the profit of his team's search, a small jumble of clothing. During the whispered conversation between the man, J and D'rosario, Marshall was able to sneak a wink to Anne unobserved, which went some way in ironing out the worry-lines on her forehead.

At J's desk the trio's secret conclave was punctuated often as they broke off to glance at Marshall or the bundle of clothing on the desk. Gibson, curious to know of their business but very conscious that he was out of favour, oscillated nervously between his position next to the girl and the group at the desk. Soon his indecision forced him to make do with a halt midway between the two. The meeting was, however, short and after drawing Ilianov's attention to the door, with a glance and a nod, J turned to face Marshall.

'I am not a patient man, Marshall,' said J without expression. 'As you are no doubt aware, we are in the midst of a large-scale operation which demands too much of my time to spend very much with you. However, being curious to know your object in coming here, I shall spend a little of my precious time listening to your story. If you fail to respond to this invitation you will be placed in my friends' hands,' he waved towards D'rosario, 'and I shouldn't doubt Gibson would like to even the score a little.'

Marshall looked over towards the mercenary and recognised a fellow professional; not on the same side, but a professional all the same. Pointedly, he looked at Gibson and, though he had no illusions that he would have more than minimal trouble alone with him, he saw that the ex-PR man had a lot of hate to work off which made him dangerous if Marshall were pinioned by D'rosario's men. The security man then turned his head slightly to the left - not quite far enough around for him to see the large frame of Ilianov, but his thoughts could be read with that gesture.

J nodded silently, watching Marshall closely. 'Well?' he said shortly.

Marshall glanced at Anne and again at the heap of bandages at her feet. 'Farewell to that story,' he thought. He needed another line if he were to turn the situation in any way to his advantage.

'You're a man who's difficult to find,' he responded, chattily. 'You've no idea of the trouble I've had trying to locate you. But I'll tell you anyway: almost a year has passed since we began enquiries......'

'Don't be flippant,' censured J, 'we are well aware of the extent and duration of your investigation. Your reasons for being here are what I want to know.'

'To meet you, of course,' replied Marshall then, noticing the tightening of D'rosario's frame, added quickly, 'and intervene in this operation.'

'What form would your intervention take?' demanded J. 'What are your bargaining points, assuming you represent the governments of this world?'

'Simply, I intend to stop the operation going any further and, in return for the complete cessation of your activities - including the surrender of your carriers - I will promise you your lives.'

For a second-or-so the air was electric. Then, as the silence continued everyone, including Anne, looked at the man who had uttered the words. It did not require special qualifications to know that each person regarded Marshall as having flipped his lid. That was until they remembered his awesome reputation and paused to consider if he meant what he said. Then even J had to suppress a shudder.

'If you refuse to treat me seriously,' said J coldly, 'I must implement my alternative means of persuasion....'

'Oh, but I do take you seriously,' said Marshall gently. 'You've proved through the inhabitants of Dent, Plomsk and Randall's Halt that you must be taken very seriously. My answer was but a serious reply to your question.'

J was not convinced and showed it by seeming to ignore Marshall as the Frenchman nodded to the large man.

'You obviously don't realise it but there is no way you can pull this off,' persisted the security man quickly.

Ilianov was already moving towards Marshall when J turned quickly to face the security man, raising his hand at the same time. Ilianov stopped.

'Show me the flaw then, Mr Marshall,' challenged J, whose vanity could never refuse the proving of his system. Marshall noted the very subtle change in tone and stored the knowledge of what it told him for further use later.

'Okay, the plan seems to have gone very well so far,' conceded Marshall, 'notwithstanding Gibson's errors.'

'Notwithstanding Gibson's errors,' repeated J, 'which, incidentally, have proved to be of no detrimental significance whatsoever. Your presence aboard this vessel alters the situation not one iota.' He looked pointedly at the large man and his two friends. 'You must agree to that. The plan is working perfectly.'

'So far,' qualified Marshall.

J said nothing.

'You have a fleet of ships which are at present, alongside in various ports around the world. You demand and are receiving the cooperation of the world's governments in obtaining a massive amount of their gold reserves……'

'Yes, yes,' put in a vaguely irritated and impatient J. 'And?'

'Against which you hold the incentive to their continued cooperation with the deployment of carriers of Marburg virus,' said the security man. 'Your vessels under this special protection will then sail for their destination.'

J's irritation mounted as he waited for Marshall to come to the point. His emotional state showed in two curt nods of his head.

'Up to this point it is a wonderful plan and full marks. But it is then, when the ships arrive at their destination, that your problems burn a short fuse to your destruction,' said Marshall, with a feeling in his voice which was meant to impress. By injecting emotion into his voice his aim was merely camouflage, for his next words were based on pure speculation which didn't quite fit in with the string of fragmented information he had received at the DOH.

'No matter where you go, no matter whichever country supplies you with a base, or even bases, your term of office as the world's most powerful bank must be considered very short indeed. Your protection, the Marburg virus, has only a limited life: tests have shown it to be capable of secondary infection up to ninety days - three months - after the primary case contracted the disease. True, we do have limited information on Marburg, but no virus in its group of haemorrhagic diseases is known to have a virulence to endure – with potency – for a period more than a year to eighteen months.

'Also true or rather, feasible, is the infection of a new carrier before the 'old' one has lost the capability to infect. In an operation as meticulously managed as this, such a procedure couldn't, with credibility, be entertained for survivability of the infected patient cannot be guaranteed - you stand just as much chance of killing off the carrier before he is well enough to infect without being noticed. Putting these two facts together; limited life and the uncertainty that re-infection won't kill your carrier, it is obvious that your protection has a life of no more than eighteen months, and that is on the safe side.

'Meanwhile, the world's governments will freeze gold levels for a predicted eighteen months which should reduce economic disruption to the very minimum.'

Marshall checked the level of interest around the room. His gaze was rewarded by a uniformity of expression, that of calm interest. He saw this as indication that he was off the mark but he had started now and he intended to finish.

'As for the gold itself during this period,' he continued, 'every military surveillance satellite whose orbit carries it over your ships, every intelligence gathering activity capable of being brought to bear, will ensure that no-one so much as ventures on the upper deck without us knowing about it. You won't be able to move your gold, correction *our gold*, one single inch in the open and, after the year to eighteen months is up, you won't have it at all.'

Marshall looked across to D'rosario, hoping for a trace of the emotion he thought J was feeling but not showing, but there was the same stone face. 'All in all,' he persisted, 'your plan seems to consist of spending a lot of time and money to achieve very little return.'

Silence again reigned for some seconds before J coughed and then uttered: 'Have you anything to add to that?'

'No,' responded Marshall, simply.

'And your role was to convince me that it was not in my interests to continue my operations?'

'Yes.'

'A little like telling the prize-fighter who is fourteen rounds ahead that you, the recipient of his wrath, had got him licked as the last round may go the other way,' said J, somewhat scornfully. 'In a sentence, you've got it all wrong Marshall.'

J glanced across to D'rosario who smiled back and even the luckless Gibson relaxed visibly. The moment of tension, whereby Marshall had sounded as if he might still be dangerous, had passed.

'Excuse me if we don't quake with fear, Mr security man,' taunted J, 'but, you see, we were all expecting some startling revelation more in keeping with the truth. Alas, it is a shame; we believed you to have superior qualities to those you have demonstrated.' Bereft of expression as J's face had been throughout the proceedings so far he could not now hide his relief and joy at regaining the initiative.

'The principal flaw in your theory,' he enthused, 'is that it rambles on into too much detail. You should remember that the simplest plans are invariably the most effective. You were one hundred per cent correct in your estimations right up to the point where you said our ships would sail for their destination. However, you must have realised that much just by being aboard a ship which is due to embark gold.' There was no mistaking the sarcasm in his voice.

Marshall ignored the tone of J's voice and concentrated more on what he was saying. His hurried cogitations, while J drew breath, came not with a premonition of the actual plan but the oddest feeling that not only was he, as the Frenchman had said, totally wrong but that whatever the plan was it was going to work.

'We fully realised the dangers of the plan you just outlined,' continued J, 'when we planned this operation. That is why we chose the only alternative which would meet with success. We're going to sea, all right, Mr Marshall. All thirteen ships : eleven OBOs, a LASH vessel and a products tanker are going to sea. And you know what else? We're staying there.'

As if Marshall's mind's eye were focussed on a computer readout screen, the indicators, once question marks troubling his overworked brain, appeared like a tote. Such excessively large ships, he had once wondered. Now the reasons why they were so large were clear. The larger the ship generally meant the better the long term sea-platform and, being OBOs, they could store vast amounts of oil - fuel oil in this case - to supply engines which need only maintain headway once ships were on station.

The next line came up in his mind. The LASH vessel, *Baccarat*, which had been taken over in an act of piracy, included not only barges in her cargo but also tugs - six of them - with which they could manoeuvre the ships when refuelling at sea and during any other transfers. Another question flickered into view in his mind, that concerning the excess of oil which even eighteen months or more at sea would not exhaust. But no answer came for this. He would need to find out.

'You would just steam around the world in convoy, is that it?' he asked.

'Once we have joined up in one fleet we will cruise - very slowly - around the deep oceans of the world,' supplied J.

Marshall saw the connection then. He knew what endless months at sea could do to even seasoned seamen. The days in the doldrums may not worry any of the crews and terrorists used to the waiting game but the periods of rough weather, sometimes violent and frightening in the deep oceans, would be something else. Rough weather at sea, though causing varying degrees of sea-sickness in most, from queasiness to miserable gut-wrenching, has one universal effect on the human body: tiredness. The constant battering, whether resting or on watch allows no time for proper relaxation and therefore rest. The few seasoned seamen amongst his crews would have developed a certain immunity to such buffeting but the majority of J's terrorists would reach the stage quickly in a storm where interest in everything but one's self became of little importance.

J had been made aware of this problem and had planned for it: the largest possible ships gave the most stable platform from rolling and pitching and, when ultimately - if a storm lasted long enough - even these ships began to see-saw, oil from the huge tanks could be used to flatten the water somewhat when poured over the side. Having decided on taking the gold for a long stay at sea, J's plans had been shaped to further accommodate the need for constant alertness amongst his men - a need fulfilled by the recruitment of such large vessels.

'Of course, we knew the virus was a relatively short-term lever but that is not the point,' said J, dragging Marshall back to the present. 'As I have no intention of spending anything like eighteen months or more on this vessel, it becomes not a question of how long we are at sea but what we accomplish while we are there.'

Once again Marshall felt a nagging feeling of unease.

'We have a very powerful radio aboard and, when the whole gold fleet is positioned in an area of very deep water, something in the order of one-thousand fathoms, we feel confident that our suggestions for the improvement in world government will meet with approval,' continued the Frenchman. 'Link the idea further, with the threat to sink a gold-ship per disagreement, and you have some notion of the persuasive influence this operation has going for it.'

'You would sink a ship each time they failed to put into force your, er, amendments to world legislation,' stated Marshall 'You would create economic chaos because they couldn't recover the gold from such depths.' He was merely thinking aloud now, seeing no-one, just reasoning the consequences of such action. 'You've probably got a manifesto prepared which will set one faction against another. With such power - and knowing the kind of people you are - your targets can only be alliances and treaties, or rather, their destruction. You could disrupt everything that is stable in this world!'

'Precisely,' responded J, cheerily. 'A much better idea altogether than that which your dowdy speculation envisaged. And now that we know all there is to know we have no further need of you or your assistant. Get rid of them,' he ordered.

'A moment,' said D'rosario and the large man once more halted in his tracks. 'We have no real idea what the authorities may have planned for us. I am, however, certain that if anything but our instructions are being contemplated, Marshall will know about them. I suggest we wait until the gold has been embarked and we have sailed before we take any action with these two.' He smiled. 'Besides, it's more convenient then.'

J nodded. 'I'm sure we can pass the time until then to our mutual interest. We could even discuss the differences between our two plans.'

Marshall felt cold. There was little - if anything - that he could say to dispute what J had said. It was a superb system and the security man could see no way once the fleet was at sea that the terrorists could be stopped. It seemed that there was no way the fleet could be attacked without severe disruption to the world economy, through loss of the gold, or tragic consequences to the world population through the use of the virus. And if they were left alone, the governments of the world would be blackmailed into making drastic changes which could, in any event, have no other consequence than their own downfall. Marshall decided that he could do nothing but probe further, with the help of J's vanity, for weaknesses in the situation aboard; an area Marshall had for long held to be the most likely to be profitable.

'You're a rich man,' said Marshall. 'Independent, as so few of us can be today. Why not enjoy yourself with this wealth?'

'But I am no longer rich,' responded J, 'I am no more than the hirer of some ships and for one voyage only. But it doesn't matter, because with or without money one cannot be independent. I am trying for independence though, in a way. You see, no-one can really be independent, obtain one's destiny with the same idealism he set out with, without there being in existence a state of change. Not insidious change, either: the real thing - rough-turmoil, strife, general panic. This is the situation upon which independence flourishes; when it is the destiny of the individual that is being sought and not that of collective mankind.'

Marshall watched the Frenchman closely. The man might have been delivering a lecture for his mannerisms and the way he delivered his voice to the room was indicative of the same mood.

'At present the state of tension, balance of power - call it what you will - which exists between the various powers – America, Europe, Asia - prevents those blocs the freedom to move politically, or to stretch themselves with the merest freedom in any way. Smaller states suffer less, being less of a threat to the major powers and in turn the balance of power, but still they watch each other closely.

'The individual is but a pawn that is tied in legislation by the state which, in the case of a lesser power, maintains its own status quo lest the superpowers be offended. So the buck - as the Americans say - is passed up and down the line from major power to lesser state to the individual and all the way up again. And all the time more and more legislation is brought in to bind more tightly the individual and the state - or should that be the other way around? Anyway, all the time, the major powers watch each other, the lesser states watch each other and the individual either fights to watch someone else or sinks beneath the surface into a mindless animal. The result of the exercise is a solid jam of deadlock.'

'You mean we need a change?' summarised Marshall.

J glared at him, suspecting the security man of levity. But Marshall held his neutral gaze and, as J couldn't work out what it meant, the Frenchman replied, calmly: 'Quite simply, yes.'

'And you're trying a different approach?'

'Again, yes,' said J. 'Peoples' movements have spent too much time in the past just fighting with words or, as terrorists, with guns. Urban guerrillas, military coups, you name it, it has been tried.'

'But it hasn't worked, has it?'

'Correct,' agreed J, responding readily to Marshall's prompting. 'People got killed. Always the wrong ones, but apart from the state having to respond to public outcry by more deployment of security forces, the status quo never really suffered. Besides which, the media are always on their side, ironic really when you consider they are supposed to be the establishment's most vociferous critic.

'I arrived upon the method I should need to employ after watching the antics of America and Russia. Prior to the collapse of the USSR, I noticed that advances in military might showed one or the other creeping ahead as each strove to perfect the weapon which had no antidote. The SALT initiative made a start at climbing down from this escalating situation but never to the point where it would make impossible annihilation of everyone on this earth.

'Then came the rise of the other nuclear states beyond the long-term other members of this elite club, the UK and France. These newcomers are the emerging and third-world nuclear powers: China, Pakistan, India, Israel, North Korea and the others threatening to ruin the world. I've watched all of this and arrived at two conclusions: one, the major powers are not only looking at their historic adversaries but also at the new kids on the block. Strategic arms reduction by the USA and Russia will reverse because the number of targets is growing as other nuclear-enabled states stockpile, and deploy into missiles, their own warheads.'

'And the second? You said there were two conclusions,' encouraged Marshall.

'That no-one in the world is prepared to do anything about this. Even the threat of Iran producing a nuclear warhead has not met with concerted action to stop it, even when the regime there has declared it wants to wipe off the face of this earth the country it hates, Israel.' J looked over to D'rosario.

'The world is in crisis and no-one is tackling the debt and the injustice and the threat of annihilation.' J was beginning to sound hysterical but he caught himself before he went over the edge. He took a deep breath and smiled. 'So this mission is long overdue. It's time see what a little private business can do.'

Marshall had seen the glance J had shot at D'rosario and he now looked at the mercenary. There was a gleam in his eyes, the first emotion Marshall had seen in him. He was surprised at D'rosario's reaction, almost shocked.

'You'll use this mission to bang heads together. Is that it?' Marshall felt it would be unwise to take a contrary stance to J's at this point. He thought J was unbalanced enough as it was.

'We'll see,' replied J. 'We'll see.'

'It's here,' said the still figure of Captain Seamark, whose vigil at the window had been unbroken since Gibson's threatening behaviour towards Anne. 'The gold is here.'

J and D'rosario looked simultaneously at their wrist-watches.

'Ten minutes early,' announced D'rosario. 'Time to go up top.'

J explained. 'We will all go to the bridge. There is no way either of these,' he said, nodding to Marshall and Anne, 'are leaving my sight at the moment.'

Ilianov moved unbidden towards the pair. 'Move,' he said, simply, nodding curtly towards the door.

Their walk was very short indeed for, once in the passageway outside the Captain's Quarters, it took no more than half -a-dozen steps before they were halted in front of a bulkhead with a large partition set into it. With a swish the partition disappeared to one side in response to the operation of a switch by one of the guards. It was a lift.

'Menswear,' quipped Marshall, though he didn't feel humorous. It was a vain attempt to lift Anne's sagging spirits and recover his own.

Chapter Twelve
(Saturday: 2300 - Sunday: 0045)

At a distance of half-a-mile from the *Orico*, and on the very demarcation-line between land and jetty, the first pair of headlights in a line which stretched away out of sight, were dipped to illuminate the arrow-straight run of oil pipes between them and the ship. The jetty was quite wide and had a clear space to one side of the pipe-lines to facilitate motor traffic along its length. Parallel to this and some distance up river was another jetty. It was identical to the first and joined to it by a jetty which connected the two at the seaward end, all three forming a giant 'U'. It was alongside the connecting jetty that the *Orico* lay.

'Makes for a fast loading rate,' said Marshall, thinking aloud.

He and everyone else who had been in the Captain's quarters were gathered inside the box-like structure, thirty feet higher up, which was the 'flying bridge' Marshall had seen from across the river. To his right, J lowered his binoculars and smiled.

'The road,' said Marshall, realizing he had been overheard and wanting to explain, 'it goes all the way back to shore after it passes by here?'

'Yes,' said the Frenchman good-humouredly, 'but it wasn't by accident that we picked this port: the jetty configuration is important.' He pointed to the large crane towering above the ship. 'So is that.'

Marshall didn't comment on this for his attention was diverted back to the jetty by the roar of what he calculated to be fifty trucks as their engines burst into life. Even across the length of the jetty the noise of the convoy of gold-trucks getting underway was loud. Slowly the head of the column came nearer and the increasing rumble, as more trucks came on to the jetty, vibrated through the steel-reinforced concrete and rubber-fended catamarans which held the *Orico* away from the jetty, to cause the merest sensation of juddering through the deck-plates of the bridge.

'When do you sail,' asked Marshall, hoping to get an estimation of the length of time needed to load the gold aboard. When the reply came, again from J, it was a shock.

'One hour?' exclaimed an astounded security man. 'That's impossible!'

'Not at all,' beamed J. 'Watch.'

Marshall watched as instructed. The first truck was now moving slowly down the jetty alongside the *Orico*, guided by a string of armed men who gestured precise instructions with the snouts of their rifles. Finally the first truck stopped and as a figure opened the driver's door the boom of the crane was already swinging its hook into position above.

What happened next surprised Marshall by being totally unexpected and also by the swiftness with which it occurred. Four men, each dragging a heavy wire, appeared at the four corners of the vehicle. Seconds later they began their individual climbs to the roof, clipping the eye of the wire onto the waiting hook when they got there. Once clear the truck was already being hoisted skywards, the boom swinging it over the side of the ship to a gaping black rectangle which marked the hatch-way of the first hold.

Wrong-footed as he had been, Marshall managed to spare a questioning thought as to why no search had been made of the vehicle even to check that the cargo was really gold. He marvelled at the sheer arrogance of the terrorists that they believed no-one would dare sell them short or, as he secretly hoped, add a few crack-troops to the cargo in the back of the trucks. But his secret hopes were dashed as the truck was lowered out of sight. Almost simultaneously there came the sound of the truck landing very heavily onto the floor of the hold and a ripple of vibration ran through the ship.

'A trifle heavy-handed,' commented Marshall.

'Not at all. Purely a security measure. We drop the trucks for the last twenty feet to shake up anything which is alive inside them,' replied J.

'A trifle dangerous, then,' persisted the security man. 'Their petrol tanks could quite easily ignite from...'

'You haven't been watching properly, have you?' interrupted J. 'There's a man with a high capacity pump down on the jetty whose task is to drain most of the diesel from their tanks. Precautionary rather than essential for, as you probably know, diesel isn't the easiest of fuels to ignite.'

Marshall looked automatically toward the jetty at this and, although he could not make out the man indicated by J, he was in time to see the next truck being given the treatment. He saw the same procedure carried out five times in as many minutes but still the line of trucks stretched back along the jetty seemingly undiminished in length. Now the crane paused in its back and forth movement to move bodily along its tracks to halt at the next hold to be loaded. He withdrew his interest into the bridge.

'So this is your control room,' he said. 'A flying bridge.'

Captain Seamark turned at the words. 'Navigating bridge, if you please,' he said. 'It's designed function is to enable better control in confined waters...'

'And selected by you to project the role of mother hen on your fleet at sea,' interjected Marshall.

'Correct, in part,' put in J, 'but it is also the one place on board which can easily be sealed against intrusion from below. At the same time it affords an excellent all-round view, the better for early warning of attack, and there is a direct link with the transmitter room should we need to activate our carriers.'

'An eyrie,' said Marshall. 'An eagle's nest.'

'Quite so,' responded J. 'The insurmountable pinnacle from which we watch and plan our next moves. You were right in what you said: we will use this platform to watch over the brood.'

Marshall gave him a sceptical look which, in the half light of the bridge, may have been lost. His tone, however, more than made up this loss. 'Insurmountable pinnacle? Repeat that line after one or two well-aimed missiles have come this way and I'll believe you. The way you will be under surveillance you may not have the time to transmit your signal before this ship is blown out of the water.'

J looked over at Marshall for a full five seconds. When he spoke again his voice was patronising. 'You would have learned all of this had you only stayed at home, Mr Marshall,' said the Frenchman, patiently. 'Together with the delivery instructions for the gold went a further tape explaining my communications organisation. Your masters already know that I keep in touch with my organisation by radio. I also added that a complicated call-up procedure and corresponding interlocking answering procedure ensure the continued security of the system. I told them that if certain pre-planned but irregular transmissions are not made from this ship - never separated by more than a few minutes - then my agents would assume interference in the system and deploy the carriers. Your people know that all the ships and all the carrier stations are involved in this system so that interference with any one will be sufficient to warn the others.'

'It's very kind of you to be so forthcoming,' said Marshall, trying to inject sarcasm into his voice.

'Not at all, Mr Marshall. Not at all,' responded J, oozing confidence. 'The underlying principle of deterrence - and deterrence is what it is - is to let your opponent know that you are in a position to hurt him beyond tolerance if he were to attack you. The East and West practiced this for forty years in the Cold War. Still are. Why not I?

'Naturally, I didn't go too deeply into detail or even give them the frequencies of these transmissions of ours. But it would hardly matter if indeed they knew our frequencies; any attempt to jam them would have the same effect as any other type of interference.'

He looked carefully at Marshall with the same unwavering stare he had used only minutes before. 'You know, either we have totally misread your ability - which I doubt - or you are putting up a smokescreen of seeming mental slowness.' J turned to D'rosario. 'A dangerous man, wouldn't you say, Lee?'

'As dangerous as they come,' uttered the mercenary.

The loading progressed with an oiled smoothness and J's mood became more and more expansive as he wandered between the large windows of the port and starboard sides. Occasionally he would glance at the digital clock on the after bulkhead or hold brief conversation with either D'rosario or Captain Seamark.

The mercenary spent most of the time sweeping the scene around the jetty and approach roads with the long barrels of his binoculars while, on the port - seaward side, Gibson spent his time in limbo doing the same. The centre spot, forward facing, was occupied by the captain whose interest in the activity on the deck stretched out below was unwavering. Even when his hand reached for the telephone to utter a quiet word he continued to stare straight ahead.

From where he stood at the rear of the 'bridge', separated from the two doors of the lift and alternative ladder by the flanked escort and the watchful Ilianov, Marshall noted every detail. Anne, whose presence made up the total of those on the 'bridge', stood only three feet away to his left. Although their eyes seldom met and only when they were certain they were unobserved, Anne found enough in them to buoy her flagging hopes above dejection.

'Last one coming aboard,' called J to anyone who may have been listening. Quickly he turned to check the time and seemingly satisfied joined the captain. 'Our tugs should already be on their way.'

'Almost in position,' supplied Captain Seamark. 'Two for'ard, two aft.'

'Good,' breathed J, before darting over to the seaward windows. 'Excellent,' he corrected, as his eyes picked out the small vessels. 'Let's get out of here, Captain.'

Captain Seamark did not acknowledge the order. Instead he reacted by talking softly into the telephone.

'Impressive, don't you think,' said the Frenchman, who, with nothing to do, joined Marshall at the rear of the bridge.

Marshall said nothing.

'Go on, admit it. Fifty-two minutes and all the gold is aboard,' said J. 'In six hours we will be well clear of the coast of your country and then....But of course, everything after that time is of no interest to you as neither you nor your lovely assistant will be with us.'

'Now I am impressed, especially by that last bit,' replied Marshall. 'It is a shame, however, to witness the execution of such brilliant plans only to realise that your obvious talents could have been put too much greater use for the benefit of mankind. Fortunately no plan is perfect.'

There was something in the way Marshall spoke his last sentence which caused J's over-sensitive antenna to switch on. But he wasn't convinced Marshall's words weren't mere bravado. 'Come now, Marshall. Haven't we convinced you? Our plan is working flawlessly,' he reminded him.

'Was,' corrected Marshall. 'As I say, every plan has a flaw. It may be only a matter of degree with just one facet not quite perfect. But there is the flaw and so it is with yours.'

The ship now having 'slipped', they were joined from the two lookout positions by D'rosario and Gibson.

Marshall was still speaking. 'Your flaw is as subtle as that. It is nothing you could have seen yourself for it is not a planning mistake. It is simply an error of attitude.'

'Attitude?'

'Arrogance, to be precise,' said Marshall. 'Arrogance - conceited presumption - which enabled me to board this vessel totally unobserved and to move around freely until I gave myself up to one of your search-parties....'

'But..'

'Hear me out,' demanded Marshall. 'It was arrogance which caused you to overlook the smaller details. For example, you recorded your messages from the same room aboard this vessel on every occasion. Through the use of an expert in the field of sound signatures we not only found out the type and name of the ventilation fan motor heard in the background, but the distance between you - the speaker - and that fan. From that little piece of information we could trace this vessel.'

'Useless information, as it turns out,' scoffed J. 'You depended on Gibson's error to get you here.'

'To the area, yes,' agreed the security man, 'but once I had arrived at Southampton it was a simple matter of contacting the Port Authority. By supplying them with the details of ship type I had been given by a shipping expert, I was able to trace her within minutes - even though you had changed the ship's name.'

'And?' prompted D'rosario, whose suspicions could be more easily read from his face, than J's.

'I knew Gibson must be headed for the ship,' continued Marshall, 'I therefore didn't need to waste time trailing him once he had arrived at Southampton Airport. I could, and did, arrive in the vicinity of this vessel before he did. I was actually aboard within minutes of his arrival.'

'Congratulations,' sneered J. 'What does that prove...?'

'Only that I had freedom of the major part of this ship for something like twenty minutes before I made myself available to your louts,' said Marshall. He was aware that both J and D'rosario were poised on the brink of asking just what he had been doing in that time but he ignored them; he would tell them anyway. Some of it.

'You remember I spoke of the fan which traced this type of vessel and the distance between the motor of the ventilation fan and position of the originator of those tape-recordings. Yes?'

Both men nodded.

'You will also remember that my clothing revealed nothing of an offensive nature when it was delivered to the captain's stateroom.'

Again both men nodded.

'It would seem the height of stupidity, for anyone hoping to change the course of this enterprise to arrive empty-handed but again your arrogance blinded you to this fact. I was carrying something.

Something very apt in the circumstances, ironic even,' said Marshall, and, though a smile flickered across his lips, his face returned quickly to serious expression. 'It was just a small aluminium tube - with a screw-top. It fitted very easily in the ventilation trunking on the output side of the fan where, taped upright for security, the draught could easily waft the contents along the system.'

'What did the phial contain,' asked D'rosario.

'Marburg virus,' said Marshall, matter-of-factly.

The security man watched impassively as Gibson reacted with an instinctive movement of his hand to caress his throat - as if to ease the asphyxiating sensation he felt at Marshall words.

'You're joking!' cried J, a note of panic in his voice. Marshall didn't reply.

'But you'll kill us all, even yourself. Are you mad?' persisted the Frenchman.

'Not mad - just immune,' supplied Marshall in response. 'I contracted the disease when investigating the break-in at our research laboratory. My assistant here has been treated with controlled doses of plasma. She should be alright.'

'If we are to die, Marshall,' croaked a frightened Gibson, 'you can be sure you will not live either.'

'Up until moments ago I had an appointment with the deep, as did my assistant,' said Marshall, tiredly. 'You would be fools to further contemplate such action for I am the life-line of any person contracting the disease; my blood carries the antibody which will kill the virus.' He turned to look at Anne. 'As for my assistant, her training will be invaluable in saving life.'

Aware that something very serious was being discussed, the captain turned from his post to join them. Holding him back from the circle of people, J acquainted him with the drift of the conversation. The captain's reaction was uncharacteristic by its ferocity.

'You've introduced these damn germs into the ventilation system of my ship?' he shouted.

''Fraid so,' answered Marshall.

'Where?' he demanded.

'Lower bridge deck,' responded the security man, obligingly.

The captain did not continue the conversation for several moments for - by his strained expression - he was thinking hard. Then he brightened visibly and turned to address J and D'rosario. When he spoke his voice was clipped in the tone of a formal report. 'The ventilation fan affected is one of three,' he began. 'Your tapes were manufactured in the passenger accommodation which is on a different line to that of my quarters. Therefore, the contamination this man caused would be confined to the passenger accommodation on the lower bridge deck only.'

It took some time for the significance of what the captain had said to penetrate into the minds of the badly shaken trio. Even when D'rosario recovered sufficiently to speak it was to seek confirmation of what he hoped he had heard. 'You mean we aren't affected - not in danger of infection?'

'Unlikely, I should think,' replied the captain. 'And, although I will check with the Chief, I should think the risk of infection even in the area served by that ventilation system is minimal now - the air-conditioning units, which take the stale air out and over the side, will have seen to that.'

'Failed again, Marshall,' taunted Gibson, somewhat shakily.

'Not exactly,' corrected Captain Seamark. 'It depends on whether anyone was in the zone of infection when the bug was released.'

'The operations centre,' supplied D'rosario. 'And, if I'm not very much mistaken, both our operators are in there.' He glanced at the wall-clock. 'I'd better check they're still there. We must contain the infection.'

While D'rosario spoke over the phone, J gazed silently over at Marshall. As usual his expression was difficult to interpret but Marshall was certain he knew what was going through his mind. He was about to make a decision, Marshall knew, and it concerned the security man and the girl: he was deciding whether to believe Marshall's story and, even if it were true, if he would be better to rid himself of the troublesome pair earlier than planned. Marshall saw that J needed prompting. He prompted.

'The situation remains largely the same,' said Marshall. 'You are unlikely to have entrusted more than two operators with the operation of your sophisticated electronics. Allow them to die and your carriers will deploy uncontrolled, you will not have the sympathy of a single faction around the world and your plan will fail.' He paused searching for the words which would form his and Anne's life-line. 'An angered world will write-off the gold so that you have no bargaining power whatsoever. I hardly think you and your little fleet would long survive such a decision.'

'Damn you, Marshall,' snarled J. 'Get them below, Leo.'

'It isn't going too well, is it?' said a white-faced Anne.

They were alone now. In a room seven-foot by four, just one of thirty-odd similar rooms in the crews quarters on the lowest deck, Marshall and a distraught Anne talked together in quiet tones. Out in the passageway, beyond the locked door, were stood two sentries.

'It is having its hot moments, I agree,' returned Marshall, breezily, trying to sound more confident than he felt. 'The time-table is a bit out, I must admit. But then, I hadn't allowed for them loading so speedily.'

'What will we do, Paul?' she pleaded, stroking his face, and once more he felt the surge of remorse at his stupidity in involving her in the scheme of things. It was against all the rules for people emotionally entangled with each other to work on the same mission - a situation aggravated by the fact that Anne wasn't even a professional agent. But, as before, the horrible sensation faded as he remembered why it was that they in particular should be on this mission. Hadn't he the best qualifications for the job? He was immune to Marburg virus, a fact which was keeping them alive. And, as for Anne, wasn't he the best person to be looking after her? He didn't just think so - he knew so.

'The plan hasn't changed, only the timing,' he reasoned. 'We will need to engineer events with much more subtlety. We must fit the variables to the constants. There are three constants; the two I've organised - and the dead-line.'

'Which is?'

'Deep-water. Once the ships are in deep water they are immune from attack. The carriers will have achieved their usefulness in safeguarding the transfer of the gold to deep-water. Thereafter the mere threat of scuttling will suffice to continue their immunity.'

'Didn't they say that would be in six hours?' queried Anne.

'No, six hours would see them safe from the coast, is what J said. The hundred fathom line - the demarcation point between salvage and total loss - is some three-hundred-and-fifty miles out into the Atlantic. This ship would need to average over fifteen knots to get there by,' he checked his watch, 00.30, 'midnight tonight.' Marshall shook his head. 'It isn't this ship I'm talking about when I say we have a deadline. I wish it was.

'When we found out the locations of all the ships in his fleet I checked the distances from the ports concerned to the nearest deep-water,' he continued. 'The shortest distance was that for Cape Town, a mere thirty nautical miles. Two hours steaming at fifteen knots. If we're to prevent a sizeable ripple in the monetary balance we must stop J before that ship gets beyond the Continental Shelf.'

'Two hours?' she gasped.

'An hour-and-a-half,' he corrected. 'All the ships sailed at the same point in time. We've been underway for the past half-an-hour.'

'But it's impossible. We can't even get out of here.'

'We will be out of here in fifteen minutes,' predicted Marshall confidently. 'Remember those 'constants' I mentioned? One of them is about to happen in just under a quarter of an hour.'

He squeezed her shoulders then trying to pass on some of his strength. 'Just do the things as I told you,' he said. 'Fortunately, I've been able to take their attention off you for a lot of the time. This should help our plans considerably. We're going to make it. Promise.'

For some minutes they were silent as they sat on the bunk, Anne held close in his arms. The gesture was automatic for Marshall's part, however, as his mind was back to planning, finding ways to direct events, to pare minutes off his schedules, and to condense an already over-filled sequence of events into his 'allotted' time. He revised his plans many times in that short space of time, trying to visualise any situation which could occur and the correct action for him to take. His final plan was hardly worthy of the name; it was a set of time-capsules into which he could fit a number of actions. He was fairly confident he could direct and control most situations but as he looked at the schedule in his mind's eye he wondered if he could do so against the constraints of time.

Suddenly Anne's head came up off his shoulder as she reacted to the noise she had heard. Marshall had also heard the sound: the flat crack of a small explosion some distance away.

'One of your constants,' she asked.

Marshall nodded and squeezed her shoulders again.

Chapter Thirteen
(Sunday: 0045 – 0230)

Their move from the cabin to the door marked 'Passenger Accommodation' was swift if not very comfortable. No doubt reacting with utter faithfulness to the emotion with which the order was issued, Ilianov helped the sentries with the task of delivering Marshall and the girl. More than once an over-enthusiastic shove sent one or the other rebounding off the metal fittings of a bulkhead. Nearing their destination they passed a blackened area of paintwork close to the deck where the contents of a cable-run had been severed, the ragged ends now fused from the tremendous heat of the explosion.

Inside the brightly-lit compartment were four people and Marshall noted immediately that something was contrived in the scene before him. The two nearest him and therefore nearest the door, were J and Gibson, while as far into the room as it was possible to go stood the two men he assumed - rightly so - to be the operators of the complicated equipment lining the bulkheads. Between the two pairs was an expanse of some twelve feet and it was across this no-man's-land that the older of the two operators spoke his report.

'Main power supply disconnected,' he said. 'Secondary power switched in automatically, of course, but it imposes limitations on the gear.'

'Such as?' demanded J in a barely controlled voice.

'The automatic sequencer, which ensures our transmissions go out on time and logs all incoming synchronised transmissions, is out of action. That means we'll be very busy from now on as everything will have to be carried out manually. It's going to get very rough - maybe impossible - if we go down heavily with this infection we're supposed to have.'

J's attention was divided at this point for a crewman entered the compartment and reported directly to him in whispered tones, before disappearing again at the Frenchman's nod.

J looked up at Marshall. It appears we have an escort - a Royal Navy frigate,' he said calmly. 'Would you care to explain her presence?'

'I've already told you,' replied the security man tiredly. 'From the moment you sailed - even before - you were the subject of a surveillance exercise only paralleled by that devoted to intelligence gathering between the major powers. The ship will be only the first of many to keep you company at sea.'

J said nothing, just nodded slowly.

'Five minutes, thirty-five seconds to the next scheduled transmission,' announced the younger operator.

273

'Five and a half minutes before we need to transmit manually what our 'sequencer' did automatically.' He pointed to the safe in the corner. 'You'd better open up quick. We need the list of the transmissions to be made.'

The safe was the usual combination type and, after J had supplied the numbers from a pocket-book, the older man bent to the task of opening it.

The short intermission this created was all that Gibson needed to concentrate on Marshall. 'Seems your error with the ventilation system might have been anything but that.'

'I'm not with you,' lied the security man.

'In one sense, you most certainly are not,' retorted Gibson. 'But you do understand what I am saying. From what our electricians tell us the severed cables fed the equipment in this compartment only. Together with the fact that the 'doctored' ventilation trunking fed only this part of the Lower Bridge Deck it does seem more than mere coincidence.'

'A trifle sinister, perhaps,' commented Marshall, blandly, and knew immediately that he had made a grave mistake.

The redness which welled-up in Gibson's face was darkening visibly as he turned to J. 'I say we get rid of him now,' he cried emotionally. 'He's far too dangerous'.'

The Frenchman, galled by the same bland comment that so enraged Gibson, momentarily lost his head. Marshall read the danger signals:

without D'rosario to steady them, the two were volatile, to say the least.

'I agree,' said J. 'I have foolishly allowed him to live. Take him away, Gibson, he's all yours.'

Marshall shot a frantic glance to the man at the safe. Now that he had the safe open he was sorting through the documents unaware of the dangerous turn of events.

'And kill these two men?' called Marshall quickly, so loud that both the operators responded by turning towards the group.

'Shut up, Marshall!' ordered Gibson. 'Move!'

'You both know damn well both these men will die unless I am around to give them transfusions of my own blood,' persisted the security man, not budging an inch.

Persevering in his attempt to get Marshall to move, Gibson moved round to confront him more squarely, indicating the door with a wave of his gun. In carrying out this action he was momentarily unsighted towards the older of the two operators who moved towards him with surprising swiftness and wrenched the gun from his fingers.

Under no illusions as to the delicacy of the position which his holding a gun on the hierarchy created, the man made sure that everyone knew they were covered. 'Now let's just calm down a little, shall we?' he said, his voice itself all calm persuasion.

Pausing only to pass a piece of paper to his colleague with a nod to an odd-looking machine close to where Marshall now stood, the man continued. 'I reckon I'm the vital link in the success of this operation. Likewise my buddy here. Now it don't make sense at all to waste the man who'll most likely be keeping me alive in the days to come.'

'He's right,' said Marshall, innocently.

'Shut up!' snapped Gibson, balling his fists.

'How do you suggest we keep him out of trouble, O'Malley?' queried J.

'By putting him and the girl in there,' he motioned to the inner room of the compartment which the men used as their sleeping quarters. 'Put two of your heavies in there on a roster basis and then I'll know they're safe. But just in case,' he weighed the gun significantly, 'there's no way he will get from there to the outer door with my life depending on it.'

'And when your infection becomes contagious?'

But Marshall didn't get the full gist of the man's reply - beyond the notion that masks and gowns could be used - because surreptitiously he was eyeing the piece of paper from which the younger operator was copying details onto the keyboard. He couldn't hope to memorise all of what was written on the paper in the period - a matter of brief seconds only - that he believed he had at his disposal. Luckily he had no need to memorise it all for most of what he saw was undecipherable. It was the last word in each of the eleven lines that drew his attention like a magnet; all were place names. Three times he ran his eyes slowly down the list of names. Then he slowly looked up but his eyes were unseeing as he concentrated on committing the words to memory.

Gradually the voices in the room broke through into his consciousness and he suddenly was aware that J was speaking.

'We'll try it, O'Malley,' said the Frenchman. 'We'll try it just once.'

The inner room of that compartment was almost square in plan with each wall some twelve feet long. Unlike the outer room of the passenger accommodation this room had not been altered in any way from its legitimate role and so it was that Marshall and Anne, sitting on one dishevelled bed, were watched continuously by their two guardians from the other.

Around the room on the bedside tables, wardrobes and dressing tables stood or lay, the indicators of male inhabitancy: electric razors surrounded by a collection of cheap deodorants, shirts, pin-ups and music player. In the more unisex vein, towels and washing-gear littered one corner - the floor as much as the wash-basin - and, within inches of Marshall's right hand, a heavy green-glass ashtray complete with a week's cigarette-ends.

The security man coveted this last object above all the other items his few seconds of 'natural' observation had allowed him. He knew, with only one glance into the eyes of the guards, that he would never get even half-way towards using it as a weapon such was the degree of their vigilance. Their single-mindedness of purpose did not surprise Marshall for he knew, as they did, that if he escaped their custody they would probably forfeit their lives.

The clock on the bedside cabinet indicated that almost forty minutes had elapsed since the explosion, an hour and twenty five minutes since they had left the jetty. It meant he had only thirty-five minutes to the dead-line when the Cape Town ship should pass into deep water and beyond salvage.

But Marshall's thoughts were on a time-scale even shorter than that: within the next five minutes. At the end of that period the next 'constant' would occur. Mentally tracing the plan of the ship's accommodation spaces he tried to calculate the distance between them and the telecommunications office, the site of the ship's powerful communications transmitter. He gave up the exercise after a brief struggle when he realised that no two places in the after-superstructure were more than seventy feet apart anyway. However, apart from a ripple of fear that things could go wrong, it gave him an idea.

The two guards whose eyes followed his every blink were, Marshall realised, the same pair who had delivered him first to the Captain's Quarters, then to the flying bridge, and finally, from the cell below to their present location. Marshall reasoned that as both had ears and eyes they would be pretty well briefed in the situation. It was upon this that he decided to play.

'Five minutes,' he said to Anne, whose shocked response, more due to the sudden breach of silence than the import of what he had said, served Marshall's plan very well.

'Silence,' rasped one of the guards automatically. Then the two carefully exchanged questioning glances before resuming their vigil.

Across from them Marshall slowly began a performance of mime which would have packed theatres; except that no such performance could have been repeated in such establishments as its unique excellence depended upon his desperation, fear and the vital importance of regaining his liberty.

The nervous tic at the corner of Marshall's right eye and the quick, urgent glance at a wall or the ceiling, were watched with visible anticipation by the two guards. Anne, as much at a loss to decipher Marshall's antics as the two men, found her already battered nerves vibrating to each symptom of a malady she couldn't understand.

Soon the three onlookers made meticulous note of each gesture as they would a clue in the parlour game of charades. Indeed, given another situation, the comical side of the scene would have been strongly evident. But the situation was serious, the man who now 'stole' repeated glances at the clock and hunched his head into his shoulders as if to escape some shattering event was dangerous, already the men had heard of 'bugs' - as they knew them - being introduced into the atmosphere and an explosion had severed vital power-cables and, more importantly, they knew that their lives depended upon this man. They therefore watched and listened.

A minute before the short-term dead-line, Marshall's movements became more obvious. He now squirmed and hugged Anne, muttering words which were, with one exception, unintelligible. The word which did come out clearly was 'explosion'.

The effect on the two guards was electrifying. Both, maintaining little of their former vigilance towards Marshall and Anne, increasingly looked about them as if hoping to see the bomb which would blow them to oblivion. As the seconds ticked by, Marshall contrived to cover Anne's head with one arm while he attempted the same thing, on his own head, with his other. The whole exercise was little more than a complete failure as he constantly changed the priorities from eyes to ears and vice versa, the covering power and angularity of an arm being impractically tasked with such a job. But it accomplished another objective with as much success as it is possible to estimate. It provided the last in a long line of incitements which had the nerves of the two guards at breaking-point; they could take no more and were almost rigid with apprehension.

When the explosion came it was nothing more than a dull, flat crack but it might have been that of a thousand-pounder for its effect on the pair. For two seconds neither moved, such was the state of their paralysed nervous systems. And two seconds, perhaps even one second, had been all that Marshall would ever need in such a situation. The first recipient of the green ashtray was already unconscious and on his way to the floor while the other was only a split-second away from the same fate.

Throwing the ashtray onto the bed Marshall turned to Anne. Let's get out of here,' he shouted, his tone occasioned by the need to mobilise her roughly, as she hadn't fully recovered from his play-acting. Harshly he pushed her towards the door. Then he picked up one of the guns which had so recently been trained on him, checked it, and followed her. Anne was soon through the door, leaving it slightly open behind her, when Marshall, stopping only to smash the telephone with the gun butt, backed through the opening and turned the key in the lock.

'Hold it,' said a voice Marshall recognised as belonging to the older operator. 'That's as far as you go.'

When Marshall turned around it was to see the man holding Anne as a shield between him and the security man. 'It's a shame,' responded Marshall, allowing the gun to fall to the full extent of his arm, 'I thought you were more intelligent than that. Remember, if I die you die. I am going through that door and you'll need to kill me to stop me doing so. We should be working together. We need each other. Let the girl go.'

No doubt remembering the Frenchman's intentions before he had intervened, the older man applied what Marshall had said and, when he next spoke, his tone had changed radically.

'That's a mighty convincing argument you have there,' he said, releasing Anne. He turned to the younger man who was blocking the way to the door. 'What do you think, Bud?'

But Bud said nothing, His eyes told a story all of their own, of indecision and apprehension, but he couldn't speak.

'You think you can stop this thing?' asked the older man, turning back to the security man.

'I'm going to have a very good try,' said Marshall, hoping that the force of his voice would help camouflage the evasiveness of his answer. But that the man's receptiveness wasn't too squeamish on this point was indicated when he ignored the words.

'We're coming with you!' he said.

'No,' cried Marshall. 'The transmissions - you must continue the transmissions at least for a little while.'

'Okay. Bud you stay and hold the fort,' he said. 'What do you want me to do, mister?'

'The scuttling-charges,' responded Marshall. 'I don't know exactly where they are but there must be some below the water-line. See if you can find them and apply your electrical experience to render them inoperative.'

The trio split outside the door: the operator went left as Marshall and Anne moved to the right in the direction from which had come the sound of the explosion. Such had been the speed of events since the noise had been heard that only two minutes had clicked by.

It was possible to get to their destination, the small compartment which housed the Telecommunications Office's emergency generator, by two routes. Marshall decided the first, most direct route, was totally out of the question as it meant having to pass in front of the Telecommunications Office, an area likely to be overpopulated at present. The other route required that they cross to the other side of the ship by way of the boat-deck which meant they would be in the open for a short distance. Then they would need to climb a ladder and enter the poop-deck and a parallel passageway to that of the direct route.

They arrived at their destination without incident but didn't enter. Instead, Marshall reached above the door, into the concealing darkness of a cable-run, and fetched out a small aluminium tin. This he handed to Anne.

'Alright. Back the same way,' he told her. 'And for heaven's sake, keep it hidden.'

Alone now, the security man opened the door. He was inside for less than ten seconds and when he came out he was holding a small transceiver. Something else was present when he emerged, in the person of Ilianov.

If Marshall had paused for just long enough to consider his physical fitness he would have given in then. To try to match his tired frame against the size and obvious power of the large man was not even an academic exercise; it was an impossibility. But Marshall did not try to calculate his chances because his mind was running to a schedule, a clock with less than thirty minutes to run. He saw the large man as just another obstacle which he must somehow get over, around or through. With his right-hand holding the transceiver he couldn't hope to get to the gun which was in his right trouser pocket. He hadn't the time in which to carry out the task. Besides, the large man was already moving towards him.

The first casualty of the fight was predictably the radio for at the large man's first lunge it was knocked from Marshall's hand to slide along the deck towards the sea. If there was one thing, apart from the welfare of Anne, which could stun the resourcefulness of the security man, it was the loss of the transceiver. Fortunately, if that is the word, he didn't have time to dwell on the problems posed by its loss for he was giving of his best against a seemingly iron man.

In the dreams - or more correctly, the night-mares - he had suffered too often after missions in the past, Marshall had sometimes found himself fighting an adversary who was so powerful as to totally negate his suddenly enfeebled efforts. Often he would wake from these dreams soaked in sweat. But this was real now, this was the 'dream' come true. He recognised this in a split-second and wondered if he would, in reality, wake-up from this one.

It was all too fast for Marshall too, and soon - very soon - the strength and speed of the other man told. Being able to fight intelligently, instead of with the blind desperation Marshall was forced to employ, the large man chose his targets well. He chose the places where it would hurt most but where it wouldn't cause unconsciousness too quickly, for he was enjoying himself. Soon enough would come his opponent's collapse; soon enough would come the time when he must throw him over the side so as not to incur the wrath his actions must bring from his superiors, unknowing as he was to their revised attitude towards the security man.

But he wasn't to enjoy himself as much as he wanted. Marshall, still conscious but going fast, was - with his back against the bulkhead, at the stage where little more than the force of the large man's punches was keeping him upright when he dimly became aware that the man had become heavier. In fact, he had stopped punching. Then, slowly, he slid down Marshall's front into a heap on the deck.

Marshall's fall to the deck was inevitable but halfway down he felt his weight being supported. With pain-filled eyes he looked at his rescuer. It was the older operator.

'I sure as hell don't know why I'm doing this,' said the man, 'but I guess it has something to do with you taking a beating. And being my life insurance.'

'Thanks,' croaked Marshall. He looked at the deck and his expression showed puzzlement through his pain but he couldn't quite put his question into words.

He didn't have to. The man saw what he was wanting to know and told him. 'Your playmate kinda fell over the side.' His tone then went grave. 'Now listen. I'm going to drag you in there,' he indicated the compartment Marshall had recently left, 'where you can recover. I have to try and find those scuttling-charges you were talking about. No luck so far.'

'No need to help me,' said Marshall. 'I'll make it myself. I could certainly do with the rest.'

'Sure thing,' replied the man. 'By the way, is this radio yours?'

Marshall brightened visibly.

'Found it in the scupper,' added the man.

Marshall raised himself to his feet and managed to stay there even if he was leaning heavily against the bulkhead. After two attempts to get himself started in the direction of the compartment had failed he turned to speak to the man. The man had gone. 'Forget it,' he gasped, looking again at the compartment door. 'I'll have plenty of time for rest later.'

After a brief check of the radio he raised it to his lips. He repeated his message three times adding amplifying information as a precautionary measure. Then he simply threw the transceiver over the side. Moments later he slid down the bulkhead again, and would have lapsed into unconsciousness but for the jolting pain which suddenly shot up his right leg.

Looking down his length to find the cause of the pain he was surprised to see four feet instead of the usual two. By elevating his eyes he traced the solution to both puzzles, for standing ever him, with the now ever-present pistol, was Gibson.

'I would find it ever so easy to kill you now,' said Gibson, calmly smiling, 'but the boss wants to issue the death-warrant personally. Get up!'

'Time has run out for you,' said J. In the semi-darkness of the 'flying bridge' only dimly illuminated to preserve night-vision, five people listened to the words directed at Marshall. D'rosario, an unmoving shadow with his back to the forward windows was the first man in a semi-circle which stretched, via J, Gibson and an armed man Marshall hadn't seen before, to Marshall and the last man, armed also, who was the other half of his guard. 'But, please, a little light on the subject. I cannot see his reactions.'

D'rosario moved to the central console and gradually the light level increased with a dull yellowness.

'Much better,' said the Frenchman. 'But it will be difficult to see any change of expression. He looks as if he has been severely mauled.' At this he shot a glance towards Gibson. 'Has Ilianov shown up yet?'

Gibson shook his head. 'No sign of him. Marshall was armed but I checked and the gun hadn't been fired.'

'So you killed one of my best men, yes?' When Marshall did not answer he went on. 'No matter. If he cannot look after himself with his obvious physical abilities he is no more than useless.'

With just two steps J shortened the distance between himself and Marshall to half-a-dozen feet but the greatest change was in his mood. Gone was the conversational tone to be replaced by an anger not seen in him before. 'It is not because of that that you will die. You die because of your own mistakes. You die after so brilliantly ensuring your existence through blackmail - because you yourself caused the removal of that blackmail.' He laughed then but it was not a humorous laugh. 'The radioman was shot while trying to get below.'

'Is he dead?' queried Marshall, genuinely worried for the health of the man who had so recently saved his life.

'Not quite. But unconscious and unlikely to be of any further use to the operation,' replied J. 'Your assistant is taking care of him.'

Marshall felt doubly worried at this last piece of information because it placed both the operator and Anne in imminent danger of death: the operator, because his life had been placed in the hands of a 'doctor' who had no practical experience whatsoever and; Anne, because if found out for the imposter she was would surely lose the 'indispensible' pretext which had until now protected her life.

Marshall found great difficulty in keeping the concern from his eyes as he thought of this and, in an attempt to hide it from J, raised his hand to touch the cuts on his face which Ilianov had caused.

But J hadn't noticed. 'With only one operator left - and one, moreover, who is likely to be prostrated with illness within three days, I am forced to revise my plans. Three days, you hear?' he insisted. 'That is my new target, for by then all of the ships will be in deep-water and then nothing can touch them save a madman. When my operator can go on no longer I shall activate my carriers and we shall see if the world will risk the loss of its gold in reprisals. Which means we no longer need you.' He smiled then. 'Good plan don't you think?'

Marshall, in constant pain from his beating, still managed to grin back in defiance. It was a lop-sided sort of arrangement which looked more like a grimace but for him it would do. 'Well, that takes care of me. Now it's my turn,' he croaked. 'I have to hand it to you that you and your crew are magnificent. No joke, honestly. If it was me I should be pretty nervous by now. But no, all of you are very brave, or just ignorant.'

'You're rambling, Marshall,' said Gibson.

'Believe that and you're crazy,' retorted Marshall, with a force which even surprised him. 'I boarded this ship carrying just over thirty pounds of explosive. Up until now you have seen the damage that just over sixteen ounces can do. As I say, you must be very brave men - especially so, this being a laden tanker. Top marks and I'll be seeing you wherever it is we all go to.'

'We've already searched the ship. There's nothing in what he says,' protested Gibson to his boss.

'You haven't had time to mount a proper search after the main transmitter went up, so you must have done so before,' said Marshall. 'That being so, it doesn't say much for your thoroughness because you didn't even find the explosive in the tele-communications office.'

He moved then to put his weight on the other foot. It was a mistake for he could feel himself going before he had got half-way through the operation. He moved back.

'Of course, you don't have to believe me,' he went on, when the mists of pain had cleared sufficiently for him to concentrate again. 'Perhaps it will go away,' he offered, placatingly. 'Perhaps you believe me. You could have another search. You might even find the stuff before it blows us all sky-high.'

It was all quiet for a short while after this. Marshall could almost hear them thinking, those who weren't getting very scared. It was predictably J who broke the silence. 'I think I believe you,' he said. 'More importantly, I believe I know how to make you tell us all about it.' He turned to Gibson. 'The girl. Bring the girl.'

'The stakes are too high for her safety to matter,' said Marshall, but he spoke just a little too quickly to sound convincing.

J smiled. 'We'll see, won't we?'

During the brief period before they heard the lift returning, an occurrence which focussed all eyes on the wooden sliding-door, Marshall was almost neglected as J and D'rosario stood at the other side of the bridge, their attention directed towards the world outside.

The object of their interest was quite plain even on such a dark night. Keeping a discreet distance away from the OBO, and on her port side, another vessel matched her speed and was holding a position relative to her. She could have been a tender or a guardian - such was the impression her unwavering position-keeping gave. But Marshall knew she was neither of these things. From her lines he could see, by the illumination of her steaming lights, that she was low and sleek and fast: the escorting frigate, her task to watch the *Orico* very carefully. With binoculars J and D'rosario could see much more and, in words that the security man could not make out, the two of them conversed on the subject.

Being unobserved Marshall took the opportunity to investigate his injuries, knowing that any change of expression was unlikely to be noted. He proved to be right in this as no comment was made as he strived to loosen muscles which had almost seized from the bruising Ilianov's hands had skilfully wrought. Even flexing arm and leg muscles sent searing pains through his body which, apart from creasing his face in agony, sent him to the brink of collapse. But through the pain he carried on moving imperceptibly as he clenched the tendons of his hands and feet, knowing that he must prevent the stiffness from going too far if he was to maintain some mobility.

Then the whirr of the lift motor invaded the quiet of the bridge and seconds later the door slid open to reveal Anne, escorted by Gibson.

All eyes were upon her as she stood defiantly erect. Marshall noticed, with a fury he fought to control, that Gibson's looks were more carnal than merely interested.

J wasted no time. 'Well, Marshall?' he said. 'The first one. Where and when will it be detonated?'

'The first one, said Marshall blankly. 'Now let me see, the first one is......situated...' Slowly, Marshall dragged the words out, his aim to draw everyone's attention from the girl. It was imperative that he should accomplish this but, although J was concerned only with his answer and looked directly at him, his distraction of the others wasn't complete for Gibson was still drooling. 'Yes, that's right,' continued Marshall, as if seeing the disposition of the explosive according to a mental plan,' I put....'

'He's stalling,' said Gibson, still looking at the girl. 'I think we should get to work right away.'

Marshall knew then that it wasn't lust which directed Gibson's attention unwaveringly towards Anne but a hate which pride, wounded deeply by his gullibility in bringing her to the ship, demanded he should vent on her. He knew also, with an increasing fear, that to distract Gibson from his purpose would require more effort than he had anticipated.

'Tell him to back off and I'll tell you,' said Marshall, hopefully.

But J was having none of it. 'You've got it wrong, Marshall, responded the Frenchman. 'You tell us - and very quickly - or we cut up your girl-friend.'

For the first time Marshall saw sweat breaking out on J's forehead. A quick glance told him that everyone else was on tenterhooks as well - quite natural when each of them thought time was running out to an explosion which would blow both the ship and them sky-high. All of which came as almost a surprise to the security man, followed quickly by the realisation that in this he had his distraction, a revelation so strong that their undivided attention would be riveted upon him for the time he needed. 'There isn't any explosive,' he said, weakly.

As if at the touch of a switch their eyes swung round to question the man who had unshackled them from the rack of fear. It was all he needed for, with all eyes on him, Anne could dig into her clothing and produce the phial he had given her.

Whether it was the speed of fear or sheer concentration Marshall couldn't guess. Nor had he the time for within half-a-second the phial, removed from the tin, was flashing across the eight or nine feet which separated them.

Marshall made no attempt to catch the object as it hit his hand but carefully deflected it to the deck near his feet. Even though he heard the tinkle of broken glass as it hit and fractured he took no chances but stamped on it with his right foot. Again, totally unnecessary as it was, he shouted out the one word that each person in the bridge knew was the identity of the phial's contents: 'Marburg.'

Things happened very quickly in the next few seconds. Gibson, determined to repay the man who had caused his downfall, raised the gun and fired. Even the very nervous Gibson couldn't have failed to hit Marshall from such a short range but the panic-stricken guard, in his desire to be somewhere other than in the presence of Marburg virus, bowled him over, upsetting his aim. The bullet ricocheted noisily around the bridge but struck nothing more yielding than steel.

With neither the time or inclination for another shot at that moment, Gibson made a very fast about-turn and was standing fear-stricken at the rear of the lift almost before the man who had passed him. Belatedly, though it could have been only by a fraction of a second, the other guard took to his heels.

He was late for the lift, as was D'rosario but for a different reason. The mercenary had dragged out a gun and aimed it at the men in the lift with a shout for them to return. But D'rosario had been a top-man too long ago and had slowed down a lot since he had needed to react so fast. By the time he had got the barrel lined up on target he was too late, the door had slid shut and the box was on its way down.

The mercenary thought fast, however, and instantly spun round to the console which housed the telephone. He had picked it up and was about to speak when they heard the scream. It was an ear-piercing scream followed by the sound of something soft but heavy bouncing off thin metal in an empty room. It was the second guard who, in panic, had found the alternate exit from the bridge, the ladder. His continued haste had been too fast for the slippery rungs and he had fallen.

D'rosario dropped the telephone receiver though not from any squeamishness he may have felt at the guard's horrible death-plunge. It was because he was discovering for the second time, within seconds, that he was too slow. It was also more painful because Marshall put all his power behind the punch which sent him across the bridge to fetch up against the far bulkhead. The gun, however, stayed in the grip of D'rosario's left hand.

It was a groggy D'rosario who rose to confront the two. To his left, J seemed to have faded to insignificance and was taking no part in the proceedings. He simply fiddled with the little black box which he had taken from his pocket.

'The neatest trick I've ever seen repeated,' said the mercenary, waving his gun at the area of broken glass.

Slowly he moved to the console and retrieved the telephone which was still hanging by its wire. 'Hello, D'rosario here. I want....' He halted as Marshall heard the crackling of a voice. 'No, we're alright up here. Gibson, the man who came aboard with the girl. Find him and hold him for me.' He stopped for the acknowledgement. 'Oh, and another thing,' he said. 'Let me know how you get on through the loudspeaker system, we're a little busy up here.' He slammed down the instrument.

'I don't think I really need to remind you of the situation,' warned Marshall, as D'rosario raised the barrel of the gun. 'You still need me. I'm your only hope. And it's personal this time.'

'Yeah, yeah,' said the mercenary. 'We've had all that. As I say that's the neatest trick I've ever fallen for twice. But you know, it isn't going to be a bed of roses for you.'

Marshall said nothing. He just returned the stare but he was suspicious of D'rosario's tone.

'The girl for instance,' he continued, 'you'll just have to learn to live without her.' The barrel shifted a few degrees to the right and steadied on Anne.

'You wouldn't kill the daughter of one of your oldest friends would you?' said Marshall quickly, moving to interrupt the mercenaries line of fire but waved back with the muzzle of D'rosario's gun as incentive.

'You're scraping the barrel, Marshall,' retorted D'rosario.

'So are you, by associating with this rabble,' said Marshall. 'But you even sent an aide to this girl with a story and a bundle of her father's belongings. Surely you remem...'

'Anne McKinnon? Doug McKinnon's daughter?' gasped a bewildered D'rosario.

'Yes,' said Anne weakly, fear showing clear in her eyes.

'The same,' added Marshall. 'She offered her help when she found out what her father had done.'

From the other side of the bridge a forgotten J was reacting to the news. It sounded like a gurgle at first, but what followed was plain enough to understand. ''Betrayed by my own right-hand man. All around me traitors.' He raised the black box slowly. 'Well it is still my plan - my operation.'

D'rosario saw it coming and reacted. Again he was too slow and couldn't stop J pressing the button. Marshall acted very quickly but it seemed that the distracted D'rosario almost gave him the gun.

'You blew the lot,' said D'rosario quietly.

'Blame him!' cried J, pointing at Marshall. 'Blame him. But for him we could have made some sense of this crazy world.

'Very good,' said Marshall. 'You'll have even me believing you next. You sound so sincere. But we both know the real reason; the real motivation which drove you after all the power you could lay your hands on.'

ANTHONY ASHPITEL

J looked up and met Marshall's eyes.

'Jealousy, wasn't it,' accused the security man. 'J for Jealousy. The green-eyed monster ruled your life from as far back as you can remember. All because you wanted to be more powerful than the man you hated - your father. Because you hadn't the business acumen or guts that brought your father his wealth you went for it the easy way. And it's an indication of the man you are that you used his money to do it. But you didn't just need to be more powerful than him. You needed to destroy him, didn't you? You demonstrated this by selling the shares he so generously gave you, and all at once, causing him the maximum financial embarrassment.

'This operation is just the next step,' continued Marshall. 'A large step I admit, where the collapse of the world's economy would destroy the very foundations of commerce and, ultimately, your father.'

J remained silent. A part of him seemed to have died in the minutes since the phial broke; since he had last been in charge of the situation.

Marshall turned to D'rosario. 'As for you, all your idealism has gone to waste. You fell for his line,' he nodded to the still silent J, 'like a callow youth. All that stuff about changing the world for the better. It was just the thing he needed to tell you to keep you on side. Pathetic.'

D'rosario was not like J. He had a history that had once been worthwhile, worthy of praise. He could still summon some pride, even in defeat. His gaze didn't flinch from that of Marshall's.

Through the windows, Marshall glimpsed the shadowy outline of the frigate. It had left its normal position and was drawing close in to the side of the *Orico*. Moments later the loudspeaker above crackled into life; 'Warship on the port-side has hailed us, sir. Says to lay down our arms and stop the ship. He is about to send a boarding party.'

J swung round at this to stare at the shadowy form below the bridge. 'Never.'

'You've no option,' advised Marshall. 'Do as he says.'

J ignored him and made for the telephone. Only a heavy-handed rap on the knuckles would dissuade him from using the instrument and he backed away, sucking the torn flesh.

'What have you got going for you now?' asked Marshall. 'You've thrown away the only card you had. No doubt the reason you have a warship alongside at the moment is because you have ordered your carriers to be deployed.'

'Impossible! They couldn't possibly know I pressed the button, so soon,' shouted J, wildly.

'You've stopped transmitting, haven't you?' argued Marshall. 'They've been listening on your frequencies ever since they found them. They've probably noted the times of each transmission and noted the pattern they make. They must have noticed the pattern was broken when you pressed that button. Otherwise, why are they alongside now?'

But J was back to silence.

'If you don't stop,' persisted the security man,' they'll simply stand off a few miles and sink you with missiles. You can be certain they will recover the gold in this depth of water. We're nowhere near the edge of the continental shelf. So everybody - what is it, fifty people? Fifty people die because you're too stubborn to see you're licked.' He turned then to the starboard windows to look down on the frigate, which was now separated from the *Orico* by a few yards only, keeping pace with her.

'Well, we won't give in so easily,' said J, continuing an esoteric pantomime which had D'rosario and Anne in thrall. 'We'll keep going. They won't sink us. So we'll keep going and fight off any attempt to board us with small arms.'

He was recovering his nerve quickly for he smiled a self-satisfied smirk of triumph. 'They won't find my carriers until it is too late and all my ships are in deep water. Then they wouldn't dare attack my fleet.'

Marshall had waited patiently during the tirade, biding his time for the most psychologically advantageous moment. With J regaining control of himself Marshall saw this as the moment. 'Except that they already know the locations of your carriers,' he said, in a quiet voice.

'What? Don't be absurd,' dismissed J.

'All eleven persisted Marshall. He watched J's eyes very closely now, his own nerves stretched almost to the point of breaking.

J's reaction was stunned silence and Marshall's sidelong glance at D'rosario revealed a similar response from him.

'Yes, eleven,' confirmed Marshall, sure now that the names he had seen on the list below comprised the total of the carriers. 'San Francisco, Sao Paulo, Mendoza, Puebla, Marseilles,' he paused then to recollect, 'Bombay....Shanghai, Osaka, Leningrad and Birmingham.'

'Very good,' said D'rosario, recovering fast while J remained incredulous. 'But the very fact that our locations are hyper-populated...'

'....will make tracing the carriers difficult - not, as you may believe, impossible. We know what everyone of your carriers looks like from photographs found in your flat,' supplied the security man. 'Forty-two in all. By concentrating on clinics we should be able to unearth them quite quickly.'

Marshall saw the doubt in D'rosario's eyes and had to agree that on the strength of what he had just said there was good reason to doubt such confidence in locating the carriers. Fortunately he didn't need to rely on such a short period of time the terrorists believed he had available for the task. 'For the moment,' he said, nodding towards the starboard windows, 'don't keep your escort waiting. I assure you his orders are quite explicit on the subject of non-cooperation.'

It was D'rosario who moved. He went slowly and carefully to the console and lifted the telephone.

With an open expression on his face Marshall looked at the mercenary over the gun. But D'rosario was playing it straight. 'Stop engines. Tell all personnel except engine-room and bridge to make their way to the main deck. They can take personal belongings but no, repeat no, weapons whatsoever,' He paused for the message to be repeated. 'Tell the gunboat what we are doing,' he added, then replaced the receiver.

The mercenary turned to Marshall. 'You know, if I'd had my way, it wouldn't have been so easy to take over this ship.'

'Why's that?'

'Scuttling charges,' he said, simply. And Marshall almost collapsed with fright at the mention of the two words he had been at pains to keep well out of the conversation over the past few minutes.

D'rosario smiled an odd sort of smile when he saw the reaction Marshall couldn't hide. 'But he wouldn't let me fit them. He though no-one would ever dare try anything that would necessitate them being employed,' he said.

'As I say,' croaked Marshall, having trouble with his voice, 'arrogance. Pure arrogance!'

Chapter Fourteen

(Sunday: circa 0600)

Benson was tired now. He had played a waiting game in a room off the offices of the Harbour Master's complex in Southampton for almost nine hours. Now, at six in the morning with the dawn a reality, it was the liberal, if careful, application of cold water which maintained his alert appearance.

But it hadn't all been waiting. There had been four notable occasions when a burst of activity had transformed him and his advisers into action. Marshall's transmission of the carrier locations had been the first, occasioning the second - to get him and Anne off the ship now that the main part of their task had been accomplished, for which he had needed to dispatch a helicopter. Neutralising the terrorist presence aboard *Orico*, through the use of the frigate's Royal Marine detachment, had formed the third occasion, and warning the security people in the carrier locations, the fourth.

They had been very lucky. Things had gone more smoothly than expected. No sooner had the frigate's boarding-party taken over the ship, with only one incident, than the helicopter had arrived to pick-up Marshall and Anne. A second helicopter, from the frigate and well provided with security men, had picked up J and D'rosario.

The debrief which followed the arrival of Marshall and the girl had taken just over half-an-hour before it was terminated at the insistence of the doctor brought in to tend the security man's wounds. Reluctantly, Benson had let them be taken to another part of the building where medical care could be better implemented. With them had seemed to go the major part of his staff for now, only minutes after the exodus, there were just five people in the room with him: the ever-present Jenkins, two rather heavy-weight 'heavies', and the two men they had just brought in, J and D'rosario.

The admiral spent some time reading and re-reading his notes from the debrief before he acknowledged the presence of the two terrorists. Then, impassively, he surveyed the two in turn. The J who looked back at him was a very different person from the one who had gazed upon the newly-captured Marshall aboard the *Orico*.

There was a fitful nervousness about him now, the cool facade having dissolved completely. But Benson saw something in the eyes which surprised him, a glimmer of defiance. It drew a strange feeling of respect from the admiral and something else, the urge to see the defiant light extinguished.

D'rosario was a different animal completely from the Frenchman. He maintained the same impassive expression as always and the eyes did not waver under Benson's scrutiny. In the mercenary's relaxed stance was an indicator to the type of man he was and to his attitude: he was a professional, he had lost and would accept the consequences without histrionics. To him, it was as simple as that.

Benson returned his gaze to the piece of paper in his hand. 'All of your ships are now in our hands,' he announced, in a quietly conversational tone. 'We stopped the Cape ship less than three miles from the deep-water line,'

'I don't believe you,' sneered J.

'Don't. It doesn't matter what you believe. It happened, anyway,' replied the admiral in the same quiet voice. 'But then, my man made the same mistake that you probably did. He calculated the time to deep water at an average of fifteen knots when, in fact, Dormon's maximum speed is only seventeen knots. He had forgotten the time it takes to get from stopped, alongside, to her max-imum speed. In the case of Dormon, this period was roughly half-an-hour.'

'So what?' challenged the Frenchman, unable to argue the truth of what Benson had just said. 'I have accomplished what I promised would hap-pen if anyone interfered with the operation. Soon the human race will know a devastation greater than...'

'You could still help avert the loss of life from this virus if you told us the exact location of each carrier,' urged Benson.

'You mean save your neck for precipitating this situation, don't you?' chided J. 'Well, no go. I've already told your security man that only the carri-ers know the information you want. Not that I would tell you, anyway.'

'Pity,' replied Benson, simply.

'A great pity,' elaborated the Frenchman, a demonic glee new in his face.

Benson remained calm. 'No matter,' he continued, 'we will have sufficient time to round them up before they deploy. Your operator is seeing to that.'

'What the devil are you talking about? Deploy? They're already deployed!' J was shedding the defiance now as his natural arrogance reasserted itself.

'Your operator,' repeated Benson, with gentle emphasis. 'The one whose close friend and colleague your fellow, Gibson, shot. He has been transmitting the codes without interruption since the automatic equipment went unserviceable. Fortunately, we have people helping him.'

J leant forward, his jaw jutting out. 'If your agent had bothered to tell you or perhaps, if you had listened, you would know that I transmitted the signal for the carriers to deploy from the bridge, through the use of the remote-control box!'

For a second there was silence in the room. Then D'rosario broke into laughter. It was several seconds before he was sufficiently in control to explain the reason for his eccentric behaviour. 'What the gentleman is saying, you clot,' he said, looking at J, 'is that without the automatic gear you cannot transmit from the remote position. Everything has to go manually, through the operator. Don't you see?' He said. 'You could press that button all day and get nothing more for your trouble than a sore finger.'

It was plain, by the time D'rosario had finished explaining, that J did see. 'But the carriers will know what has happened,' he blurted, trying to win something from the argument. 'They'll hear the news from the media....' But he didn't even believe what he claimed even himself. A mental image had prompted the sudden halt in his excited babble. It was the image of the *Orico* as he saw her from the helicopter, course and speed unchanged and, apart from the terrorists, the injured operator, D'rosario and himself, an unchanged crew.

He knew then just what was happening. He could see that the media wouldn't even get the story until it was too late, until the carriers had been located and the ships returned to harbour. He saw then that his long months of preparation and the expenditure of his fortune had accomplished nothing. If Marshall's intervention aboard the *Orico* had caused him anguished frustration it was nothing to what he felt now. Five people watched as first the arrogant set of his jaw melted and then the light in his eyes went out as he looked vacantly at the blank wall.

'What happened to Gibson?' asked D'rosario, remembering where most of the blame lay for the collapse of J's plan.

'Dead,' answered the admiral, still watching J closely. 'He wasn't quick enough in surrendering to one of the boarding-party.' There was no feeling in the way he said these words - it was just a flat statement.

He turned then from looking at J to nod towards Jenkins. It was just a signal for him to take over. Then he moved to the door.

'Tell me something else,' D'rosario called after him.

Benson turned back, a quizzical expression on his face.

'The Marburg virus,' prompted the mercenary.' There never was any aboard the ship. Right?'

Benson nodded.

D'rosario chuckled to himself again. 'Quite a man, your Marshall, he sighed, shaking his head. 'Quite a man.'

As the admiral walked slowly down the corridor he heard again D'rosario's laugh and suspected he could detect a rough edge beginning to creep into it. Still, he was tired now. Perhaps he was imagining it. It didn't matter, anyway.

As he approached the room in which Marshall and Anne were receiving treatment he slowed to a halt. 'Quite a man,' he said, under his breath. And perhaps the only man who could have pulled it off? Possibly. And now gone forever. Lost to married life. Or was he, thought Benson, not one to lose a good man without a fight.

He got as far as placing his hand on the door-knob before he remembered Marshall's physical health and dismissed the thoughts uppermost in his mind. Then he withdrew his hand hastily and continued down the corridor. 'No-one should even try to convince a man he is needed just after the completion of a mission, especially in front of his woman!' he murmured.

Suddenly he had the solution and increased his walk to a brisk pace. 'Give him a few days to mend,' he said aloud, to an empty corridor. 'At least, until after the wedding!'

THE END

www.ingramcontent.com/pod-product-compliance
Lightning Source LLC
Chambersburg PA
CBHW060532180626
46817CB00002B/535